RETURN TO NEWEDEN

He'd taken a flitter from Sterka Port to the city, deciding impulsively to walk its streets again. For the most part, it seemed the same: cluttered, narrow streets made for pedestrian traffic and not groundcars, rich and poor dwellings side by side. Sterka was nothing like the sleek and clean lines of OldinHome, the ordered beauty of its buildings and parks. It gave Gyll grim hope that he could accomplish his mission on Neweden—to take Hoorka Guild away from the Alliance, to lead them again, under the Oldin Family flag.

As he walked, something nagged at him, some vague feeling of unease. A prickling at the back of his neck: *danger*. Something in the net of shadows about him made him hesitate. Gyll took a false step forward, waited, pulled back.

The feint saved him. A hand holding a dagger stabbed air where he should have been.

A QUIET OF STONE
by Stephen Leigh

A QUIET OF STONE

Stephen Leigh

BANTAM BOOKS
TORONTO · NEW YORK · LONDON · SYDNEY

A QUIET OF STONE
A Bantam Book / February 1984

ISBN 0-553-23894-9

Published simultaneously in the United States and Canada

Bantam Books are published by Bantam Books, Inc. Its trade-
mark, consisting of the words "Bantam Books" and the por-
trayal of a rooster, is Registered in U.S. Patent and Trademark
Office and in other countries. Marca Registrada. Bantam
Books, Inc., 666 Fifth Avenue, New York, New York 10103.

PRINTED IN THE UNITED STATES OF AMERICA

O   0 9 8 7 6 5 4 3 2 1

TO THE FAMILY:

—Walter and Betty Leigh, for more than can possibly be expressed here. They are ultimately responsible.

—Eva Kohnle. Gigi, for gentle and uncritical encouragement.

—Sharon and Pam, because they insisted.

With much love to all.

A QUIET
OF
STONE

1

McWilms never let his hand stray far from the sheathed dagger's hilt. He knew the gesture for the nervous habit it was, but he'd long ago convinced himself that the feeling of proximity gave him confidence.

"How many are there, and what have they got?" he asked the apprentice brusquely, staring at the building before him. In the wan light of Gulltopp, it looked formidable enough. He was willing to bet that they'd need a disruptor to batter down that doorshield.

McWilms hated this contract, this night.

The apprentice was nervous. It showed in his skittering eyes, the restless shifting of weight. "We're not sure..."

"Then stand still, boy, and think. Your frigging uncertainty could cost us kin, and I'm not going to lose someone because you didn't do your job. I'll toss you back in there first." Moon-shadow hid his gaze, but the apprentice could feel the anger in McWilms's voice. "Now tell me what you saw, and do it quickly. It's getting late."

The boy nodded. "We trailed Vasella here, and there were at least two others already inside—we saw them, a man and a woman, when they opened the door to let Vasella in." The apprentice grimaced and swallowed hard. "That's when they used the sting on us. I ducked and rolled, like in the lessons, but when I looked up again, Elzbet was still lying there in the street. There was a lot of blood. A lot."

The boy stopped again, sniffing. McWilms made no move to hurry him, but waited as the apprentice wiped at his nose with the sleeve of his nightcloak. "I didn't know whether to try to get to Elzbet or stay behind cover. It was like I was frozen there..."

There was more than a hint of hysteria in the boy's voice.

It softened McWilms's anger. "She'll live, Steban," he said. "The Hag won't have her yet." She'd been badly hurt, though; seeing Elzbet had made McWilms recall the months he'd spent recovering from a cowardly assault after an offworld contract. Eight standards ago, now, yet he could still feel the weakness in his right arm, the budded one, and the skin of his chest was hairless and glossy with scars he hadn't bothered to have removed. Elzbet would be a long time regaining her health, and the pain would never entirely leave. He knew that too well. "Don't worry about her," he said to Steban. "Worry about your kin that are here now. What else did you do?"

Steban inhaled deeply, let the breath out in a trembling sigh. "I used my relay to call Thane Mondom and get the full kin here early. Then I went out and pulled Elzbet back here. I tried to stop the bleeding; there were people around—lassari—but none of them would help," he said, bitterness tinging his voice. "I may have missed someone coming in or out of the building then. I don't think so, but I can't be sure."

"But there are at least three of them, and they're armed with projectile weapons?"

Steban nodded. "I'm sorry I don't know more..."

"It will do. I doubt that anyone could have done much better." McWilms's gaze had gone back to the blank darkness of the house. The uproar in the street had caused the curious of the neighborhood to assemble. Around the Hoorka assassins, intent faces peered from windows, and a crowd jostled elbows on a streetcorner a judicious distance away. Not too near, for the Hoorka were known to be less than gentle with those deigning to interfere with their contracts, but close enough to see the blood if there was to be any. Their faces were strained with an almost happy anticipation. McWilms cursed the morbidity of the onlookers. "I want you to do one last thing, Steban. Go and bring d'Mannberg here—he's to the back of the building. Then you can head for the flitter; Felling's put a good meal in there for you.

"I don't know that I'm hungry."

McWilms pulled Steban to him, hugging the boy firmly. "I can understand, believe me. Get d'Mannberg here, then tell the flitter pilot to take you directly to med-center. Go see Elzbet."

Steban smiled. "Thank you, sirrah." Then he was gone, his nightcloak (with the red slash of the apprentice) blending into the night's shadows.

McWilms paced restlessly as he waited for d'Mannberg. His fingers tapped an erratic rhythm on the dagger's hilt. He hated nights when the victim barricaded himself in with companions and weapons. It was dishonorable, an insult to the demands of Dame Fate, and wasteful of life. And it was becoming far too common. *A shame to their honor, but the lassari and low kin don't care. And these cows will be here watching, counting the bodies as they come out. Smiling and talking.* The fact that the contract was another of the Li-Gallant Vingi's didn't help his mood. Politics again: McWilms knew that without reading the sealed contract in his pouch. The crowd knew whose house the Hoorka had surrounded, and he could hear the whispers from the spectators. *The Hoorka are doing the Li-Gallant's dirty work again. He points, and they kill, and only those with power benefit.* Vasella was reputed to be one of the leaders of the insurrectionist group known as the Hag's Legion, a group of low kin and lassari—those unguilded and without kin. If rumor were true, the Legion was responsible for the sabotage of the transport *Five Winds.* The ship had gone down over the Dagorta Mountains. Its cargo of ippicator bones had been ruined or lost, and its crew had all died in the crash. The kin demanded revenge, the kin-lord calling for bloodfeud, but there had been no answer to her challenge.

Cowards, all of them, with no honor.

McWilms shook his head. Bloodfeud was the accepted custom of settling affairs of honor between guilds, but the Hag's Legion ignored custom, turning their backs on the gods of Neweden. McWilms didn't care for the Hoorka to appear as vassals of the Li-Gallant, but if a man deserved to be sent to Hag Death, Vasella was that man. He hoped Dame Fate and She of the Five would not allow Vasella's escape at dawn, when the contract ended.

The situation made his stomach sour.

The whispering throng parted abruptly, and d'Mannberg strode through the cleft. The Hoorka was a huge man, both tall and massive, and the crowd gave him wide berth, as if his touch might contaminate them. A scowl lurked in d'Mannberg's

3

reddish beard. He came up to McWilms and spat toward the house. "Shields," he said. "I *hate* wearing a shield, especially the worn-out things we have. They're too frigging stiff and constricting. And too damn hot, as well." His voice boomed in the night, heedless of anyone overhearing. "Well, Jeriad m'boy, there's not a way around it, is there? Damn; we always seem to get the nasty ones." He shrugged. "If that's what the Dame wants, I'm just as glad the rotation paired me with you."

"I'm glad that makes you happy."

"Don't go patting yourself on the back, now. There's still things I can teach you on the practice floor, youngster." D'Mannberg grinned at his companion. "One lesson I can think of is humility, Jeriad."

McWilms smiled briefly. D'Mannberg was his kin-father, the one who had sponsored his transition from apprentice to full kin, and McWilms enjoyed the man's bluffing good humor. It did a little to alleviate his feelings of foreboding, that bad luck seemed to haunt this contract. "Thane Mondom's sent over another of the kin—Serita, she said. The com-unit at Underasgard said that'll even up the odds."

"The bastards inside should be so honorable." D'Mannberg's voice held disgust. "I swear, sometimes following the code can be galling, when it seems only to benefit the victims."

"The victim must always have his chance to escape."

"I can quote the code better than you. I've lived with it longer." D'Mannberg flashed a grin. An oddly dainty hand prowled his beard; delicate fingers twisted hair. "I want nothing more than to take a long, hot shower, Jeriad. And Vasella's holed up in there so tight we probably won't get near him until dawn, if at all. They're going to wait until light, then laugh at us. Damn them." He spat again.

"I don't think they're going to be that lucky, Ric. She of the Five isn't going to be kindly disposed to them after what happened to Elzbet and Steban. That was on the far borders of honor, though I'm sure they'll claim that they didn't see the apprentice-slash, and that they shouted a warning first."

D'Mannberg grunted. "Shit. That's what that is." He let out a deep breath. "Well, are you ready?"

"As soon as we see Serita's flare."

The signal came a few minutes later. A hissing, spluttering

gout of blue-white arced into the sky; Gulltopp, startled, had
hidden its face behind the roof of a nearby building. Long,
dark shadows moved in the street as the flare rose, fluttered
at zenith, and fell. The watchers in the street murmured.
"Now," d'Mannberg said.

They moved toward the house, swiftly and quietly, like
shards of night themselves in the gray-and-black Hoorka
nightcloaks. McWilms expected at any moment that the sting
would bark again from one of the shuttered windows, but the
house remained silent. The two assassins pressed themselves
against the wall on either side of the doorshield. With little
hope, d'Mannberg touched the contact for the shield. A bell
chimed inside, distantly, but the shield remained up.
D'Mannberg shook his head, McWilms grinned. D'Mannberg's
hands moved in the silent code. *Disruptor?*

Yah. Quickly.

D'Mannberg reached behind him for the device, an ugly,
plain box strapped under his nightcloak. He pressed a switch,
and a rank of lights shivered from scarlet to emerald. They
pulsed. D'Mannberg pointed the smaller end of the disruptor
toward the shield. Sparks—violent, sputtering—danced from
the doorway to the pavement as erratic light played over the
Hoorkas' features. The empty darkness between the door-
frame began to glow an alarming orange-white. It throbbed
like an uncertain heart, then—suddenly—was gone. The
disruptor wailed, its serried lights gone amber. D'Mannberg
touched the end of the device, winced silently as it burned
his forefinger. He set it down. The air smelled of ozone.

McWilms went to his knees and leaned forward to peer
into the interior of the house. He could see nothing of
import: some furniture too small to hide behind, a carpet that
looked half-dead, all lit by a hoverlamp near the ceiling.
Everything looked well-used and rather shabby. He nodded
to his companion. *In. Fast.*

D'Mannberg unsheathed his vibro, McWilms his dagger.
They entered.

A corridor led off the room through an open archway.
There was no other exit. McWilms glanced about, looking for
the formal warning required by Neweden law that a weapon
other than one requiring proximity was being used. There

5

was none. McWilms knew that d'Mannberg had noticed that lack as well—a scowl creased the larger man's face.

The corridor (narrow, paint falling from the walls in long strips) was empty. A few doors led off its length, another was set at the end. McWilms didn't like it: the place had the smell of a trap. Too many possibilities for ambush, and these people were too dishonorable to ignore any possibilities.

D'Mannberg signed to him: *bodyshield*. McWilms touched his belt and felt the sudden rigidity as the shield snapped into place around him. The shield would repel slugs from a sting or similar weapons, though it still left them vulnerable to slower attacks, such as a vibrofoil or dagger. The borders of the field slowly exchanged outside air for that trapped behind it, but the shields, overused and much in need of expensive repairs that the Hoorka guild could not afford, were both hot and uncomfortable. Once supple, they now constricted movement. McWilms could sympathize with d'Mannberg's often-voiced distaste for them; still, they were needed protection if Vasella decided to use the sting again. Neither Hoorka was foolish.

The assassins moved slowly down the corridor, one to each side, hugging the walls. McWilms nudged the first door with a foot. It swung open, revealing a stairway leading down into darkness. He listened, heard nothing, and shrugged to d'Mannberg. Too many choices: *separate?*

Neh. D'Mannberg pointed with his chin. *Keep going.*

McWilms clenched the hilt of his dagger. D'Mannberg had yet to activate his vibro—the whine of the weapon would have screamed of their presence. They continued down the hall, McWilms now slightly ahead of the other Hoorka. He couldn't shake the feeling of wrongness that had afflicted him from the moment he'd seen Elzbet. Dame Fate was looking away, She of the Five was somewhere distant, attending to Her own affairs with the ippicators. Hag Death cackled softly nearby. His muscles ached, fighting the gelatinous resistance of the bodyshield. His breath was too quick, and the air about him was tainted with his exhalations.

It happened quickly.

A woman burst from the door at the end of the hall. McWilms saw little of her but the sting she held. She shouted, her face a rictus, but he could make out no words.

She fired twice, rapidly. McWilms felt his shield go rigid, locking up his body as the pellets ricocheted about the corridor, gouging the walls, tearing loose chunks of masonry. He strained toward the woman (the sting down now, unprotected, yet her flat, plain face was curiously triumphant) but the shield held him, slow to release. In the second before he could move again, he heard footsteps and the characteristic high keening of vibros.

Behind. Behind.

McWilms could even admire the plan while abhorring the dishonor in it: force the Hoorka to use shields, fire the sting, and then attack in the instant before the shields became flexible again—a small advantage, made larger by the condition of the equipment the Hoorka used. The skin of his back crawled in anticipation of the blade, then the shield relaxed and he let himself fall with it. A vibro whined over his head (moving in the slow-time thrust of shield-fighting— his assailant knew the technique) as McWilms rolled and kicked blindly up. He was lucky: the man—it was Vasella, he saw—howled in pain, clutching his groin. McWilms slashed with his dagger, and the howl became a wail. Vasella looked surprised and almost sad as McWilms thrust again, the edge of his weapon going deep. Vasella went to his knees, a dark stain spreading out on his clothing. He gasped, fish-mouthed, a hand grasping for the vibro he'd let fall. McWilms, on his feet again, kicked the weapon aside.

A clatter behind him: McWilms, cursing the slowness forced on him by the shield, turned to face the new attack, grateful only that the shield forced his opponent to move a touch slower with his thrust. A vibrofoil slapped ribbons of paint from the wall as McWilms ducked aside. The foil, backhanded, gashed his leg. McWilms could feel the warmth of blood, and he had time to wonder whether the leg would support him as he moved to defend himself. It was all instinct—Ric's training, Ulthane Gyll's training. Everything had happened too quickly for a measured plan; he could only react. There was a blur of a face, an intricate pattern of blue and white on a shirt, a grimy wall and something dark and mounded lying on the floor a few meters away. McWilms parried the foil with his dagger—wishing now that he'd chosen a vibro himself. The man (he had a twisted nose, a

frown on thin lips) beat the dagger aside easily and thrust for
McWilms's chest. The man was too eager this time. The
shield deflected the foil slightly, the blade scoring his side.
McWilms grimaced, twisting aside. He touched his belt
control, felt the shield go.

(Somewhere, a shout in a voice he knew, the cough of
the sting, and a shrill cry of pain.)

McWilms forced himself to move as if the shield still
constricted him, waiting for the man's next thrust. When it
came, the Hoorka suddenly leapt aside and around the
lethargic attack, moving at his opponent. Echoes of Ulthane
Gyll's old teachings: *In a real fight, don't go for half-
measures or worry about etiquette or technique. Do what
you need to do and worry about style later. And kill, don't
wound.* McWilms felt the cut in his side tear further, felt the
throbbing of his leg as he bowled into the man. Grunting, he
slammed the dagger into the man's chest. He wrenched it
back out, sheathed it again under the ribcage, thrusting up.
The vibrofoil slid from nerveless fingers, the body went slack
under him. McWilms let him crumple to the floor.

"Jeriad?"

At the sound of his name, McWilms glanced back at the
doorway. Serita Iduna stood there, the sting now in her
hands, the other woman—moaning—sitting against the wall,
holding an arm that dangled at a wrong angle. "Ric," she
said. With the sting, she gestured behind McWilms. He did
not like the look on her face.

He turned. D'Mannberg was on the floor, the nightcloak
tangled around his large frame. There was a stillness about
him that made McWilms's throat constrict, his breath catch.
He hurried over to him, glancing at Vasella. The victim was
still alive. Dark eyes stared back at McWilms. "I'll deal with
you in a moment, bastard," the Hoorka said, and went to his
kin-father.

He grasped d'Mannberg's shoulder, turning him. The
vibrofoil had come from behind, cleanly. There was very little
blood. "Ric?" he said, knowing there would be no answer.
D'Mannberg's light eyes stared at nothing. With a guttural
curse, McWilms brought the eyelids down. He made the star
of She of the Five over him.

"How is he, Jeriad? I've the relay for the flitter. It can be here in two minutes. Less." Serita's voice was full of her concern.

He glanced at her, still kneeling. His face was stony, his voice did not sound like his own. "Call the flitter, but tell them they don't need to rush." Then: "Oh, *damn!*" His voice caught on the word, almost breaking.

Serita's shoulders sagged with sudden grief, the sting wavering in her hands. McWilms shook his head at her. "Later, kin-sister. We'll mourn him later." There was a wavering in his sight. He felt weak, fatigued. He nearly stumbled when he rose to go to Vasella. He cleared his throat, blinked quickly.

"You don't deserve the quickness I'm code-bound to give you, Vasella. You're lassari shit that doesn't deserve the rights of guild-kin, and I hope the Hag gnaws at your soul for the rest of eternity."

"Do you talk all your victims to death, Hoorka?" The man's eyes were clouded with pain, his fingers knotted into fists against the hurt. Blood had pooled beneath him, seeping into the wooden floor. "Tell your master Vingi that I'll be waiting for him."

"The Li-Gallant isn't Hoorka's master." McWilms didn't bother to deny that it was Vingi's contract they worked—it would have fooled no one, and he was too tired. He wanted to sit down, wanted to weep. "We'll be the weapons in anyone's hands."

Vasella laughed. It was a hoarse, phlegm-loud rasp of sound. "Tell that to the lassari and low kin the Li-Gallant beats down." The man paused, coughed once more, bringing up bile. "Tell it to the ones he kills with your blades."

A sudden heat of anger filled McWilms, turning his sorrow to ash. Ric's death, Elzbet's wounds, the cowardly attack, and Vasella's taunts: all goaded him. "*Bastard!*" He kicked the prone man, nearly falling as he did so. The soft thud of his boot was surprisingly loud. Vasella howled, the lassari woman sobbed in sympathy.

"*Jeriad!*" Serita shouted. "Stop it, man! Kill him and end this Hag-damned contract, but don't torture him. You're Hoorka, kin-brother. Remember our code."

"*Damn* the code," he replied. "The code and our frigging broken equipment killed Ric, didn't it?" He swung around to face her. The hall seemed to sway slowly around him. "Look what it's gotten us. Insults from scum like Vasella."

"You just feed the misconceptions of those like him, Jeriad." Her voice was soft, pleading. "I know how you feel, Jeriad. Ric was *my* friend, too, and a lover as well. And he wouldn't want this from you. You foul his memory."

McWilms wanted to shout back at her, but the weariness had returned, worse this time. His leg seemed to be on fire, his side gigged him whenever he breathed. The hallway wouldn't stay still. His hand threatened to lose its grip on his dagger, and he clenched harder, closing his eyes for a moment. He took a breath; pain lanced him. Serita was staring at him, concerned. He shook his head, glancing down at Vasella again.

"Sirrah Vasella, your life is claimed by Hag Death. I can make your way easy, if you prefer. The blade or a capsule: the choice is yours." McWilms forced himself into the role of the aloof Hoorka once more, a distillation of cold neutrality caring only for the contract and guild-kin. His voice was stiff with ritual. Vasella, huddled in a fetal position below him, simply grimaced.

"Do it however you want, Hoorka. Whichever way gives you the most pleasure." Vasella coughed again. His eyes closed. "Just end it." He spat, bright red.

McWilms nodded. He knelt before the man, but his leg betrayed him. He staggered, bracing himself with his right hand. Serita came over to him, but he shrugged her hands away from him. Scowling, he steadied himself. His dagger flicked out, came back running blood. Vasella gasped, then was still. McWilms let his weapon drop. He sagged.

"Jeriad, you're hurt." Serita's strong hands gave him support.

"I'll be fine. Get the flitter here, let the woman go, and take Vasella's body to the Li-Gallant. Just let me rest a moment first."

He blinked. The hallway danced about him. It seemed

to be getting darker, but he could keep his eyes open no longer to see why.

"They all look good from here, Gyll. That's the trouble. You can't see the filth until you get close and stick your nose in it."

Gyll turned from the port where Neweden's reflected glare snuffed out stars. One of the world's two moons, Gulltopp, leered around the curve of the world like a small child over the shoulder of its mother. Sleipnir, Gulltopp's companion, rode between Neweden and *Goshawk*, Gyll's ship. Its curve filled the bottom of his view. Gyll found the scene entrancing enough, but he smiled back at Helgin. "And you smell the stench already, neh?"

The Motsognir Dwarf was perched on the leather seat of Gyll's floater, petting Gyll's bumblewort. The animal purred satisfaction as Helgin leaned back and put bare feet on the desk in front of him. The ship's gravity was set to OldinHome norm—the movement stirred flimsies set there. The paper moved sluggishly, as if under water, rising and settling slowly. One of Helgin's hands stroked the bumblewort's furred shell, the other played in his thick, long beard. "If you could open the port, stick your head outside, and take a good whiff, you'd lose that delightful dinner we just had. And I'd have to assign someone to clean the side."

"If I could do all that, they'd have to rewrite all the physics texts in existence, Helgin. That scenario's utterly impossible."

"What's impossible is the thought that I've been crazy enough to be talked into coming back to Neweden. I didn't like it here the first time, and I doubt that eight standards have improved the place at all."

Gyll laughed, Helgin frowned. The dwarf's thick fingers pressed too hard on the wort's shell. It mewled a protest. Gyll turned back to his contemplation. "It's my homeworld, Helgin. FitzEvard Oldin is interested enough in it, and so am I." Gyll stared at the planet, giving names to the places he could glimpse below the ragged cloud cover. Neweden's main continent faced them, and he searched for the once-familiar landmarks, following the path of the largest river through haze to where he knew the city of Sterka lay, then south to the mountains. There: that was where the caverns of Underasgard hollowed the earth. Hoorka-lair.

"Lots of memories?"

"Yah, a few." Gyll spoke to the port.

"Sentimentality is a disease, Gyll," Helgin grumbled behind him. The Motsognir shifted to move the wort from his lap and scratched at his beard. "It eats into you and turns your mind to cold oatmeal. It can make you think that a shrieking harridan is the woman of your dreams just because she once let you into her pants. I never let sentiment interfere with my feelings."

"You keep telling me you don't *have* feelings," Gyll replied mildly. He gazed at the slow ballet of planet and moons.

Helgin's feet thumped the deck. "I lied." It seemed he was going to expound at length, drawing himself up to his full height of a little over a meter and striding toward Gyll, but the holotank chimed. Both men turned. "Yah?" Gyll said.

The holotank sparked into life—the figure of Gyll's aide, Fischer, bowed to them through greenish sparks that gradually faded. The aide was dressed in the plain, loose clothing of the Oldin-Hoorka. "Sula," he said, addressing Gyll by his title, "there's a transmission from Diplo Center. The Regent d'Embry would like to speak with you."

"In a moment, Fischer. I'll call you. Give her the stall while I settle myself first. Off."

The holotank darkened once more. Gyll glanced down at Helgin; the Motsognir was grinning under his beard. His rough voice sounded gleeful. "You see, the unpleasant memories make their first appearance. There you were, getting all misty-eyed about Good Old Neweden, and—poof! Welcome, the bitch woman of the Alliance. Might've thought she'd be dead by now."

"Helgin . . . " Warningly.

The grin would not go away. "Just don't go telling me that I didn't warn you, Gyll. I'm going to take great pleasure in giving you the 'I told you so' routine. Now, I'll simply stroll down to the pharmacy and get a Nopain tab ready for you. You'll need it for the headache." Helgin reached down and picked up the wort again. Then, with the rolling gait of the dwarves, he went to the door. He punched the contact on the floor with his big toe, stepped through. "Give her a kiss for me," he said as the door shut behind him. Gyll could hear Helgin's roar of self-amusement as the Motsognir walked away. He was singing in an off-key bass.

Gyll sat at his desk. His smile faded as he shuffled flimsies into a neat stack, swept stray acousidots into the drawer, and set the com-unit terminal to one side. He sighed deeply, closing his eyes, willing himself to relax. He straightened the sleeves of the simple cotton tunic he wore, the Family Oldin crest sewn at the breast dragging at his skin. *You're more nervous than you should let yourself be, old man. She's just another one of the bureaucrats that keep nagging at the Oldins, another obstacle. Look at the challenge and be calm. Calm.* Finally Gyll checked the view of the transmitter, made sure that the impression was one he wished d'Embry to see. He nodded to his camera-self in the monitor: a gray-haired, rather thin and chiseled head inclined in answer.

Not bad. Ascetic, but not too stern. "Fischer," he said aloud.

"Yes, Sula?"

"I'm ready now."

The holotank seethed with aquamarine interference, then cleared. For a moment Gyll and d'Embry stared at one another, looking for the changes wrought by nearly a decade. D'Embry was still thin, still tinted at earlobes and eyelids and mouth with the bodytints (a vivid scarlet, this time) that had gone out of fashion well before Gyll ever left Neweden. She'd acquired, somehow, a dowager's hump: it took a moment before Gyll realized that the bulge behind her shoulders was a symbiote. She was in ill health, then. The symbiote would have taken over most of the automatic functions of the body, its well-being dependent on hers; the symbiotes were stupid creatures, but possessed of a high instinct for self-preservation. Gyll wondered what it would be like—the bloodroot lancing her spine and connecting her to the parasite, always feeling just below the surface of her thoughts the presence of the creature. He'd seen symbiotes before, knew what they could do medically, but the sluglike appearance had always made him shiver with distaste. If he had to choose between the parasite and death, he wasn't sure the symbiote would be his choice. He didn't envy d'Embry her decision, and he wondered idly how Neweden reacted to the blatant evasion of Hag Death. *No, that's the old religions. Let them go, those gods infecting this world. And don't judge so quickly, fool. You've made choices you'd never thought you would make, when they became necessary.*

D'Embry had finished her own inspection of Gyll. She nodded as if what she saw confirmed her expectations. Her voice was as reedy as he'd remembered, but softer. "Ulthane Gyll," she said.

He knew, he *knew* that she used his shorn title deliberately to goad him. He tried to control his expression, but the words jabbed inside. He'd walled up the pain of the day he'd left this world and Mondom and the Hoorka, all his past, but the old title gouged a hole in that wall. It hurt.

Helgin was right. He was beginning to remember why he disliked the woman. "You told me so," he muttered.

"Hmmm?"

"Nothing. Regent. And I'm *not* Ulthane Gyll," he said carefully. *Tread lightly, and don't show anger—she may only want an excuse to rescind the trade agreement.* "'Trader,' perhaps. Or 'Sula.' That's my title among the Families." *The bitch knows it damned well, too. That was the way I signed the request for* Goshawk *to enter Neweden orbit.*

D'Embry smiled. It was a slow, surface movement of the lips and nothing else. Her voice was slow as well, careful. She seemed tired. "My apologies, Sula. My seneschal—not merely an aide, mind you; he's to be my eventual replacement as regent..." She hesitated an instant, the faintest hint of a scowl crossing her mouth. Gyll wondered what in that last statement irritated her so, and how he might use it. Then she took a breath and continued. "...told me that you'd prefer 'Sula,' but we ancients sometimes slip into old habits."

The self-mockery was unlike her. Gyll began to see that there had been changes in her beyond the mere physical. "The apology is unnecessary, Regent."

"I give it to you anyway. You've changed, Sula, but not as much as I might have thought. Grayer, thinner, but you look healthy and fit. Better than when you were Hoorka-thane."

Again, the chipping at the wall. "Thank you, Regent.

14

The life with Family Oldin is better for me than Neweden was. You've changed also, m'Dame."

When he said nothing more, her smile became genuine for the first time. The heavy-lidded eyes brightened, and she nodded. "And you aren't about to say whether it's for the better or worse. Good, a point to you. You've gotten other things than health from the Oldins, it would seem. And you needn't be so superficially polite. I know all too well how I look. I know what the symbiote does for my figure." She half-turned in her seat, so that he could see the ridge trailing halfway down her back. "It's not been a good time for me, but I'd advise you not to mistake physical frailty for anything else."

"I wouldn't make that blunder with you, Regent."

"That's intelligent of you." She sat back in her floater with a sigh. A thick-veined hand came up to brush at dry, wispy hair. "When I received your request to enter Neweden space, I was sorely tempted to refuse it. My seneschal— Sirrah Santos McClannan—was adamant about doing so. Were he in my place, you'd be off to Longago or some other world with your cargo. He may even be right. The Trading Families have brought nothing but trouble, in my experience."

"We sometimes bring benefits, as well."

"What? Devices that glow and sing, all bound with promises of health and well-being, but which do nothing?"

"You have a symbiote sharing your blood, Regent. That came from the Families. Two decades ago, the Family MacGuire brought them to Niffleheim."

She hadn't known that—Gyll could see it in the deepening of the creases between her eyes. Then she shrugged. "And I dislike the monster intensely. It's a parasite; it uses me, and I'm always aware of its presence. I'd almost rather have the bulky machinery and the tedious drugs, Sula, but my doctor insisted that the symbiote would be better. I'm not sure I can believe someone who's lived far less than me, but I let him convince me. Had I known who brought the symbiotes to the Alliance, I might have been less gullible." She paused, and closed her eyes for a moment. Gyll began to speak, but she cut him off in mid-word. "I gambled with the parasite, though. I'm gambling with you, as well."

"That's kind of you, Regent."

"It has nothing to do with kindness," she barked suddenly. The effort cost her. She coughed violently, a spasm that bent her over. Her body shook, racked, and the symbiote shivered beneath the glowcloth tunic. Then, still hunched over, she cleared her throat, dabbed at her mouth with a tissue. Slowly she sat up again. Her gaze was angry, as if she dared him to comment on her weakness. "I know you damned Traders, and especially the Oldins. You'd have started spouting the fine clauses of the Alliance-Families Pact, then cried 'foul' to Niffleheim Center. You'd've caused me more trouble than I want to think about, and in the end I still might have had to endure your presence. I'm a realist, *Sula*." She put more emphasis on the title than was needed. "I don't believe in giving myself the aggravation, not at my age, not in my situation. You're here, and that's bad enough. But I can deal with you."

"Regent—"

"No, please indulge me. I don't know why you've come back to Neweden. I'd like to think that it was merely to see your old homeworld again, but I don't believe that. You're with the Oldins, and they don't work that way. I *do* know that I won't tolerate disruption here. There's enough of it already, with Renard and his Hag's Legion. This isn't the same Neweden you left. Be very careful, *Sula*." Again, that strange inflection, as if d'Embry mocked him.

She allowed Gyll no chance to retort. With a harsh gesture, she broke the contact. The holotank swirled with jagged color, then collapsed into darkness. With the dimming of the room, the globe of Neweden pulled at Gyll's attention. He contemplated it for a long time in reverie, leaning back in his floater. He shook his head.

"Welcome home," he told himself.

16

2

The Li-Gallant Vingi's office was as Gyll remembered it: large, shaped so as to channel the eye to the Li-Gallant's desk and the massive floater behind it, the walls crawling with ambulatory colors of mobile tapestries. Ostentatious, and too rich for the world. The expansive window to one side gave a view of the keep's gardens, a landscape of topiaries and intricate beds of flowers. The grounds were a buffer separating the Li-Gallant from the tiresome sight of his lessers, a vista of fertile soil, none of the products of which were at all anything but decorative.

A waste on a world where people sometimes starved.

The Li-Gallant reminded Gyll of those gardens. Bloated like a puffindle, and ornamental. Flesh, only thinly concealed, hung from his ponderous frame. His body shook with each movement; he wheezed, his chin was trebled. Rings adorned each of his thick fingers, his manicure was immaculate. The eyes, small and almost lost, were clear and alert, and the tiny mouth was set in what might have been a smile, might have been a smirk.

The Li-Gallant didn't rise from his floater behind the desk as he would have been compelled to do if Gyll had been guilded kin—as he had done before when Gyll was kin-lord of the Hoorka. Vingi remained seated, hands steepled just below his mouth. "My secretary gave your title as 'Sula,' Sirrah Hermond. Is that correct?" Vingi asked the question without preliminaries, without the amenities that, on Neweden, marked the beginning of a conversation between equals. It was, Gyll realized, another small statement. Not quite insult, not quite blatant enough to give cause (to another Newedener) for bloodfeud, but fixing the parameters and giving notice to Gyll of his status.

As familiar as he was with the tactic, a spark of anger began to grow inside Gyll. *As antagonistic, as predictable as*

17

ever, the Li-Gallant. The man has damned few attacks, but he's not loath to use them. "The title's correct, Li-Gallant," Gyll answered. "It marks me as head of the Oldin military arm." Gyll smiled back at the Li-Gallant and, with a trace of satisfaction he could not help feeling, pulled a floater from near the wall and sat without invitation before Vingi's desk. He crossed his legs, laced his fingers around his knee.

The Li-Gallant's reaction was pleasing. Gyll knew what buttons to push in this society—it was one of the few advantages of living in a static and formalized system; emotions were easier to manipulate. Vingi's face reddened, his flabby arms pushed his bulk back from the desk, the mouth began to open. Gyll, still in his relaxed pose, shook his head into the beginning threat. "Li-Gallant, remember who I am and what I do. And who I was. We're both past our physical primes, but I've kept in training. No matter how fast you think you can call your guards, you'd be dead before they arrived. I've made that threat here before to you, Li-Gallant. You know I meant it then. Do you want to take the chance that I'm bluffing now?"

Gyll spoke blandly, slowly, while Vingi stared. The Li-Gallant's hands made a short convulsive movement. He swallowed. Then he sat back once more and pulled his floater to the desk. He smiled a predatory smile.

"You still know the Neweden mentality, Sula, but you speak like an offworlder. No guilded kin would be that blunt, not to me."

"I'm not guilded kin."

"True. You're lassari, unguilded. I remember Thane Mondom appearing in council to announce your ouster from the ranks of kin. She spat on the floor when she spoke your name." A pause. "She seemed very angry."

"She had reason to be," Gyll replied. *He's trying to provoke his own reactions, searching for a weakness to exploit. Don't let him see it.* "Li-Gallant, let's start over again. I think we can both respect one another's positions, even if we're no longer part of the same culture. You're much more intelligent than you pretend to be at times; you know as well as I that Neweden's ways are not the ways of the rest of humanity."

Vingi nodded. He twisted a ring around a finger, watching

reflected light flare in the gemstone. "And that was spoken like the Oldin woman, not the old Hoorka-thane. Which are you, Sula: kin or trader?"

"Both," Gyll said. "And neither. But more trader than kin. I've renounced citizenship in the Alliance, and Thane Mondom left me no alternative but to leave Hoorka. I'm of the Family Oldin, Li-Gallant. They have my allegiance."

Vingi seemed not to have heard Gyll's reply. He was still staring at his ring, as if lost in the facets of the stone. "I use the Hoorka quite a bit, Sula. I've heard it whispered that the lassari consider your old assassins to be my hirelings, my own elite guard. And of course that feeling has its roots back when you were Thane, when you failed twice to kill my rival Gunnar on my contracts—the guilded kin thought then that you'd allied yourself with Gunnar. When Gunnar was killed in a cowardly murder, *then* they thought I'd finally paid you enough to join with me. Now your Thane Mondom fights against the image, trying to prove that the Hoorka are indeed neutral, but it's more and more difficult, since the Hoorka are poor, except when *I* furnish them funds via contracts."

"I've heard those rumors as well, Li-Gallant. The part of me that was kin hates them." *He's still looking for your sore points—tell him some of the truth, but not all of it.*

"You hate it, neh? And do you intend to do something about it? I wouldn't like opposition, Sula." His tone was almost jovial as he said the words.

Gyll said nothing for a moment. He wondered if it would be this way for the rest of his stay on Neweden. First d'Embry, now the Li-Gallant. *Always chipping at the wall, always trying to provoke a reaction, always trying to hurt.* "That's all past, Li-Gallant. History. One can't change that."

"Well, Sula, because of Hoorka's history, the guilded kin view your old assassins with much suspicion; because of the whispers that Hoorka—under your direction as well as Mondom's—from time to time ignored the code of neutrality you built for them, has led to a decline in their status and wealth. They may be feared; they're no longer respected."

"As I said, Li-Gallant, my loyalty is now to the Oldins, not the guild Hoorka. Not anymore."

"Not even though they're your own creation?"

Despite himself, Gyll felt irritation roughen his voice,

pull his mouth into a frown. "Li-Gallant, if I felt that Hoorka were a corruption of all that I'd set out to create with them, I'd be happy to destroy the guild, or let them be destroyed by you. I don't know that such is the case—I haven't been on Neweden for some standards, and I haven't kept in contact with Hoorka." He'd unlaced his fingers and put both feet on the floor, leaning forward slightly from the waist. *Fool, you're giving yourself away. You're showing him just how much you are interested in Hoorka, in Neweden.* He made an effort to calm himself, to put his back against the floater's cushions.

The Li-Gallant looked pleased with himself. "So you've returned to meddle in Neweden's affairs."

Calm. Gyll made himself smile. "No. The Family Oldin survives by selling our goods, and I know Neweden. I came to see you because it's only good policy to speak with those in charge of the worlds we service—it smooths potential problems. Kaethe Oldin told me of the, ahh, arrangements she made while she was here. I'm prepared to double that fee—and the exact amount of the stipend will not be disclosed to the council. Your guild, and you as kin-lord, will be the prime benefactors."

That had been Kaethe's suggestion. She'd gauged the man well. The Li-Gallant's eyebrows rose slightly, the lips pursed, contemplative. He made no attempt to conceal his satisfaction. His greed was almost palpable. *That bastard's more avaricious than you'd imagine, Gyll. I knew him better than you in that sense, and his drive for wealth overrides the rest. That's the key to him.*

"When Kaethe Oldin was here," Vingi said, "she sold me an alien trinket: the Battier Radiance. It's broken."

"And it will be repaired without charge," Gyll replied. "The Family Oldin honors their commitments, Li-Gallant. If you recall, it wasn't by choice that we left here last time."

"Nor will it be this time, neh?"

Gyll shrugged. Vingi laughed.

"Ah, well. The Oldins brought me luck—I rule Neweden unhampered now, Sula, except for a few paltry groups of malcontents, and I have the Hoorka to take care of them, neh?" He laughed again. Gyll smiled, hoping that he looked convincing. He didn't enjoy deceit, wasn't particularly good at it when he tried, no matter what d'Embry might think he'd learned from the Oldins. Kaethe used to laugh when he tried to hide anything from her—*Gods, you're so transparent, Gyll,* she'd said. It took all of his effort not to rise and leave this corpulent vulture. The thought of Helgin's mocking taunts stopped him more than the surety of FitzEvard Oldin's displeasure.

"Fix the Battier, Sula, and have the funds you've spoken of transferred to my account. My secretary can handle the arrangements." Vingi shifted position in his floater as if restless. Gyll, taking that as a sign that the interview was at an end, rose. The Li-Gallant's gaze stayed with him, speculative. Gyll inclined his head. "Yah, Li-Gallant?"

"I'm not given to intrigue and circumspection, Sula. You know me well enough to expect bluntness. In fact, you probably consider me too direct, too readable. To an extent, you're right. I'm not overly devious. Even my enemies give me credit for that." Pause. The Li-Gallant put his fingertips together under the swell of chins. Reflections stuttered on his rings, shivered on the walls. "Why are you really here, Hermond? I'm not a fool. You're a hell of a lousy salesman— Kaethe Oldin had a much better patter and was better-looking, as well. You're too dour and agreeable. I doubt that you're on Neweden entirely to sell Trader junk. Why, then?"

"You're mistaken, Li-Gallant."

"You're the Sula, head of the military, by your own admission. Why send *you* on a simple trading mission?"

"You misunderstand the structure of the Families. Yah, I'm Sula, but the Families don't segregate along occupational lines as strictly as we"—Gyll smiled at his unintentional slip—"as *you* here on Neweden. There are no guilds as we know them. Everyone, even the soldiers, even the leaders such as FitzEvard, take their turns on the ships. I was sent to Neweden because I knew the planet, knew the society. And, as FitzEvard told me, there's not a whole lot for me to foul up here."

"That was almost plausible, Sula." Vingi nodded. "It was even fairly well said, well rehearsed. But Kaethe Oldin hinted to me of plans that the Family Oldin had for Neweden, and she said that I might well fit into them."

"Then she's neglected to tell me of them. I seek only trading opportunities, Li-Gallant."

"I think not."

21

"Li-Gallant, all I can say is that the Family Oldin finds Neweden quite satisfactory. For trade. Or they wouldn't have sent me here."

Gyll smiled at the Li-Gallant and bowed in salutation—the bow of equals, of kin. Vingi slowly rose, with a groan of exertion. He stared at Gyll, measuring him for a long moment, then returned the bow.

"You *will* keep me informed of your progress here, Sula. And we'll talk further, I'm sure." There was no interrogative in his voice.

"Certainly, Li-Gallant. I can assure you that you stand very high in the estimation of Family Oldin."

"As you are in mine, Sula. Just remember who it is that controls this world."

The Regent d'Embry wished that Santos McClannan would shut up. Too many things about her seneschal annoyed her. His voice was mellifluous and pleasant—that annoyed her. He was handsome in a superficial, cosmetic manner despite (she told herself that she wasn't simply being petty) an odd asymmetry to his long face. That annoyed her as well. He was efficient, if somewhat prone to overstepping his limits of authority, and he was invariably polite, no matter what he was saying to her.

That annoyed her most of all.

"I know it's not my place to criticize, Regent, but I think you're going to find that allowing the Traders, *especially* the Family Oldin, back on Neweden was a tragic mistake." McClannan had been staring out the window toward the port, where a *Goshawk* shuttle was unloading cargo. Now he turned back to d'Embry, a smile of inoffensive apology touching the corners of his full lips. She returned the smile—if he wanted to play the game of excessive politeness, let him; she wasn't inexpert herself—and sipped from the cup of mocha on her desk. The dark liquid shivered with the involuntary tremor of her hand. She wished she could lean back in the floater, but the chair's back was high and contacted the hump of the symbiote. She was afraid of hurting it, fearful that she might dislodge the bloodroot despite the doctor's assurance that the symbiote was quite unfragile.

"There's the slight problem of legality," she answered.

Her voice was soft; she didn't seem to have the energy to speak more forcefully anymore. "By the Alliance-Families Pact, the only captain I can refuse is Kaethe Oldin. Not unless I have due cause."

McClannan's smile widened, showing white and perfect teeth. He sat on the edge of her desk—another annoyance—and beamed down at her. "Ahh, but that's an easy thing to acquire, that due cause. We both know that—a little money spread in the right places, a violation of the Pact swiftly enters the records, and this Sula Hermond is gone. And so are our troubles."

"But it still wouldn't be right, and it wouldn't be that easy, despite all your assurances. The Li-Gallant, for one, would scream in rage. I know that the Oldins bribe him with a percentage of their profits, and FitzEvard would never allow Sula Hermond to leave until every legal and illegal channel had been pursued. We'd only give ourselves more aggravation." She looked at him, blinked slowly. "There *are* chairs in the room, Seneschal."

"Pardon me, Regent." He stood slowly, seemed to hesitate, then extruded a hump-chair from the floor. He sat again, crossing his legs. Over steepled hands, he regarded her. "M'Dame, what's better, pragmatically? To follow the regulations blindly, or, by a bit of selective blindness, avoid larger potentials for trouble? The Oldins are interfering bastards. Despite the Pact, they stick their noses in the politics of every world they visit. They undermine our influence, subvert the locals, and do us no good whatsoever."

"Damn it, McClannan, *I* know the Oldins better than anyone!" D'Embry's breathing stuttered with her outburst. The symbiote squirmed on her back in response. She covered her discomfort by picking up her cup and pretending to study the contrast of her fingers (tinted lime green today) against the delicate porcelain. "And are such quasi-legal questions the things they ask in the Academy nowadays? Seneschal, I know the Oldins, and, believe me, you underestimate them."

"Yet you've allowed them to return." McClannan shook his handsome head carefully, his hair staying delicately in place. "When the Oldins came here last, they helped the Hoorka assassins kill a head official of Moache Mining. Gunnar, Vingi's rival, was killed, and Vingi was able to seize dictatorial powers. The lassari organized under the unknown person Renard—whom we still haven't captured—and lassari attacks on the guilded kin increased tenfold." He continued to gaze at her, still without much expression, as if talking to himself. She sniffed, set the cup down, and tapped her fingers near the switch for her com-unit, hoping he would take the hint.

He didn't. "Niffleheim Center had to explain to Moache Mining why nothing was done to catch the persons responsible for slaying their man, and this whole planet's social system was rocked. It's still rocking. You were nearly removed from this post. You had to call in every last political favor you've earned over the decades to keep this regency—and if the Legat Gioneferra weren't your friend, it *still* wouldn't have been enough. I *know* that, Regent. You were the talk of Niffleheim that standard. Now tell me about legalities, about why we should let Sula Hermond and the Oldins back here."

He looked as nearly smug as he ever allowed himself to look.

"There are these things called ideals, Seneschal. Did you talk about them in between gossiping about me?" She really did not feel well. She told herself that it was the company and not just her body. "I pledged myself to follow the laws of the Alliance because I felt that, even if not perfect, they were for the most part just. I don't intend to follow that oath only when it's convenient for me, nor do I think myself wise enough to alter the laws I follow because I might not be comfortable with the results. Now, that's an old woman talking, mind you; I haven't your sophistication or education, Santos. But I *am* Regent. As long as I am, we'll do things according to my wishes."

"Some of your accomplishments are in the textbooks at the Academy, Regent; your work on Thule, for instance. But"—he smiled again, as d'Embry thought that, somehow, she'd known that particular word was coming—"everyone, even the best, can sometimes make a mistake in judgment."

"We should both remember that, shouldn't we?" She'd raised her voice to say that, and the weakness of her lungs betrayed her. She doubled over in a paroxysm of coughing. Dull, insistent pain throbbed in her stomach and chest, the symbiote moving uneasily. The attack subsided slowly. D'Embry reached for a tissue, spat into it and folded it in her fist, wishing she hadn't given in to anger. It made her look weak, feeding the pity she sensed McClannan felt for her.

"Have you heard from your daughter lately?" Had he said it in anything but the carefully neutral voice he used, she might have been provoked again, sensing in his indelicate change of subject a placation for an old used-up woman and a none-too-subtle suggestion that she should retire.

"No, I haven't," she replied tartly. And just as well. Every time, Anne would try to get her to come back to the estate on Aris, to give up the Diplos. The last time d'Embry had been to Aris, it had taken only a week of sitting, surrounded by four generations of offspring, to become bored and surly. Anne hadn't enjoyed the visit, nor had d'Embry. She wondered how Anne contrived to forget the horrors of each visit and invite her again.

"Aris is a beautiful world," McClannan ventured.

"They spent several fortunes taking everything dangerous or unsightly out of it."

"You have a lot to look forward to when you go there." The prodding in his voice almost made her laugh scornfully.

"It's an antiseptic, artificial place. It's like living in a museum with all the exhibits chosen by someone else. After the first enthusiasm wears off, it's dreadfully stultifying. I'm never comfortable there."

McClannan pursed his lips, almost—but not quite—looking disappointed. He shook his head slightly. "Have you ever told your daughter that?"

"Many times. Every visit." She felt a quick shudder of pain in her abdomen. She willed herself not to show it. The symbiote twitched; d'Embry felt a flooding of relief as it released some chemical of its own into her bloodstream. Her discomfort passed, but a faint fogginess remained, calming her but dulling her senses. She could not seem to care much about McClannan's slick criticisms. They still irritated her, but she didn't want to do anything about them. *Damn it, you parasite! Don't do this to me. Leave me my feelings even if it means pain.* "You'd like Anne," she said. "She resembles you. She listens to what's told her, then selectively ignores what she doesn't want to hear."

It pleased her to see a hint of peevishness in McClannan.

His fingers tightened, a faint redness touched his cheeks, and his lips pressed together, whitening. Another time, that would have been enough to make her feel childishly gleeful at having broken his facade. But this victory wasn't as sweet as it should be. She couldn't summon enough energy to care.

"Well, Regent, I really didn't think I had much chance of persuading you to change your mind, and I see you're in a bit of pain today. I doubt that you want to be bothered with Neweden affairs or idle chatter."

Meaning that I ignore my responsibilities as Regent, you son of a bitch. Even as she thought it, the lethargy slid back over her, making everything seem distant. She fought the tiredness, forced herself to smile.

"I probably shouldn't be bothered with useless and stupid second thoughts on decisions already made," she said. She waited a moment, watching the flash of anger behind his eyes. "Let me get some work done here, Seneschal. I'm sure you have duties to attend to as well. Duties other than mine."

He rose primly and bowed slightly to her. "Always, Regent, always. If I can help you, though, please let me know. I won't hide what I feel—I believe that you've made a mistake in this. Sula Hermond is an enemy of the Alliance, as are all the Oldins."

"I knew the Sula when he was Thane of the Hoorka, Seneschal. He might have been proud, arrogant, and stubbornly blind, but he was a man whose word you could trust. He tells me he's only here to trade."

"He's been eight standards with the Oldins. What if he's changed, or what if they're using him as a dupe? I saw the record of your talk with him—I don't like the man, Regent."

"I wouldn't think you would, Seneschal. Sula Hermond speaks his mind freely, without guile, and I've always found that he keeps to the spirit, not just the letter, of his own morals." She stared at him, he looked steadily back. "We disagree on most things, the Sula and I, but I find that I like the man."

"Then I pray that you don't discover your affection for him to be your downfall, Regent."

"I'll manage, Seneschal," she said.

"I'm certain you will," he replied, with absolutely no conviction in his voice. "Are you certain you don't wish me to pursue this further? A thorough check of a ship's log inevitably unearths some discrepancy..."

"I think you know my answer."

McClannan nodded. He strolled leisurely to the door, stroking the replica of a d'Vellia soundsculpture as he went by—it moaned in the wind of his passage. He waited patiently for the door to open. He went through.

D'Embry sighed, leaning back gingerly in her floater. She closed her eyes. After a few minutes, her breathing deepened and became more regular. The head lolled back.

She slept.

He'd taken a flitter from Sterka Port to Vingi's keep. Stepping from the gate of Vingi's grounds into the overcast day, Gyll indulged a whim. He waved away the flitter's pilot, deciding impulsively to walk and see Sterka again.

For the most part, the city seemed the same: cluttered, narrow streets made for pedestrian traffic and not groundcars, rich and poor dwellings separated only by a street of small shops, residences and businesses mixed hodgepodge. Chaotic. It brought a smile to his face, born of memory and amusement at what he now saw as archaic and haphazard planning. Sterka was nothing like the sleek and clean lines of OldinHome, the ordered beauty of the buildings and parks there. The scenes gave him hope that he could accomplish his mission on Neweden, the true reason that he'd kept from d'Embry.

He would take Hoorka away from Neweden, away from the Alliance. He would lead them again, under the Oldin flag.

(And as he walked, something nagged at him, some vague feeling of unease, a prickling at the back of his neck: *danger*. He stopped, turning this way and that, but he could see nothing out of the ordinary. Just a street crowded with people, that was all; a noisy conglomeration, most of whom seemed to be kin intent on their own thoughts. Gyll continued walking.)

He'd badgered and cajoled Grandsire FitzEvard, telling the wily old man that he could not give the Oldins a viable military force without a nucleus of trained people—his own old kin. Oldin wanted them too fast to start from scratch.

27

Oh, yes, the Trader-Hoorka he had already were good people, but the Neweden Hoorka would serve as a larger training force, and the work would go that much faster. Let me go back to Neweden, Gyll had said. Let me go back and get them.

It had taken time and much argument, but FitzEvard, under pressure from Gyll, Helgin, and Kaethe Oldin—Gyll's lover and FitzEvard's granddaughter—had at last relented. Kaethe was banned; she could not go, but Gyll and Helgin would return to Neweden. FitzEvard had even smiled when he told them. Gyll would be in charge of the ship, and it would operate as any Oldin trading mission—except that Gyll would seek to recruit his old guild as well.

Gyll knew what he had to offer—far, far more than squalid Neweden, the world Gyll had once thought as all. Far more than the Alliance offered. Gyll could see now why all the Trading Families disliked the Alliance. If the Alliance died, Gyll would not grieve. If what Gyll did here helped to negate its influence, he would be pleased.

Gyll had found several truths about himself in the time since he'd left Neweden. Paramount among them was that he enjoyed being a leader. *The* leader, the one who commanded, who created. He'd given that up when the guild of Hoorka had faced political problems on Neweden, when it seemed that he had dealt with them poorly—and he had found that he was bored and restless, and that he could not keep his hands away from the reins of leadership. That had led to his conflict with Mondom, to whom he'd given the Thane-ship. It had driven them apart, driven Gyll from his kin, and the troubles of Neweden had given the Hoorka less and less work.

He would amend that all now, if he could.

He could not change Neweden, but he could change Hoorka. It would have to be slow, have to be careful, but he was confident. He was Sula now, not Thane, and the title suited him better.

If d'Embry knew, *Goshawk* would swiftly be seeking some other port. Meddling, she would call it, interference with Alliance business. Gyll did not enjoy lying, but he was slowly finding that it was sometimes necessary. If he had to lie to get Hoorka, he would do it.

As he walked, Gyll let the impressions soak into him, comparing them with remembrances of standards past. He strolled slowly (though the small uneasiness he had felt earlier would not go away), observing. It seemed to Gyll that it was the people as well as the city that had changed. Yes, much was still similar: lassari still drew back from him, as they were supposed to do, the guilded kin nodded politely even as they stared at his clothing and the strange emblem on his belt where the holo of the guild insignia should have been. It seemed that there were perhaps more lassari now, more low kin whose shabby clothing proclaimed the poorness of their guild. And the churches—Neweden had always been haunted by piety and a multitude of gods from which to choose; that trait seemed to have become more pronounced in the time he'd been gone. Neweden was, as the scholar Cranmer had written, "surprisingly rich in gods for a damned poor place; it must be the cheap rent." Gyll was most surprised at the number dedicated to She of the Five Limbs, goddess of the extinct ippicators and also patron of the Hoorka. It seemed that a cult had sprung up around Her. Whatever, every block he walked had its church, of one god or another.

Gyll could only speculate on what that might mean, whether it was due to the solace provided by religion in bad times and the promise it gave of eventual reward, or because, by becoming a member of the clergy, a person became something between guilded kin and lassari. To become a minister of the gods had always been one way of improving your lot if you were lassari, and that was why the regulations regarding the establishment of churches were strict here: high taxes, an avalanche of paperwork, and a constant proof of a sufficient congregation.

He knew FitzEvard Oldin would be pleased either way. It meant that things were not all well on Neweden.

There was something odd in the way Gyll was regarded by those he passed, something subliminal. He could sense hostility from the lassari even as they stepped out of his direct path, and the guilded kin seemed wary rather than strictly polite. Twice, he saw the green-robed Magistrates of Justice judging a duel, a crowd gathered around the conflict— that had always been a rare scene when he'd last been here.

And though kin had always gone armed on the street, the weapons were now more prominent, placed boldly at the hip as if in defiance and challenge. Guild-kin walked together in bands, as well, traveling with companions rather than alone. The sense of worry came back to him, stronger now. He stopped and glanced behind him: guilded kin went in and out of the door of a bakery, a pack of jussar youths lolled against a wall, two women argued prices with a vendor of sweetmeats, a group of kin (the Sterka Jewelers' Guild, by their buckles) scowled their way around the obstacle of his body. Nothing there to feed his paranoia. Gyll shrugged and continued his aimless strolling.

A building he did not remember blocked his path. He turned left, found that the street died after a few blocks, forcing him to go right, down an alley to another street. He knew where he was, roughly if not precisely; somewhere on the edges of Dasta Burrough, one of the lassari sectors. Gyll didn't care for the sights or the smells, and that nagging feeling of being pursued still insinuated itself. The street was less crowded now. He stepped around a sated wirehead sprawled near the central gutter, moved into shadow and out again, now making his way up a series of wide steps. He kept his hand near his dagger even as he cursed his uneasiness, then justified it by recalling what he had taught his new Hoorka. *To an extent, fear is good. Only a fool is truly unafraid, and fools tend to die quickly in a crisis. Don't allow fear to cripple you or make you change your tactics, but don't shut it out, either. Listen to it.*

He turned left at a crossing street, then left again, trying to find his way back to the street of shops without admitting defeat and retracing his steps. He came to the mouth of an alley. The houses near him were empty and dark, ruinous, and the street was oddly deserted. Something about the scene, something in his fear and the net of shadows around him made him hesitate. Maybe the scent of rotting garbage and dampness welling from the alleyway: Gyll took a false step forward, waited, thinking that in a moment he would feel rather foolish.

The feint saved him.

A hand holding a crowd-prod stabbed air where he should have been—that first glimpse of the prod showed Gyll that the weapon had been altered, and the ugly blue-bronze scorch marks at the tip indicated that the alteration was likely to be deadly. Gyll caught sight of his attacker; a thin, sallow face, a gray bodysuit with a tear at one shoulder. The man took a quick step from the alley. A dagger held in the left hand followed the prod, slicing at Gyll. He sidestepped, feeling cloth tearing as the dagger's edge slid along his side; in the same motion, Gyll grasped the man's dagger hand at the wrist. He twisted, hard, and brought the hand down and his knee up. The weapon went clattering away as the man yelped in pain. Another lunge with the prod; Gyll went with the move, falling backward and bringing up his legs sharply into the man's midsection, propelling him back over Gyll's head. Gyll lurched to his feet, sliding his own dagger from its sheath, crouching, watching as his assailant groggily regained his footing. It took the man several seconds, but Gyll did not move toward him. He waited, breathing quickly but easily.

There was no guild holo on the man's buckle, no identifying insignia anywhere on him. The ripped bodysuit seemed to be plain dress available anywhere. "Back off now and this won't go further, lassari," Gyll said. "Think about it, man; if I'd wanted you dead, I had plenty of time."

The lassari grimaced, whether in pain or answer, Gyll could not tell. He shuffled his feet, his fingers loosening and tightening on the prod's handle. "You're bleeding, offworlder."

"Don't mistake a scratch for anything else."

The lassari straightened, the crowd-prod now held down at his side. He nearly smiled—the edges of his mouth curved upward. "You were almost Hag-kin. You're quicker than you look to be, old man."

"For a frigging coward who'd attack without warning, you don't move nearly as quickly as you need to. With your skills, you'll be Hag-kin yourself soon enough."

The smile vanished. Thin shoulders shrugged under frayed cloth. "Give me another chance, offworlder. I'll be glad to show you the ways of Neweden. A personal introduction to our gods, neh?" The man spat on the pavement between them. In another time, that would have sent Gyll into a rage: Neweden reflexes. Now it almost amused him, a futile, empty insult. It didn't touch him, didn't mean anything. "You're blocking my way, lassari," he said simply. "I'm not really interested in proving to you that I'm good with this blade, but I am. Very. It's your choice."

The lassari shifted weight from one foot to the other. He seemed to turn the decision over in his mind; thought twisted the narrow face into a mask, a snarl. Gyll braced himself, certain that he'd be attacked once more—*when you were Thane, you wouldn't have hesitated when the man was done. You'd have finished it, and not had to. worry.* He hoped the man would back down, was afraid he wouldn't. He had no real fear of the man—he was inept and clumsy—but he didn't want to begin his stay on Neweden with another death. He'd killed too many here already. On the bad nights, they crowded his sleep.

The lassari took a step away from Gyll. Then, as if that movement broke the stasis of confrontation, the man fled, turning and running. The sound of his flight echoed from the buildings.

Gyll straightened. The muscles of his back were sore, and he tried to convince himself that it was a result of the unaccustomed drag of Neweden's gravity that made him ache. He examined his side—the dagger had barely broken the skin, though now that the adrenaline surge was gone, he could feel the pain. He frowned. The dagger the lassari had lost was stuck halfway in a pile of garbage the wind had gathered against the curb. Gyll picked it up—a cheap thing, the blade filed from some stock metal, the hilt just tape over the bare steel. Rough, but effective enough; a lassari weapon like a thousand he'd seen before. Gyll stuck it in his belt. He began walking.

There were people around him before he'd gone two blocks. He mused on the attack. Once before, such a thing had happened after leaving the Li-Gallant. Coincidence? Gyll shrugged back the phantoms of speculation and looked about him. He could see the spire of Tri-Guild Church transfixing clouds. He moved toward it, ignoring the stares his torn, bloody tunic caused.

He wasn't really aware that he'd slipped back into the old Hoorka aloofness. It didn't matter what others might think: let them stare if it pleased them.

McWilms was noticeably bursting with some news. He smiled, his eyes danced, and though he feigned nonchalance by leaning up against the cool rock of Mondom's chambers in Underasgard, his body didn't seem to be at rest. His hands fidgeted with the clasp of his nightcloak, his boots scuffed the packed earth of the floor. Mondom, pushing the hoverlamp away from her desk, looked up at him with a quizzical smile.

"Fine, Jeriad. I'll bite. Has the Li-Gallant overpaid his last contract and not noticed? Or did Nisa finally agree to go to bed with you?"

"Gods, Thane, she did *that* weeks ago. You're not very observant." He laughed, and Mondom could not help but join his amusement. McWilms hadn't been smiling much in the past few days, since the death of d'Mannberg. He'd limped about the caverns in dour silence, keeping to himself, accepting solace from no one. She was glad to see the sorrow beginning to come to some proper perspective. Hag Death was a harsh god—She struck often here, and Dame Fate wouldn't interfere. Grief was good, a needed release, but she didn't care to see one of her best kin-brothers disabled by it.

"Weeks ago, was it?" she said. "Really? And was the reality better than the fantasy?—everyone saw you lusting after her."

He simply grinned. "I didn't come in here to tell you about my love life—but she didn't complain."

"That's hardly a tribute, simply discretion. So, what's got you so bouncy? Come, Jeriad, you can't wait to tell me—I see it in your eyes."

"Hah, you're just jealous because I got to Nisa first." McWilms shouldered himself from the wall and came over to the desk. He still favored his wounded leg. He picked up a crystalline ball with a piece of polished ivory set inside—an ippicator's bone—and hefted it from hand to hand. "The Trading Families have sent another ship here. It's in orbit, and their shuttle's docked at the port."

The depth of her reaction to his announcement shocked Mondom. The words brought back unwilled, unwelcome memories, none of them pleasant. She ran a hand through dark hair cropped close to her head and tried to keep her expression in some semblance of normalcy. *The frigging Families. I haven't thought of them for ages, haven't thought of what they did to Gyll and me.* She attempted a smile that felt tentative and false.

And which did not fool McWilms. His own buoyant satisfaction dissipated instantly. He frowned, set the ball down. "Thane, I'm sorry. Damn, I didn't think..."

She waved a deprecating hand. "Don't worry about it, Jeriad." She affected unconcern. "What about this Trader's ship? It's not the *Peregrine*, is it; Kaethe Oldin's craft?"

Suddenly she could see that he was reticent to continue. He slipped back into the hesitant lethargy that had followed the Vasella contract. It was more than simply Ric's death; all the Hoorka were experiencing it to some degree—the hardly veiled intimations that the Hoorka-kin were the Li-Gallant's minions in all but name was at the root of the depression. The other contracts with guilded kin had slowed. Vingi's name was on most of their work, and their treasury was pitifully low. The fact that their code of neutrality—Gyll's code—forced them to these straits didn't reduce the gall. Mondom nodded to McWilms. Her dark eyes encouraged him. "Out with it, Jeriad. You were aglow with the news a moment ago. It can't be just the arrival of a Trader ship. What's the rest of it?"

"No, Thane." He gathered his nightcloak around him as if the cool air of Underasgard chilled him. The cloak was bulky around the bandages lacing his side. "And if I wasn't such a damned idiot, I'd've realized how you'd feel about it."

He grimaced and sat on the edge of the desk.

"You going to tell me or just keep going around it awhile longer?" She smiled again; slow, gentle. "I don't have all day, Jeriad. And I'm a big girl. What are you holding back?"

He sighed. "Yah. Well, I thought it was interesting enough that the Family Oldin owns the ship. Not *Peregrine*, though. *Goshawk*. When I heard, I checked with Diplo Center, and learned two more interesting items about the ship. First, there are paramilitary people aboard her, ostensibly the ship's guard. At least that's the rumor."

"I doubt that's so unusual. The Families don't trust the Alliance. They'd keep their own guards."

He didn't look at her. He examined his hands closely. "They call themselves Hoorka, these guards," he said.

McWilms heard the intake of breath, but when he looked at Mondom, her face was emotionless. She returned his gaze flatly, with little emotion in her voice. "That's indeed one interesting item, kin-brother. What's two?"

He took a breath, looking away from her again. "Ulthane Gyll is in charge of the ship. He calls himself Sula now, but it has to be the same person—Gyll Hermond."

Mondom looked down at her desktop, feeling McWilms's gaze on her again. She fiddled with an acousidot holder and sat back in her floater. She looked up at him from under her eyebrows. Her eyes had an unusual sheen. "Damn," she said huskily. "He's back."

"I thought," McWilms ventured, "that maybe you'd be glad to hear that."

"Hag's *teats*, Jeriad!" Mondom slapped the desk with an open hand. "I had to strip him of his kinship when he left. He didn't leave me any choice. Why should I be happy to see him again?" Abruptly she laughed, a quick breath, and glanced at McWilms bemusedly. "I'm a fine example to you, neh, losing my temper like that. I'm sorry, Jeriad. I guess I wasn't ready for it."

"I understand. And I didn't bother to think about how you might feel. I'll take half of the blame, anyway—easier to share it, neh?"

Mondom smiled at him, and phrased a question even as her lips turned down again. "Are *you* glad he's returned?"

"He created Hoorka, even if he later left us. And he was always fair with me. He taught us all a lot, and I'm grateful for that at least."

"But do you want him back?"

McWilms shrugged. "It's not my decision, is it?"

"He'll cause trouble, that's all." Then she laughed once more, fully this time. "Listen to me, talking about my old lover as if he were an enemy, as if he weren't once kin." She shook her head. "Leave me alone for a while, will you, Jeriad? I want to think about this, so I won't be so startled when someone brings it up next time."

"Whatever you wish, Thane." McWilms rose. His nightcloak fell around him, swirling. "I have to do the blood-duty for Ric, anyway." He faltered a little on the last words. He swallowed too hard. Mondom looked up at him.

"We all miss Ric, Jeriad."

"Yah." Sharp, quick. "It's the damned Li-Gallant and his

contracts. He enjoys making us appear to be his hirelings. Ric hated that."

"He feeds the Hoorka. How many other contracts do we get?"

"He makes us look like his lackeys. Ulthane Gyll hated Vingi."

"Enough, Jeriad," Mondom said warningly. She softened her tone. "Do the blood-duty for your kin-father." She stared at him, at the shadows the hoverlamp threw on his lean face. "If you're not too busy with Nisa, would you want to keep your Thane company tonight? I know it's been some time, but I ..." She stopped, wondering why she felt that she had to explain it to him.

"Yah," he said before she could speak again. "I'd like that."

"You're sure you're well enough?"

"If you don't mind a slow lover." He indicated his chest, his leg. "I can't support myself very well."

"A slow lover sounds preferable, and there are ways around having to have you support yourself." She rubbed at the back of her neck, smiling faintly, stretching in her floater. "Thank you, Jeriad."

"You don't have to thank me. I don't expect the pleasure to be quite that one-sided."

His grin made her laugh despite herself. "Get out of here."

She was still smiling when the door slid shut behind him. Slowly the smile slid into frown. She closed her eyes, forehead propped on hand.

"Damn that man," she whispered. "He would come back."

Helgin glared at Gyll from under thick-ridged brows. Pupils shot with yellow regarded the Sula, taking in the grimy pants, the slashed tunic, the stain of dried blood at his side. "For a person with a hole in him," the dwarf growled, "you're damned cheerful."

"Just a scratch, Motsognir. You've given me worse in practice." Gyll glanced back at the prickly skyline of Sterka. Around them, the port was busy in a thin drizzle. A tram clattered past full of trader goods from the hold of their shuttle. "How's business?"

"That's what you're supposed to be worrying about, rather than looking for ways to kill yourself." Gyll started to speak, but Helgin interrupted. "I know. We've received an invitation to a costume ball, and you're going as a corpse."

"Helgin . . ."

"Business is well enough, I suppose." Helgin squatted on the tarmac in the shadow of their craft. Rain was spotting the pavement around them. "Is the Li-Gallant responsible for the scratch, or did you just stumble into thornbushes?"

"You don't give me enough options. It was a lassari attack."

Helgin raised his eyebrows in mock surprise. "A damned strange thing to have happen, your first day back here." The dwarf picked a pebble loose from the field, flicked it away with a stubby forefinger. "Of course, it's probably just coincidence—they *do* have a god here for coincidences, don't they?"

"Don't make more of it than it is, Helgin." By his tone, it was obvious that Gyll didn't care to elaborate on the incident any further. Helgin chuckled.

"Which means that you're worried about it, too." The roar of his amusement was blunted by the shriek of a transport leaving the field. Helgin raised his voice to carry over the tumult, shouting. "Face it, Gyll. Neweden's not going to look upon you with a friendly eye; not the Regent, not Vingi, not your precious Hoorka-kin. Nobody. All those too many gods you have here are going to be pissing their bedsheets, worried about what you mean to do here. They ain't gonna like you." The Motsognir chuckled again as a frown deepened the lines of Gyll's face.

"I don't particularly like the idea, either, Helgin."

"But you're willing to go along with it because you know that Oldin, despite his personality flaws, is right."

"I suppose."

"Then sharpen your knives, Sula." Helgin spat on the ground. He stared at the result critically. "You're gonna need 'em."

3

The light of Gulltopp, like some silvered liquid, flowed over the figure of a man moving in the forest near Underasgard. The nocturnal creatures were making their nightly chorus of chirps and howls; the intruder added little noise to the concert. He moved swiftly, quietly, sure of his ground. He halted once near the end of the broadleaves. Staying to the whispering darkness of the shade, he peered into a clearing beyond. There, a tall, slender column of stone stabbed the sky, a cluster of glass-eyed receptors at its summit: the dawnrock of the Hoorka assassins, the announcer of life and death. Beyond the dawnrock, the opening of Underasgard loomed like a gaping mouth half-hidden in a fold of hills. From the darkness of the caves, he could sense watchfulness, eyes regarding the night. The man crouched under the broadleaves for long minutes, breathing softly, staring at the maw of Underasgard, rubbing a pliant leaf between thumb and forefinger. After a time, he let the leaf, torn and broken, fall to the ground. The faint scent of the foliage clung to his hand.

He stood, dappled with Gulltopp's brilliance. His clothing echoed the night, and a hood left his face in eternal shadow.

In time (always carefully, always with deliberate slowness), he moved to the western side of the clearing, staying just inside the cover of the trees. There, he spent a few minutes arranging a small pile of dead leaves and twigs, leaving it sitting inside a circle of bare earth. Turning his back to Underasgard, he puffed a thin cigar alight—he'd found them off-world; the tobacco addiction wasn't well-known on Neweden—and placed it carefully in the twigs. He took a small pouch from his belt and added a pinch of dark powder near the cigar. A thin coil of smoke was already curling upward. As carefully as before, he made his way back to the other side of

38

the clearing. Once more, he crouched, waiting. A ruddy light flickered among the trees where he'd left the cigar. It faded, then pulsed again before becoming a steady, wavering glow. He could smell the sweet smoke. He watched the entrance of Underasgard.

Someone stepped from the tumble of rocks into the clearing, wearing the black-and-gray nightcloak of the Hoorka. The man could hear the faint whine of an activated vibro; moonlight shuddered on the vibrowire. The Hoorka stared at the fire, turned and said something toward the cavern mouth, then ran quickly across the clearing into the broadleaves' shadow.

The man smiled, rising to his feet. Still in a half-crouch, he ran toward the entrance. He paused momentarily, in a listening attitude, then vaulted over a boulder into Underasgard.

The Hoorka on duty—an apprentice—reacted far too slowly. The intruder kicked aside a vibrofoil that, belatedly, the apprentice drew from its sheath. Unactivated, the hilt clattered away into darkness. A swift hand movement followed the kick, without delay, and the apprentice slumped, wobble-kneed. The intruder caught him, laid the boy down gently. His thin, gnarled hands pulled up an eyelid, felt the flutter of heart underneath the cloak. Then he stood. Under the cowl of his hood, his eyes stared, watching for movement in the twisting corridor leading back into the caves where the Hoorka lived.

Nothing. Empty, silent night lay there. With a glance back at the apprentice, he moved deeper into the Hoorka-lair.

Twice, he had to disable lone assassins walking the maze of tunnels; each time, luck was with him. He had no difficulty, and his attacks were as silent as he could have wished. He skirted the brilliance of the common room, with its sounds of many voices. Finally he came to a doorshield with the Hoorka-Thane's insignia set above it. He stood there a second, contemplative, as if suddenly unsure of himself. It was at odds with his previous demeanor.

And at that moment, the alarm sounded, a hooting ululation like Hag Death's wail. The intruder bounded into shadow—thankful that Underasgard was always shadowed—not waiting to see the woman that rushed from the Thane's room. Instead, he moved deeper into the labryinthian system of caves, away from the areas frequented by the assassins, away from the welling uproar.

He smiled, as if with some secret amusement.

"You're sure no one saw you?"

Helgin took off his cloak with a sweeping motion that stirred a small breeze in the dankness, and threw the garment into a corner of the room. He glared at the speaker and the two people sitting in shadow behind the man. "What do you take me for, Renard? When I don't care to be seen, I can be much more elusive than you—after all, who did Kaethe send to do her dirty work here? It wasn't you, was it? She knows your abilities."

Renard grimaced. His skin was the color of tea; he was stockily built, but rather tall. In the wan glow of a half-shuttered hoverlamp, the outline of his figure was indistinct, but Helgin could see the thorny spines and thick coil of a plant-pet around his shoulders. Renard stroked the thing as he talked.

"Keep your voice down, Motsognir."

"Are you worried, Renard?" The dwarf grinned lopsidedly at him. If anything, Helgin's voice was a trifle louder, raspy as always. It carried well. "I saw the people you had hidden outside. One on the roof across the street, another down the way pretending to be casually leaning from a window. Right? You need to teach them better, but they'll keep away any of Vingi's guards. And I lost the two others that trailed me from the port, lost them way back on the outskirts of Dasta."

"Vingi's people?" It was the woman behind Renard. She stepped up into the light. Helgin looked at her appreciatively—then decided she looked too serious.

"No," he said curtly. "Diplos. The Regent's lackeys."

He could see the relief pull at the woman's face. "Good."

"Don't deceive yourself, m'Dame. What the Diplos know, Vingi will eventually find out. He has a better intelligence network than you might think." Helgin turned back to Renard. "Do these two have to be here?"

"They're part of my cell."

"Tell them to wait outside."

Renard stared at the Motsognir, one hand idly petting

the beast around his neck, smoothing down the fleshy spines. Helgin looked back at him blandly, one hand on his hip. The tableau held; then Renard jerked his head in the direction of the door. "Micha, Alex. Please."

The two gave Helgin appraising glances as they passed him. The dwarf waited until the door had shut behind them, then went over, opened it again, glanced outside, and latched it. He pulled a chair from the side of the room to the table behind which Renard stood. He sat.

"How long have you been here this time, Renard?"

The man's eyes narrowed. "Three standards, almost. I was gone for nearly five. Why?"

"FitzEvard worries about his hirelings, that's all. Doesn't want them to become too involved in their work and forget who's ultimately the benefactor of all you've been doing."

"Are you making an accusation, or just noise? I don't frighten that easily, man."

Helgin's eyes widened in mock surprise. "Frighten you, Renard? Me try a silly tactic like that?"

"Just tell FitzEvard I haven't forgotten."

"I understand you lost Vasella."

Renard grimaced. His hand left off its stroking; a tremor ran the length of his living collar. "Yah, the damned Hoorka..."

Helgin shook his head in exaggerated sadness. "Now, you see, that's just the problem—you shouldn't let yourself get so perturbed. Your job is to see that the low kin and lassari stay angry. What's going to anger them more than losing a folk hero? You *want* Vingi to do exactly what he's doing. And you could certainly stand to have a martyr to play with, especially when it's not you."

"I understand that, Motsognir. You needn't lecture me. But I could have used Vasella—alive—awhile longer."

Helgin nodded into Renard's irritation. He crossed his legs underneath him on the seat. "The woman's your lover, or the man?"

"*Damn* you and your frigging useless questions!" Renard slapped the table; the plant-pet quivered. "Dwarf, did you come here deliberately to irritate me? I tell you—I know what I'm doing."

"I don't mean to irritate you, Renard. That's just my outgoing personality shining through my dour exterior. I came to find out how things are progressing for you here in the dregs of Neweden society. You haven't sent reports lately; FitzEvard's slightly curious. I can't say I really blame him, considering what he's paying you."

"I haven't had the time for paperwork." Renard didn't bother to disguise his growing anger. "Nor the chance. I can't very well send them by the legitimate routes, now can I? In any case, why should *you* be the one so concerned?—you've a Sula in charge of *Goshawk*."

Helgin frowned. He tugged at his beard. "The Sula Hermond doesn't know everything. He knows what FitzEvard Oldin wants him to know. He's not here for the same reasons you are." Helgin glanced critically at a hair plucked from his beard, then let it drop to the floor. "FitzEvard wants the reports to go only to me, not the Sula."

"So he's just another pawn in the game."

"One metaphor's as good as another."

"Pawns are cheap, easily lost, and sometimes it pays to sacrifice them."

"I hope not. I like this one."

"I could use him, Motsognir." Renard looked thoughtful. His hand had gone back to stroking the plant-pet. He paced to the rear wall and back. "Think of the conflict it would create if your Sula were to die in the right manner—say, by lassari rebels. Vingi would be furious at the loss of potential profit, and embarrassed because of the way it happened. The Diplos wouldn't raise a finger, and old d'Embry might just get thrown out of her job because of the backlash. . . ."

Helgin had risen, standing on the seat of his chair. In another, the posture would have been ludicrous, but the wrath twisting the dwarf's face forbade amusement. "You'll leave him alone, Renard." His voice was uncharacteristically low; it seemed more sinister because of that.

Renard only smiled. "*Now* who's emotionally involved? You like him, Motsognir, neh? Is he *your* lover?"

Helgin spat. His hands curled into fists. "I'm telling you to work with what you have here. Do you understand that?"

"Are you giving me a choice?"

"No."

Renard shrugged. He waved a lazy hand in acquiescence. Slowly, his face still ruddy with anger, Helgin sat again. "So long as we understand each other, Renard."

"I understand what I need to do. I know who pays me, and that's all I need to know."

Helgin nodded. His expression relaxed in stages. The grin returned; he cracked his knuckles loudly. "Good. Then let's get your friends back in here and tell me what you've been doing and what you plan to do."

As Renard moved toward the door, Helgin put his bare feet up on the table and leaned back dangerously in the chair. "And get rid of that damned thing around your neck," he said. "It's ugly and it stinks."

She could see him sitting before the headless skeleton of the ippicator. Light from a handflare barred the walls and ceiling of the cavern with beast-shadow. He didn't turn to look at her, though she knew that her approach, over the broken, treacherous stones of the empty caves far from the normal haunts of Hoorka, had hardly been silent. She stopped, hand near the hilt of her dagger, her nightcloak thrown back over her shoulder, out of the way.

"Hello, Gyll," she said. It was not what she'd been rehearsing in her mind.

Now he turned. A hand swept the hood back from his head, revealing hair well-laced with gray. Gyll half-smiled, nodded. "Mondom, it's good to see you again. I knew you'd figure that it was me, and that you'd know where to look."

"You take a damned lot for granted, then," she replied gruffly. She'd thought she'd known how she felt; now, seeing him, she was no longer certain. Emotions warred inside. She kept her hand near the leather hilt—Hoorka's comfort, she thought, like Jeriad. "I have three kin being attended to for your bruises, and Underasgard is in an uproar. I'll have to take disciplinary action that none of the kin—including me—is going to like. I could have sent kin back here to kill you for an intruder."

"You didn't." His attitude conveyed a studied relaxation: one arm propping up the body, the other across the knee of a flexed leg. "Hell, Mondom, none of the kin were really hurt beyond their pride and a bruise that'll be gone in a week. I'm

43

good enough to have made sure of that. It'll be a good lesson, especially to the apprentices you had guarding the entrance. It was too damned easy, m'Dame. Way too easy."

She continued staring at him, but her weapon hand relaxed, fisted on her hip. "Once, you were good enough to have made it look that easy. You're telling me you're back to that shape?"

Gyll laughed, a full-throated amusement that rolled across the folded walls of stone. Mondom didn't share the laughter, didn't move at all. *I should hate him. I should hate him for what he did to me, did to his kin, did to Hoorka—for abandoning us as if his own damn restlessness were more important than the welfare of guild-kin. I should be angry with him. So why is what you're feeling closer to jealousy?* Her flat gaze watched him as Gyll leaned back to vent his pleasure, watched as the laughter slowly faded to a chuckle, watched as he stretched and rose. His loose clothing had the look of a uniform, but she saw no weapons. His face was as craggy as ever, etched with yet more time-lines, but the eyes were alight and restless, gleaming in the harsh light of the flare.

"It's good to hear you say that, Mondom," he said. "It must show a little, then. Yah, I feel much better now. You always told me that I was losing my tone. I was horribly out of shape those last few standards here."

"You could have managed to get back in trim," she answered. Without leaving, she almost added.

He knew. "Leaving was one of the best things I could have done."

"Not for Hoorka." A pause. "Not for me."

"You did miss me, then." His voice was very soft.

"I've never taken lovers or made friends easily. You were both."

A look of something akin to sympathy came to his eyes—Mondom knew only that she didn't like the expression. Its very empathy repelled her. Gyll took a step toward her, holding out his arms in the welcoming attitude of kin to kin. The gesture rekindled Mondom's anger. She glared at the proffered hands. After a few moments, Gyll let them fall to his sides. "But you still harbor the grudge, neh?"

"What the *hell* do you *think*?" Fury goaded her into

shouting, the patronizing tones of his voice fueling the emotion. Gyll watched her, that cool sympathy/pity on his face, not saying anything, not reacting much at all. Mondom forced herself into calm again. *Hoorka show their inner faces only to kin—that's how the code-line goes. Remember, he's not kin. Not any longer.* Her face became blank, neutral, a mask of flesh. With it, Gyll's expression altered as well. The shoulders fell slightly, his lips clenched, and he seemed to sigh.

"So that's the way you're going to play this?" he said. "As Thane to a dishonored kin-brother?"

"Gyll Hermond is not a kin-brother, dishonored or otherwise. Gyll is nothing. He's lassari, kinless. I do not hear him." Mondom spoke scathingly in the impersonal mode. Such a callous and deliberate insult would provoke a Neweden native to rage, and Mondom readied herself, widening her stance for his attack.

When he didn't react at all, she knew just how much he'd changed in the intervening standards.

"You needn't speak that way, Mondom," he said mildly. "I wanted to see you again, sit in the quiet of the caverns with my old friend the ippicator, to see if the beast still made me feel close to She of the Five."

"Do you?" she asked, despite her anger.

"I don't know. I think maybe I do. The ippicators were always sacred to us, inviolate relics and not something to be sold as the rest of Neweden would do. I feel something looking at it." His head turned back to regard the great ribs, the sheen of the bones, the five legs sprawled in collapse. "I think about how they were the pets of the gods and how the gods took them away from Neweden to live with them. And I look at the Great One here and I think about how much those bones would be worth, cut and polished." He looked back at her. "You didn't have to speak that way to me, Mondom. I wanted to see you again most of all. I didn't want us to scratch open all our old wounds."

"You could have communicated with me in the time since you left, but you didn't."

"You could have initiated it just as easily."

"It wasn't *me* that came back to see if he still felt Her presence in the bones of the ippicator."

Gyll exhaled loudly. He shifted his weight, and rock

clunked dully under his feet. The sound was loud in the cavern's stillness. "We're both damned stubborn, aren't we? Neither of us was ever willing to bend much."

"I don't know that I'll ever bend in this, Gyll. What are you here for? I hope you didn't think to begin our relationship again." Saying it stirred memory. The ghost of their affection and love was still there, underneath, battered and broken. It nagged at her. She glanced from Gyll to the five-legged ippicator's skeleton, not wanting to look at him. *She of the Five, why did You bring him back here? Why couldn't you have kept him away?*

"Mondom, there was a lot of feeling between us. That's never really altered for me."

So careful he is. He makes it sound so easy, as if the rift were simply a crack easily plastered. "You've a hell of a durable set of feelings, then. You disobeyed a direct order from me as Thane, you made me declare you unguilded. You left me. You chose the Oldins over the Hoorka, Gyll. What's the matter, don't your Trader-Hoorka satisfy you? Doesn't Kaethe Oldin open her legs for you, or don't you have a pretty underling there you can seduce?"

His smile was unsure. It flickered across his lips. "Mondom, let's be fair. I know I hurt you, I know I hurt the kin, but it seemed to be something I had to do. And I'm glad I did, in most ways. The Oldins are good people, Mondom, and the Trader-Hoorka is an organization with great potential, not constricted like we were becoming here." His eyes narrowed suddenly, and his gaze traveled her body. "Your nightcloak is tattered, the uniform is thin in places . . . I've heard tales since I arrived, Mondom—they say that Hoorka is poor, that you don't get many contracts anymore, and those you do work are always from the Li-Gallant."

"Nobody's starved yet, Gyll. But, yah, we don't get the contracts, and d'Embry won't allow us offworld. What of it? It means we have to wear our clothes longer, means we don't eat as well, means that some of the equipment can't be fixed as soon as it breaks. You going to blame that on me, too? It wouldn't have been different if you'd stayed Thane."

He didn't believe that. She could see it in his eyes, in the way his mouth tightened. "The rumors have truth, then," he said.

She knew what she wanted, suddenly. "I don't think talking with you is what Hoorka needs, Gyll. I want you gone."

"Mondom, I left Neweden because—whatever you might believe—I thought I could do something for Hoorka. For us. I think I do have a future to offer, having seen the Families' society." He spoke with a fervor she remembered all too well. It engendered the same reaction in her that it always had. She shook her head into his words, and he began to speak rapidly, as if speed could alter her denial. "They can offer Hoorka much, far more than Neweden or the Alliance. Gods, Mondom, you don't know how suffocating the Alliance really is, don't know how much they keep out from paranoia or some false elitism. Hoorka could be . . ."

He stopped, realizing that she wasn't listening to him. "Mondom—" he began.

"Gone," she said. "And don't talk to my kin, Gyll. Stay away from me, stay away from Hoorka."

"Talking isn't going to harm anyone, Mondom. There's so much I wanted to tell you, so much I want to hear from you; how the kin are . . ."

"Kin have died. You weren't here to mourn them, weren't here to give blood-duty."

The words hurt him. Seeing the pain in his eyes made her feel simultaneously pleased and repentant. She didn't enjoy the ambiguity.

Still, he persisted. "I don't want us to be enemies, Mondom. Maybe talking will change things, at least vent some of the bitterness you seem to feel."

She forced herself back into the Hoorka aloofness. "Maybe that's exactly why I'm telling you to stay away, neh?" She turned her back on him, strode into the darkness of the corridor leading back to the Hoorka caverns. Her voice, disembodied, came back to him. "I'll have my people away from the entrance in ten minutes, Gyll. I want you to leave. If you're still here in half an hour, you'll be considered an unwelcome and dangerous threat, and I'll make sure you're treated accordingly."

He could hear her footsteps moving away.

The endless, mocking silence of earth and stone returned.

*   *   *

The next day the confrontation was still in the forefront of his thoughts. He mused on Mondom and the Hoorka as he helped one of his crews unload crates from the shuttle hold, his shirt off like the rest of the laborers despite the Neweden chill.

"Sula?"

Gyll turned. The woman who'd addressed him was of moderate height, rather plain of face, and her clothing was that of a lassari. Yet she stared at him without the humility that should mark a lassari addressing a social superior. Her hands were on her hips, her head cocked at an angle in challenge. "I'm Sula Hermond," he said, wiping his hands on his pants. "And you?"

"My name's unimportant," she answered. She seemed nervous despite her air of arrogance. Her gaze moved about, and she licked her dry lips. "Can we move over by the other end of the shuttle, Sula? I would like to speak with you privately."

Gyll was tempted to refuse her, this no-name lassari. Yet his curiosity prodded him. *You're reacting with the vestiges of Neweden mores. This reluctance to talk to her is only because she's lassari. Remember that you're not a Newedener anymore, but an Oldin.* "All right," he said finally. "Marko, take charge here for a few minutes, will you?" The man grinned back at Gyll, glancing knowingly at the lassari.

"Certainly, Sula. My pleasure."

Gyll smiled at Marko, shaking his head. He picked up his shirt, then walked with the woman toward the nose of the shuttle, putting on his shirt against the cool breeze. When they stood in the shadow of the nose, the thick strut of the landing gear beside them, he spoke to her. "Well, m'Dame? They can't hear us here."

She glanced about once more. "I don't like being here," she said. "It's too open. Too many people could be watching." She looked back at Gyll and shrugged. "But I needed to contact you, Sula. From everything I've heard, everyone's attention is centered on you: the Li-Gallant's, the Regent's. They want to know what you're doing here."

"Just what it appears I'm doing—trading." He could not keep a faint hint of condescension from his voice. "And which of those watchers do *you* represent?"

"The Hag's Legion and Renard."

Gyll knew that she watched his face for a reaction. He didn't know if he was successful in keeping the shock and disgust hidden, but then, he did not particularly try. "What does the Hag's Legion care about the Family Oldin?" His voice had turned colder, more distant. It hardened her face, made her step back away from him.

"You were guilded kin once, Sula. We know that. You were Thane of the Hoorka, the scum that kill lassari for the Li-Gallant. They cast you out, Sula, those Hoorka. Thane Mondom had you banned from the company of all guilded kin; she made you lassari—no better than me as far as Neweden society's concerned." She paused, glancing about once more. Two people were walking toward the shuttle from the Sterka gates of the port. The woman kept her gaze on them, speaking faster now. "We need to know where you stand, Sula. Do you support the guilded kin who spat on your name and discarded you, or will you help the truly needy ones of this world, the lassari that look to the Hag's Legion for support? You could aid us greatly."

"I'm a Trader, m'Dame. I don't dabble in politics."

"You can't avoid that here, Sula. If you deal with the Li-Gallant, you tread on the backs of all lassari. All we ask is that you consider that. There are things that the Hag's Legion could use that wouldn't involve your visible support: money, material, perhaps arms..."

The two were still approaching, and Gyll could see that both wore uniforms—one that of Vingi's guard, the other that of a Diplo staff member. The woman saw them as well. Her nervousness increased. She shifted her weight from side to side uneasily. "Sula?" she said. "I need an answer to take back to Renard."

"Then tell him no."

The woman scowled, baring her teeth—they were not good teeth; discolored, broken. "Sula, you're not kin, you're lassari. One of us."

"No."

She hissed, drawing her breath in between snaggled incisors. "Very well, then. You've made a mistake, Sula. I hope you don't regret it later." She looked at the guards, then back to Gyll. "I can't argue with you any longer."

"I understand, m'Dame," Gyll said. His voice had softened

despite himself—he felt empathy for her, for the risk she had taken to come here openly, for the obvious passion of her convictions. "M'Dame, I bear no grudge at all against lassari, believe me, but I don't intend to endanger my trading mission here."

"Then you've made your choice, Sula. As I told you, all the forces here look to you as a part of the solution to Neweden's problems. You can't avoid the politics: whether there's a reason or not, those in power all look to you. Their thoughts center around you. You're involved, Sula, despite your protests."

The two guards had increased their pace. One pointed to them. The woman slid around the bulk of the landing strut and ran. Gyll heard her footsteps, watched as Vingi's guard took flight after her. The Diplo waited for a moment until pursuer and pursued had disappeared into a maze of idle machinery, then sauntered over to Gyll. The Diplo nodded to Gyll pleasantly. The badge on his tunic had the name Vorman inscribed on it—a miniature Vorman leered up at him from the holo ID. "Think he'll catch her?" he asked.

"I don't know," Gyll answered. "She seemed fast and agile. Bet she has better wind, too."

"Who was she?"

"She didn't say," Gyll said flatly. He'd already decided that he did not like this Vorman. "She was looking for a handout." Gyll elaborated no further. Vorman nodded, staring at Gyll.

"My friend from the Li-Gallant seemed to think she might be Hag's Legion."

"I know the woman was lassari. She might have been involved with the Legion, I suppose. It *is* largely lassari."

"Ahh." Vorman nodded again. He smiled; it touched only his lips. "I don't know how the woman got out here, Sula—as you know, all Neweden natives are restricted to the public area of the port."

"Then shouldn't you be chasing her as well?"

The smile became wider and still did not reach his eyes. Gyll's dislike for the man's false camaraderie increased. "It's a purely internal problem for Neweden, isn't it, Sula?" Vorman said. "At least as long as she was just here to ask for charity. Perhaps we'll find out more if she's caught."

Gyll glanced back the way she'd gone. "My money's on the woman," he said. "Care to wager?"

"I think not." Vorman shrugged. "I'll have to make a report, though. The Regent insists on knowing what happens inside the port." He glanced at Gyll and the smile vanished. "Especially where it concerns you, Sula."

"It's nice to know she cares."

The smile returned. "And I'd been told that you had very little humor in you, Sula. Well, I'll leave you to your work."

Vorman walked away, moving toward the gates of Diplo Center. Gyll watched him leave. "Gods damn all officious assholes like you, Vorman," Gyll muttered.

Then, puzzling over the incident, he went back to his crew.

4

The funeral of Vasella was held in one of the hundred or so small churches dotting Dasta Burrough—the Church of the Vengeful Ippicator. Renard had chosen it, whimsically, for its name; certainly not for its grandeur. It was an uncomfortable choice in most ways, though that made Renard feel pleased rather than the opposite. Too many people were crammed into too small a space. The interior was hot despite the autumnal temperatures outside, and it was crowded. Renard's clothes were sticky and damp. He'd left behind the plant-pet as rendering him too conspicuous, but was glad now that the creature's burdensome weight didn't add to his discomfort. Micha and Alex pressed beside him, too close. Still, the scene made him smile. Little annoyances bred anger, and the child of anger is violence.

Only the corpse of Vasella had room. Shrouded in plain glowcloth, it lay on a bier between the congregation and the altar, bedecked with flowers and small burial gifts. The mourners were almost entirely lassari and low kin, the residents of Dasta Burrough and Oversector and the wretched areas like them in all of Neweden's cities. Squirming in his seat in the front pew, Renard could see them, filling the ranks of seats, lining the walls and clogging the aisles, seemingly about to overflow the balcony. *Good, good. They're already edgy and bitter, and this poor excuse for a church feeds their irritations. Good.* The mourners shifted, fanned themselves, shouted across to friends, all under the cartoonish glare of a rendering of She of the Five that filled the rear wall. Behind the poorly drawn goddess, a simplistic sky tossed thunderheads jerkily from left to right. Renard smiled up at the visage, mockingly. He fingered the rough cloth of the hood on his lap—he'd brought the Hag's Legion here with their faces concealed, for a squadron of Vingi's guards had been just outside the church, filming all those who entered. There had been muttering and covert insults, but no trouble. Not yet.

The Li-Gallant plays into my hands. Again. As always.

The crowd quieted as the Revelate Brotsge walked slowly from the sacristy to the bier. Brotsge was old, frail of body, and foul-tempered, an old-line lassari who preached of eventual rebirth and reward for those who followed the mores of Neweden society. The revelate had been absurdly happy at receiving the overlarge tithing for the funeral service. Seeing the church, Renard could understand: it needed repair. It seemed to be held together with erratic strips of paint and prayer. Whatever the revelate's usual congregation, they were neither large nor generous with what little money they had.

The revelate shuffled forward and put a trembling right hand on Vasella's shroud. At his gesture, the lights in the church dimmed—haphazardly, for some went entirely dark and others stayed nearly full—while the sky behind She of the Five became twilight with a flickering of scratchy lightning. The Revelate Brotsge's voice was as palsied as his hands. It reverberated tinnily through the church.

"We have gathered to send the soul of Urbana Vasella to our gods and their mercy." He leered out to the people in what Renard assumed was Brotsge's interpretation of a sympathetic smile. Renard frowned back, properly respectful and sad at this death of a friend. Micha leaned toward him slightly, speaking in a whisper. "I wish we could have done this outside. My pants are itching from all the heat." Renard nodded back, still looking at Brotsge.

The revelate took his hand away from the bier and made the sign of the star over the body. "Sirrah Vasella prepares to meet She of the Five, who will snatch him away from Hag Death and prepare him for his next life here. She will take his *j'nath*, his essence, and mold it in a new form, one that mirrors the worthiness of his past lives. We should not grieve here, my friends, for Urbana is dead only for a little time, as the Gods count such things."

"He's dead! That's all that matters, Revelate!"

The shout came from the packed rear of the hall, followed by scattered shouts of agreement. Restless, the congregation mumbled to itself. Heads craned to view the source of the interruption. Renard sat, silent and still, hands folded on his hood, ignoring the sweat and the heat and the closeness, watching the consternation in the face of the revelate. The man peered myopically out into the crowd, seeking the taunter. Brotsge blustered, scowling, the sound system amplifying his spluttering ire. As the gathering settled once more into restive, uneasy quiet, Brotsge gathered together the shreds of his composure once more, drawing himself up and glaring down at the assembled, his chin high. Renard leaned back, not letting the band of wetness down his spine bother him. This would be interesting.

Brotsge had motioned to his acolyte—a boy that could have been no more than ten. Obviously hot and uncomfortable in his voluminous, heavy surplice, the boy came over to the revelate, bearing a tray on which sat censer and spices, a flask of holy water. The boy kept glancing at the crowd, especially at the solemn rank of the Hag's Legion. Brotsge cleared his throat, said something to the acolyte in a whisper. The child blanched, blinked heavily. The tray shook, but his attention was now entirely on the revelate. Brotsge took the flask and walked once around the corpse, now and then sprinkling the liquid inside over the shroud, all the while intoning the litany of She of the Five. Renard watched, impassive, biding his time and listening more to the whispers of the people behind him than to the ritualistic mutterings of the revelate. He wiped sweat from his forehead with his sleeve, folded his muscular arms at his chest.

Revelate Brotsge faced the congregation once more. Sweat had made ragged strands of his white, thin hair. Dark circles of perspiration were visible under the sleeves of his outer garment. He bowed his head: Renard watched a droplet of sweat fall from the revelate's head to the floor.

"We send Urbana on with our prayers and the blessing of She of the Five. We pray he will return soon, his *j'nath* purged by his passage." His head still bowed, Brotsge waited for the traditional response: "All praise Her." It came only from his acolyte. The crowd began the refrain, but came to a ragged halt as Micha—at a nudge from Renard—rose from her seat and spoke loudly.

"You're quite mistaken, Revelate." She had a strong, firm voice. It carried well in the mugginess of the church.

The revelate gaped at her, his mouth open comically. At his side, the acolyte giggled nervously. Brotsge flung a hand sidewise; it struck the boy on the cheek, silencing him and rocking the utensils on the tray. The revelate shut his mouth, straightened. He fixed Micha with a squinting glare. "M'Dame—" he began severely.

"Revelate," Micha interrupted. Her audacity snapped shut his mouth again. In his seat, Renard grinned to himself. *Good.* The church was utterly silent, everyone's attention drawn to the conflict. Even the swishing of improvised fans had stopped, forgotten. Micha's words fell into the quiet like stones. "Vasella was a lassari, like most of us in the Legion, like most of those here today." She swept her hands wide to include the gathering. "He had no wish to return to this miserable life on the vague *chance*"—she paused, as Renard had taught her—"that in this mythical next life he might return as guilded kin."

"M'Dame—"

"No, Revelate. Vasella will return to us when the ippicators return, as all our lore tells us they will do, when the time has come to destroy this society the guilded kin have built to serve their own needs." Another pause, and as Brotsge began to make some comment, Micha shouted over him. "Vasella would not *want* to be kin, not when it would mean defiling all he believed in. He would not turn around and spit in faces of the lassari and low kin, who were as a family to him."

At that, there was scattered applause and sounds of

agreement from around the church. Only the row of the Hag's Legion sat silent, unperturbed. Renard was pleased with the response. *A little heavy-handed with the words, but she's doing it well. Good and better.*

Brotsge clapped his hands together. The sound, amplified, rang through the hall. Slowly the crowd settled before his obvious anger: a revelate, after all, was a person touched by the gods, an institution they had all been taught to respect. Only Micha stood, defiant, with the presence of the Legion behind her.

"Woman," the old man said, "why do you persist in this blasphemy?" His use of casual address caused Micha's face to tighten into a scowl. At Renard's side, Alex started to rise, and Renard quieted him with a harsh gesture. He didn't like having to do that—it showed his power over the Legion to a careful observer, and his safety lay in anonymity.

"Is it blasphemy to speak truth, Revelate?" Micha trembled, but she held herself. Renard leaned forward in his seat, ready to interrupt if he had to, but hoping it would not be necessary—it was not his intention to have the lassari anger vented here, in private.

"I speak the truths of She of the Five." Revelate Brotsge nodded to her. "And I apologize for speaking to you so rudely, m'Dame. I only wanted you to listen."

Renard sighed in relief. He slouched back.

Micha bowed to the revelate, the deep bow of equals. "Your apology is accepted, Revelate. Vasella was a devout man in his own way, and we of the Legion knew he would want the blessing of She of the Five. But he also believed that She meant for us to be more than chattel, that She didn't want the lassari to vanish like Her ippicators. The guilded kin would like us to be content with the belief that we will someday be kin ourselves. They hope that will keep us in line, underneath them. And we *will* be kin, Revelate: we of the Hag's Legion have pledged that. But we won't receive recognition by being docile and waiting for that eventual reward."

"My dear child," Brotsge began—not an insult, but merely the perception of the elderly toward the younger.

Still, it caused Micha to toss her head back. She laughed, loudly, almost joyously.

"We're not children, Revelate. None of us. We lost our innocence a long time ago, in the blood the Li-Gallant, the Hoorka, and all the kin have taken from us."

"I know that this man's death"—Brotsge indicated the bier with a grandiose gesture—"has bereaved you greatly."

Micha smiled. "You'll never suspect what his death means to us, Revelate."

"Let us mourn him, then, m'Dame. Calmly, and without rage, as She of the Five would wish it."

"His whole life was rage, Revelate," Micha persisted. "He wanted a revelate's blessing to take with him to the Hag. That's all."

"He has that," Brotsge growled. He gripped the flask of holy water tightly, then seemed to realize for the first time that he was still holding it. He placed it back on the acolyte's tray. "I've given him that blessing."

"Then," Micha said, "we will take him."

At her signal, the Hag's Legion stood and came forward, ignoring Brotsge's protests. They took hold of the bier, lifting it to their shoulders. Petals of flowers littered the floor in a slow, bright rain. Brotsge, shouting, grasped at Alex's arm, next to Renard. Alex grinned at the revelate as if amused and, with a shrugging motion, flung Brotsge aside. The acolyte, with a cry, abandoned his tray and clutched at the falling revelate's robes. He did little good. Brotsge struck the floor hard, his head thudding against tile. The boy shrieked in fear; Brotsge—echoed by the sound system—howled in pain. "You can't do this," he screamed, holding his head. Bright, thick blood welled between his fingers. "You make a mockery of my church."

Renard, adjusting the weight of the bier on his shoulder, glanced down at the man, at the boy holding him and attempting to stanch the flow of blood with his surplice. "You're exactly right, Revelate Brotsge." With his free hand, he placed the hood over his head. His voice muffled, he continued. "And we'll continue to do so as long as the churches serve the guilded kin and not those who need comfort the most." Renard's eyes, cold and unsympathetic, stared from the ragged holes in the hood. "You've given Urbana his blessing. That was all we required of you."

The bier lurched forward, Renard moving with it, his attention leaving the plight of the old man. Moving slowly, they stepped down into the main aisle and were immediately surrounded. The church was noisy and chaotic now; shouting faces, sweat-slick brows, raised hands. A rock arced over Renard's head and the bier; behind him, he heard a crack as the missile struck the animo of She of the Five, then the bright clatter of shattered glass striking the floor. Around him, people cheered, jostling him. He grinned, the dangerous excitement of the crowd filling him with energy. A man near him shouted: "Down with kin!" Renard shouted back in kind, gleeful. The bier seemed very light; those nearest were reaching out to aid the Legion bearers. Above Renard, the bier rode like a raft on an uneasy, living sea. Someone ahead of them thrust open the doors to the church—they slammed back against their supports, askew; behind, to the side, there were more sounds of destruction, glass breaking, wood splintering. Renard could feel the chill touch of outside air.

Clamorous, moving; the crowd spilled from the church, down the wide steps to the street. As they came out into the night, into the soft illumination of the hoverlamps, Renard could see the squad of guards, still watching from across the way. They looked worried. Their hands stayed close to the handles of their crowd-prods, and one fidgeted nervously with a relay button on his lapel. The bier tilted dangerously as they came down the steps, and Renard had to give all his attention to the unseen footing beneath him. When he could look up again, he could see very little above the bobbing, restless sea of heads on every side of him. It didn't matter. Events had, so far, gone the way he'd planned. He knew what would happen, knew what *must* happen.

He waited for the first sounds of chaos.

Afterward, descriptions of the events (and, of course, the official assignment of the blame for the incident) would vary according to the sources consulted. The Hag's Legion would hold that one of Vingi's guards struck the actual first blow. The Li-Gallant's Domoraj, before the interrogators of the

Neweden press, would just as vehemently contend that it was a vile lassari who first made the confrontation a physical one.

Neither side would deny that what precipitated the fray was a photodot. One of the guards raised a camera to record the scene—all agreed on that point. Certainly the lassari were quite sensitive toward Vingi's interest in Vasella and the Hag's Legion, and especially the mysterious figure of their leader, Renard, who was rumored to have attended the funeral. Certainly (as well), the lassari were in a foul, bitter, and angry mood, especially concerning full kin. And (certainly) they felt the security of numbers, the pressure of their peers, no matter how well-armed the guards. There were a few hundred of the lassari mob, only twenty of the guards: ten-to-one odds tend to make even the most cowardly people brave.

Whatever.

Within a few moments of the photodot being taken, a melee had begun between the guards and the mourners around the bier. The guards reacted with the ingrained ferocity of guilded kin toward the social canaille: they fought viciously, with all the power at their command, and without restraint. That only incited the lassari further, fueling their anger.

The first sound Renard heard was the cough of a sting at close range, followed by a mass wailing as the crowd-creature of lassari shouted alarm and pain. People bucked back against the Legion members, the bier tossing alarmingly. Renard screamed at them to back away. "Put the bier down! Gently, gently—and get the hoods off. They only mark you now."

Micha was shoved up against him. He grabbed at her sleeve, and she twisted to hug him quickly, her face a mixture of fear and pleasure. "It's going as you said it would." Someone ran past them, yelling wordlessly, blundering into the bier. Alex, cursing, pulled the man free.

"We have to get ourselves out now," Renard answered Micha. He could not keep a quick smile from his face. The night was loud around them, alive with pain and fright. "Tell the others to leave. Go separately, then stay in hiding for the next few days. I'm going to stay here for a few minutes, then go myself. Move!"

"Not without a kiss."

"If this excites you, m'Dame, then you're a disgusting creature." But he smiled again as he said it.

"I'm disgusting."

He kissed her, quickly, roughly, then thrust her away. "Now, get moving."

"I'm gone." She laughed back at him, her eyes crinkling in delight. "I hope Vasella doesn't mind being left here."

"He's being comforted by the Hag. He doesn't care. Now, will you go."

She left him without another word, slipping her way through the pushing, milling throngs. Vasella's flowers were being trampled underneath; the shroud had slipped to reveal the face of the corpse, shining with the funeral oils for the cremation. Renard nodded to Vasella's body and moved away, back to the steps of the church where he could survey the scene.

The fighting had spread, the nucleus of the conflict still in the streets. At least two of the guards were down, dozens of lassari lay still on the pavement. It was no longer simply lassari against kin—it was simply riot. On the opposite side of the street, Renard could see a knot of people around a storefront. The holo-display had been shattered, looters moved through the wreckage. A sting spat once, then again—screams came from around a corner of the church. Renard ducked behind a pillar. A group of lassari came running up the steps toward him. They flung some noisome, pungent liquid in a bottle at the broken doors of the church. Glass splintered, the liquid splashed. Renard, suddenly frightened, ran, as a crude torch, flame guttering, was tossed into the spreading pool. The front of the building exploded with light and heat, bright searing flame. Smoke roiled up, billowing, hiding the moons. Over the roofs of the nearest houses, Renard could see the flashing strobes of approaching cruisers. Reinforcements had been summoned.

Renard wiped at his pants—some of the oil had splashed onto him. He no longer wanted to stay: this mess would continue just as well without him. He made his way around the church and into the warren of dark streets.

The mob howled at his back. Sirens shrilled in answer.

*   *   *

"*Damn* you, Santos, I can't believe you just sat here and watched this without waking me."

D'Embry was furious, and fury made her weak. The symbiote wriggled on her back, restless, no doubt pumping sympathetic chemicals into her to leech that rage, and she wanted none of the parasite's solace. Not now, not when the screen of the com-unit showed her Dasta Burrough in flames, not when she could look out her office window and see the smudge of smoke in the sky and the distant smear of erratic light.

McClannan was at the window now, gazing out. He turned to face d'Embry, who sat in her usual floater. "Regent," he said far too calmly, "I contacted the Li-Gallant's office. No one there wanted our assistance in any way, not even our fire-fighting apparatus. That ties our hands—we aren't allowed to interfere in local affairs without the Li-Gallant's explicit permission. We didn't have it, so I saw no reason to roust you from a comfortable bed."

He seemed eminently logical. He looked handsomely innocent. He even smiled, an offer of reconciliation. She despised his easy manner. "I don't believe this," she said again. Yellow fire spat at the viewscreen, and glowing sparks coiled heavenward. "Death and destruction on this scale hasn't been seen here since that typhoon six standards ago. There's a small-scale battle being fought between lassari and kin, and *you* didn't think it warranted awakening me." She let sarcastic amusement lash at him, a bitter marveling at his stupidity. "McClannan, my dear Seneschal, what *would* impel you to get me out of bed? Does Diplo Center have to burn first? And wherever did you get the idea that you were competent to make *any* kind of decision?"

McClannan's face took on a pained expression. It still looked like a regal mask. "I'm sorry you feel that way, Regent. Believe me, I only had your comfort and well-being in mind."

"*I don't want comfort!*" She shouted the words, and the effort reminded her that, indeed, she was still tired and that it was early in the morning. She sagged back in her seat, mindful of the hump of the symbiote on her shoulders. She put her hand on her forehead, her elbows on the padded arms of the chair. She closed her eyes and concentrated on breathing.

"Get me the Li-Gallant," she said wearily. "Not his office, not some damn underling, but Vingi himself."

"Regent—"

"Do it." She didn't have the strength to do more than whisper the words. *Come on, parasite. Do your job and give me some help.* She could feel its faint movements, could— somewhere under the surface of her consciousness—feel its presence, tandem with her own. A soothing coolness spread through her chest; she could breathe without pain. She kept her eyes closed. In the background, she could hear McClannan fidgeting with her com-unit, then his low, too-pleasant voice speaking. Someone replied, he spoke again. D'Embry stopped listening, her attention on her body, on her breathing, on all the small pains that added up to a nagging uneasiness.

"Regent?"

Maybe it is getting to be time. Maybe this next visit, Aris wouldn't be just a pleasurable prison but a home.

"Regent?"

She started. The hands came slowly down to rest on her desk; she opened her eyes. "Yes?"

McClannan was staring at her quizzically. "The Li-Gallant will be on in a moment."

"How do I look, Santos?"

"Perhaps you'd want me to talk with him," he ventured softly. "You *do* look as if you've been awakened in a rush."

"Good. I'm ready, then, Seneschal."

The Li-Gallant looked almost jolly. He nodded at the screen and pursed thick lips at d'Embry. "You look tired, Regent. Surely a small problem such as a fire in Dasta hasn't kept you up? It's a task for the local government, neh?"

"Frankly, Li-Gallant, I slept through the beginning of it."—with a glance at McClannan—"I assume the initial problem was Vasella's funeral?"

Ponderously Vingi nodded. Behind him, d'Embry could see his office and the shadowy figures of his guild-kin bustling about. "That's not exactly a difficult supposition to make. Yah, it was Vasella's funeral. The lassari—unprovoked, I might add—attacked the guards I'd sent there to protect those very same lassari from any harassment. But then, you can't teach gratitude to the lassari, Regent; they'll just turn and bite you."

"How many of them did you have to kill for their ingratitude, Li-Gallant?"

Vingi nearly smiled. "I see that your lack of sleep hasn't blunted your tongue, Regent. There *has* been some loss of life, I regret to say. Two of them were my kin." The Li-Gallant, abruptly, looked quickly and impossibly sad. It nearly made d'Embry laugh. For once, she was glad of the numbing effect of the symbiote.

"I'm sorry for your loss," she said. "But I pray that you haven't let it affect your judgment. You *are* dealing with the problem calmly, I trust."

"I want the people responsible for this outrage, Regent. The Hag's Legion, as you must know, are the ones to blame, not me."

"Still—"

"Your humanitarianism is well-known, Regent, if perhaps a trifle misplaced in this situation." A hand bright with rings came up to brush the Li-Gallant's hair back from his forehead. "And, in any case, at this moment my people are doing very little."

"You can't just let Dasta burn, Li-Gallant." Anger and dread rose in d'Embry's throat. Adrenaline banished fatigue. "I won't let you do that. We have both the equipment and the people to work it here in the Center. I'll send them down."

"That won't be necessary, Regent." Again, Vingi smiled. "I've already received another offer of assistance, and I've accepted it."

"And who might that be?"

"Sula Hermond of the Traders, Regent. He and his Trader-Hoorka. They've offered to secure the area, snare any of the rioters they find, and be certain that the fires are contained."

"*Traders?* Gods, Li-Gallant, Hermond was *kin*. He'll kill them . . ."

"Just as I would?" Vingi finished the sentence for her. "You forget, Regent, that I've decided that I like the Neweden Hoorka. Maybe Hermond's people will be just as helpful to me, neh?"

A vague burning knotted d'Embry's stomach. She clenched

her teeth against it. Her breath was shallow and unsatisfying again. "Li-Gallant—"

"M'Dame, why do you persist in trying to do my job as well as your own? I've given Sula Hermond the task, not your Diplos; we'll see how well he does. Without interference."

"You're indeed right, Li-Gallant. We *will* see. I hope for his sake that I enjoy the scene. Good morning to you, Li-Gallant."

With a feeling of childish glee, she slapped the disconnect contact. The Li-Gallant's startled face faded into darkness. D'Embry rose slowly and walked hesitantly over to the window. She leaned there, hands against the sill. Smoke was light against the backdrop of the night sky. It threw a pall over the city-glow of Sterka. "Santos, get a flitter readied. We're going to Dasta."

"Now, Regent?"

"Now."

"Regent, please, the exertion..."

"It won't kill me, Santos. And if it does, you can bungle the regency to the best of your ability. Get the flitter, Seneschal."

"I just don't see—"

"I know you don't. Get the flitter."

She remained silent to the rest of his protestations. Finally, with a sigh of resignation, he called for the vehicle.

"Hey, Gyll! Enemy approaching behind us."

Helgin shouted loudly enough that d'Embry and McClannan heard the bellow. The Motsognir swung off his perch on an overturned flitter and strode toward the bank of screens where Gyll stood. Gyll glanced up, startled, then laughed when he saw the Regent and her Seneschal making their way toward him, flanked by Trader-Hoorka guards. "Damn it, dwarf," he said. "You had me thinking there was a horde of lassari bearing down on us."

"Lassari you could handle. The Regent's more trouble than that." Then the Motsognir bowed low to the approaching d'Embry. "Good morning, Regent. Out for a stroll? A little too warm for Neweden, don't you think?"

D'Embry didn't appear to be amused. Her face was pinched, drawn. She frowned, and her walk was stooped and halting. Gyll stepped forward to greet her, dismissing the escorts with a hand signal. The Hoorka nodded to him and walked away. "Regent, Seneschal," he said, bowing. "I can only assume that you've talked to the Li-Gallant."

"You're quite right, Sula." D'Embry's voice was husky. Gyll had never heard her sound so weak or tired. "It worried me enough that I felt I had to come here."

"What would you like to see first?" Helgin had taken a seat on one of the consoles. LEDs flickered angrily under him. "The torturing of the prisoners, the maiming of children, or the despoiling of the dead?" He grinned.

Gyll glared at the Motsognir, who shrugged, then turned back to the Regent. "You're welcome to look, as long as you stay out of the way of my people." He gestured widely to indicate the area. They were set up in the middle of Charing Cross, a main intersection just outside Dasta. A bank of five large screens stood in an arc before them, each displaying a different scene. Before the screens was a maze of wiring and the bulwarks of the consoles. Several people in the uniform of the Trader-Hoorka sat before them, intent. Hoverlamps, full open, bathed the area in brilliance, making the darkness around them dense in contrast. Traders moved about, shouting, talking, rushing, but all with a sense of order, of studied calm. The stench of smoke was in the air, heavy and suffocating. Flames flailed at the sky far down the street. Just overhead, a firebus shrilled past; the wind of its passage buffeted them. Gyll did not speak until it had passed.

"What can I show you, Regent?"

"How many lassari have been killed?" If her voice was weak, her eyes were not. At her side, McClannan shifted uneasily. He seemed uncomfortable.

"Forty, possibly more," Gyll answered. "It's difficult to keep an accurate count in all this confusion, and there may well be bodies in some of the buildings that have burned and collapsed. We won't have any kind of accurate count until the fires are out and my people can get in there safely."

"How many will you kill before then?"

Gyll took a deep, hissing breath. Behind him, he heard the slap of Helgin's feet on the pavement as the dwarf jumped down from the console. "How many innocents has your Alliance killed, old woman?" the Motsognir thundered.

"On Longago, on Heritage..." McClannan looked as if he were about to step up between d'Embry and the Traders. "Oh, good," Helgin said, now standing alongside Gyll. "That's it, McClannan. I'd love to splatter that noble beak all over your face."

"Helgin!" Gyll shouted. He placed a hand on the dwarf's shoulder. Helgin glowered, but subsided into low muttering. "Regent, before you start making remarks that make you sound like an idiot, please let me show you what we're doing. Make your judgments after you're aware of the facts."

D'Embry's face was more sour than before. She coughed suddenly, and Gyll realized that some of her evident irritation stemmed from the environment, that she was uncomfortable. The symbiote shivered under her tunic—the sight made Gyll slightly ill-at-ease himself. He wondered, again, how that would feel, to be linked with the parasite. D'Embry cleared her throat liquidly. "My pardon, Sula. Please conduct your tour—it seems that the Li-Gallant wants you in charge here."

"With good reason," Helgin commented.

If d'Embry heard, she made no answer. Gyll led them forward into the glare of the hoverlamps. "The fire's starting to come under control," he said, gesturing at one of the screens. A firebus hovered in the midst of flame and smoke, a demon from hell; as they watched, it loosed a cloud of its own that fell into the inferno. The fire gouted, then began to subside. "A flame inhibitor we've developed, Regent. We've sold it to several of the Alliance governments. We could have stopped a lot of this destruction if the Li-Gallant had called us in earlier. Several blocks of Dasta will be leveled, but it won't spread further. My Hoorka made a sweep of the critical areas first—we've set up aid stations for those burnt out of their homes. We're not killing *them*, Regent."

He didn't give her time to reply. He swiveled, pointed at another of the displays. "There's still some minor skirmishing going on with lassari rioters, but it's all disorganized and scattered now." The screen looked down on a filthy, wreckage-strewn lane. Several men and women, lassari or low kin by their clothing, were running from a phalanx of Trader-Hoorka. The group halted suddenly in mid-flight as another squad of the Hoorka turned a corner before them. Tanglefoot bombs went off; the lassari fell in a writhing, fouled heap. Gyll's people, using neutralizing sprays carefully, separated them one at a time and led the lassari away. "We'll be taking them to the building just to your left. Some of the Li-Gallant's guards are there, and the captives are checked against a master file of known insurgents. If they aren't matched, and if we've no actual evidence of any unlawful acts, they're taken to one of the aid stations. If they *do* match . . ." Gyll shrugged. "Vingi's people are in charge past there. They take them, and if you've a quarrel with that, talk to the Li-Gallant. Neweden has its own legal codes, after all. But no one's being killed here, and none of the Trader personnel are doing harm to anyone unless we're attacked first. I'm not going to lose *any* of my people if it can be avoided, Regent, but I'm also not starting a vendetta against the lassari."

Gyll turned away from the screens. A woman hurried over to him, said something to Gyll in a low tone. He answered her, slowly, quietly. She left. Gyll stared at d'Embry.

"And unless I'm mistaken, Regent, I'm owed an apology."

D'Embry gazed at the bank of screens, at the rush of people, at the dwindling shroud of smoke. She seemed to breathe too quickly, but she nodded. "You have it, Sula. I spoke far too hastily. All I can say is that Neweden does that to a person."

"Oh, hooray," Helgin said without inflection or excitement. D'Embry's sharp stare flickered over the dwarf. "That's a *good* look," Helgin remarked, hands on hips. "I'd be quaking in my boots if I were wearing them. Keep working on it." He flexed his toes on the pavement. They cracked.

Unexpectedly, d'Embry smiled, even as McClannan scowled. She laughed. "Sula, Motsognir, you don't know how *relieved* I am to see this. I expected . . . Well, let it go. You're going to cause me royal headaches with the Li-Gallant because of your damned efficiency, but at the moment I don't care." She laughed again. McClannan stared at her in amazement. "I really don't care," she repeated, shaking her head.

"Regent, perhaps we'd better leave. The Sula is busy here, and tomorrow's schedule's rather hectic." McClannan came out of his stunned silence, bending over d'Embry like a solicitous nursemaid. Gyll thought for a moment that she would snarl at him, but she glanced at the man with an odd tolerance. *The symbiote, some sedative it put in her? Every-*

one knows she can't stand McClannan. Or is she truly pleased with what she sees here?

"All right, Santos," she said. "We'll leave the Sula to his duties. But let me first ask if you, Sula (and Sirrah Motsognir as well), would dine with me. I'll be having a supper with the Li-Gallant in a few weeks."

Startled, Gyll still managed to smile and bow. "Certainly, Regent."

"Well, then, we'll leave you to your tasks." She turned to go, always slowly, stooped under the hump of the symbiote. Two Oldin guards materialized to escort them back to their flitter. Gyll watched them disappear in the smoky night.

He turned back to find Helgin grinning up at him. "I'm really a charmer, neh?" the dwarf said. "She didn't know what hit her."

It was nearly dawn before they'd finished. The sunstar's rising made Gyll feel strange, as he'd not felt since returning to Neweden. False dawn chased the stars, and memories came with the light. They were not all pleasant.

The streets were empty. Most of the onlookers had left far earlier, after the worst of the fires had been dealt with—there is only so much crowd appeal in ash and soot. Only the Trader-Hoorka were left, disassembling the portable screens, coiling wires, packing equipment into padded boxes. Only one screen was left untouched, a small one with a privacy shield set to either side. Gyll stood before it. The view was not of Dasta Burrough, not desolate ruins and scorched rubble, but a green-cloaked peak, the sunstar just now touching the summit. As Gyll watched, a fume of dark smoke came from a hidden vent near the peak's jagged top. It rose straight in the air, spiraling, puffing; then a breeze snatched it, smearing it eastward. There was nothing else to see: no people, no wildlife, no flame. Just the slow pulsing of the dark cloud from the trees. Gyll sighed.

"That's near Underasgard." The voice came from behind him. Helgin.

Gyll turned. The Motsognir stood between the privacy shields. He looked tired; his broad shoulders slumped and he rubbed at one bloodshot eye. "Yah," Gyll replied. "The peak is Caladriel, above the Chamber of the Dead. There's a natural chimney leading down into the caverns. That's where we burned our kin."

"There's smoke now."

"I know." Gyll shook his head. "I almost feel like I should be there."

"Why? Because you're on Neweden again? Come on, Gyll; you've missed a lot of funerals since you left."

A smile touched Gyll's lips, and left quickly. "I know that, too. Mondom reminded me of it. Not very gently, either. And you're right, Helgin. It's been a long night, neh? Let's get back to *Goshawk* and get rid of the stench. Fischer can finish up here."

"Sounds fine. We smell like the guests of honor at a barbecue, and it's going to take more than one drink to get rid of the smoke in my throat."

They walked away. At the opening of the shields, just before they went out into sunlight, Gyll glanced back at the screen.

Snagged in trees, a fume of woodsmoke sagged against the sunrise.

5

The victim was Kirllia Mechem, temple harlot for the Church of Bazlot in Henima, halfway across Neweden from Underasgard. Bazlot was a minor demigod in the Neweden pantheon; most of the Hoorka knew little about Him except for His existence, though Steban ventured that he thought Bazlot was the god of cloth-dyers. None of the kin knew why a god of cloth-dyers would need a temple harlot, but the speculation was varied and amusing. It seemed that Kirllia had somehow contrived to blackmail one of the priests of the temple. She'd been clumsy; the revelate was not inclined to take the punishment into his own hands or to go through the authorities. "Let Bazlot decide through Dame Fate," he'd said. "She's not worth the money for your contract, but the church has it and it saves me trouble. If she lives, she'll be more docile, and, who knows, it may be good sport."

Mondom had found that she did not care for the man at all, but that was not a matter for Hoorka. They needed the money. She'd taken the money and swallowed her misgivings. She sent the apprentices.

The alternatives had been offered—Kirllia had no wealth of her own, and Bazlot's revelate forbade any church member to lend her funds. She would run. Watch was set, and the full kin readied.

Serita Iduna did not care for her partner. Meka Joh was new to full kinship; he'd been a low apprentice when Ulthane Gyll had left the Hoorka. Joh was competent enough, Serita admitted, but there was an eagerness to him when he was working a contract, an enthusiasm that bothered her deeply. It wasn't present when he practiced—he was rather far down on the unofficial rankings of practice matches—but Joh became animated and excited with a contract. There were others in the Hoorka like him: blood excited them, the thrill of the hunt coupled with a modicum of danger gave them a pleasure akin to sexual arousal. Serita avoided Joh and those kin he emulated, and she disliked being paired with him. Serita looked across at Joh's sharp profile as they circled Henima, preparatory to landing. He was leaning forward, his nose just touching the flitter's window, peering down at the small city anxiously. He seemed to notice Serita's stare; he pulled back and smiled as the craft banked and descended. "Should be fun, Serita. I've never run anyone in Henima before. Have you?"

"No," she said, simply. She moved her gaze away, glancing at the windshield as they landed near the Church of Bazlot. The overhead rotors churned air.

"I took a glance at the maps before we left. There's quite a large lassari sector here. The revelate and his people are half-lassari anyway. My bet is she'll hole up with someone from the church."

"Could be." *Shut up, shut up. Why couldn't it have been McWilms or Bachier, somebody I like?*

"You're awfully quiet. Not feeling well? We could still call Underasgard and tell the Thane—"

69

"No," Serita interrupted. "I'm fine. Let's just get this over with, Meka."

His face brightened slightly at that. He swung his door open; the cool air of Henima, far north of the equator, lashed at them. Serita pulled up the hood of her nightcloak. Even the presence of the sunstar, high in a thin net of clouds, didn't seem to affect the chill. Serita shivered.

An apprentice met them before they reached the church. "Easy one, this woman," the apprentice—a boy by the name of Relka—said. He was a tall and lanky youth, cocky and sure of himself; too much like Meka Joh, to Serita's mind. He laughed. "She's unarmed, unshielded, and running. You'll have the hunt of the knives; a quick one, at that. She's slow and she's stupid. Go down this street to the first corner, turn left. Mala should be there to meet you and point out the victim. When I left her, the idiot was in a market, trying to pretend that she was just one of the locals, shopping."

"Good job, Relka," Meka said. He slapped the boy on the shoulder. "Head for the flitter, then. Felling's got a stew packed in for you."

Serita merely nodded to the apprentice as he passed her. He shrugged at her silence and left them. The two Hoorka followed his direction. In the daylight, the city was dingy and active; mostly low houses huddled close together as if for warmth against the northern breezes. The Church of Bazlot stooped over them like a stern parent. A persistent wind shuffled papers in the gutters. The people milling about gave the Hoorka their customary wide berth, caution due them for their reputation. There were unguarded sour stares from the men huddled around small fires on the porch steps; long assessing glares from women leaning, elbows on sills, from the grimy windows. It was like any poor district they'd seen before, but there was nothing to balance the image. They saw the busy, noisy filth, and they saw the whole of Henima. "Worse than Dasta before it burned," Meka commented as they walked. "And damned colder."

Mala waved at them as the Hoorka entered an open square crowded with shoppers and tiny stalls crammed with produce. The open market was loud, chaotic, and filled with smells. The Hoorka went to the apprentice, and found themselves standing in an inviolate circle around which all passersby moved, scowling but unwilling to risk the anger of Hoorka. Mala shook her head. "They hate us," she said, holding out her cloak so both Hoorka could see the purple stain spreading over the cloth. "A rotten sweetrind—someone threw it at my back. Just be glad you'll get out of here quickly. The woman's down this row, the second one over. She's wearing a blue scarf on her head, and a dragon-patterned tunic. Can't miss her; she looks absolutely terrified. She'd never have made it as an actress."

"It's really going to be that easy?" Meka Joh looked disappointed; that disturbed Serita more than her kin-brother's previous eagerness.

"Let me take her, then, if it's not interesting enough for you," she said, more sharply than she'd intended. Joh glanced at her strangely.

"You're the elder, Serita. You rule the contract, not me. Tell me how you want it done."

Serita shrugged. A gust of wind made her squint, threw dust from the street into her eyes and flapped the canvas tops of the stalls. She stared at the passing crowds—*they know we're on a contract, and they wonder who we hunt. And they hate, even if they say nothing and are careful not to offend.* "Go around to the end of the row she's in—I'll give you a minute or so to get there, and then we'll work in toward her. You know the woman's face?"

"I'll recognize her. There won't be a mistake."

"Good. Mala, you can go back to the flitter. You've done well, girl. Our thanks." Mala nodded to the Hoorka and moved away. Joh, after another glance at Serita's noncommittal face, swiveled on his toes and strode off. People bumped and shoved each other to get out of his path.

Serita was left alone in the circle of fear. Now they stared at her, the hateful eyes; wondering, cautious. She tugged at the collar of her nightcloak, trying to bring the hood farther over her face. Only her eyes could be seen. She reached for her belt, felt the comforting, worn hilt of her vibro. The gesture made the watchers stumble back, and when she strode forward, a path cleared for her. No one spoke; her silence was herald enough. All would leave off haggling to watch her pass, holding a forgotten melon or swatch of cloth. The strident cries of the vendors trailed off in mid-pitch.

Hoorka. Serita heard the word: a curse, a whisper. They crowded again behind her, spectators now at this deadly amusement. She could feel them pressing at her back, filling the lane between the stalls. *Hoorka.* They might hate, but they would watch, would feed on the death.

Serita returned their hate.

The crowd parted before her. Serita saw the woman a fraction of a second before the victim noticed the Hoorka. She was indeed painfully obvious, her gaze never resting, never stopping to examine the wares around her. When that wandering glance found the assassins and saw Serita staring, her face paled, and Serita could hear the intake of breath. Far too late, Kirllia noticed that everyone had stepped back from her, leaving her and the Hoorka in the center of the lane. She tried to follow the crowd's example belatedly, clumsily, half-stumbling. Serita halted, waiting. She pulled again at the nightcloak's collar.

"Kirllia Mechem, your life is claimed by Hag Death and She of the Five," Serita said, her voice low and soft. Kirllia's eyes closed; she moaned. Serita thought she might fall.

Then, abruptly, Kirllia slashed out at those next to her with hands curled into claws. She ran, but she did not go far. A few meters down the way stood Joh. Kirllia was trapped in a narrow tunnel walled with people, death at either end. A high wailing escaped her clenched lips.

"That's it, woman. Run right to me." Joh's vibro flickered from its sheath, its throaty growling loud. "Let's see if you can get past me."

"*Meka!*" Serita took a step toward the woman. She glared at Joh, then back to Kirllia. "There are other ways of death," she said. "We have a capsule that will bring you laughter and sleep. This doesn't need to be painful if you don't resist. But my kin-brother is right; you can't escape us." Closer, always closer. One step, another. The crowd watched, rapt, silent.

"No . . ."

Step. "You can't deny the Hag with words, Kirllia." Step. "She won't listen, or She'll make it more difficult for you."

"Let her run to me, Serita," Joh said loudly. "Why waste an expensive capsule on *this*?"

The sneer in his voice was entirely too audible. With

Joh's words, several things happened at once. Serita began to speak—angry words—but someone in the crowd acted first. A frozen puffindle from the fishmonger's stand arced toward Joh's back. The Hoorka, with preternatural awareness, seemed to sense the missile; he ducked, and the puffindle struck ground. Kirllia was already moving, trying to make her way past the crouching Joh into the mass of people. It was a foolish move. Joh tripped her with an outthrust leg and, in nearly the same motion, brought his vibro down and over in a slicing motion. Kirllia died with the sudden screams of the crowd. Blood splashed and seeped into the dirt between the stalls.

Joh ignored the body. As Serita ran toward him, he picked up the puffindle and brandished it before the faces near him. "Who's the coward that threw this? Will he stand up and admit it, or is he the typical lassari?" Joh used the impersonal mode scathingly, his gaze raking the spectators. His vibro gleamed red; a droplet shivered on its tip.

"Meka…" Serita said warningly. She knelt beside Kirllia; the woman was dead. She made the sign of the star over the body.

"I didn't throw it, Hoorka," a man said. He pushed his way to the front of the crowd, a burly, tall lassari with close-cropped hair and an ugly, pocked face. "But I might've, if it had been closer to me. What of it, neh? What's wrong with giving the woman a chance?"

"You interfere with Hoorka, man, and you risk your own life."

"Insult lassari as you do, and you risk yours, as well. Look around you, assassin; how many of us are there? And there's only two of you, and all you have are vibros—a stick might serve as well, neh? I mean no insult"—the man's voice bordered on sarcasm—"but you might consider where you are before you open that stinking mouth of yours again."

Serita did not let Joh reply. She felt suddenly cold and frightened. "*Meka*," she said, sharply. The Hoorka stared at the lassari. His hand twitched around the vibro hilt; Serita could see muscles bunching in his forearm, and she thought he would cut at the man. "*Meka*," she shouted again. "I need your help wrapping the body."

Joh stood motionless; then, angrily, he flung the puffindle

back to the ground. His vibro flicked off and he shoved it into his sheath. He stalked over to Serita as the crowd watched, as the tall lassari chuckled deep in his throat. The Hoorka began wrapping the body in a spare nightcloak.

"If you *ever* behave like that on a contract again, I'll see you flayed before all the kin, Meka," Serita whispered harshly as they worked. "Believe me, kin-brother, the Thane will be told of this. Your silly theatrics could get us both killed. I won't have it. Not again. You insult the victim, her people, and Hoorka with your attitude."

His eyes narrowed dangerously, but his voice was soft. "Why, kin-sister, one might almost think you *like* these scum."

"They're people. Like you or I might have been. Give it a thought, Meka. Maybe She of the Five will see that you come back as the lowest lassari scum yourself."

"I'd still like to knock that bastard's laughter down his throat, along with his teeth. He's still there, still watching us."

"All it would prove is that you're a stupid fool who courts the Hag."

"I won't take *your* insults either, Serita." His voice was still soft. "I'll call for first blood on the practice floor in satisfaction."

"You've got it, then. First blood, Meka, when we get back. And I hope you enjoy being cut." Serita stood, wiping her hands together. The crowd had thinned, going back to the day's tasks, but the lassari man still watched, leaning against a corner of a nearby stall. He smiled, gap-toothed, at Serita. She gave him the barest of nods in acknowledgment. "Let's get this body back to the revelate, then," she said. "Afterward, we'll settle our differences."

Gyll thought he recognized him. Taller, yes; a man, not a boy anymore, changed. But the face, the walk . . . "McWilms?" he called. "Jeriad?"

The man across the street, in the sable-and-gray nightcloak of the Hoorka, turned at the sound of the name. The face went from aloof neutrality to a shocked smile. "Ulthane? I'll be damned . . ."

Laughing, they embraced in the middle of the street.

Those around them stared curiously: the Hoorka never show affection, never smile except at death; conversations that night would be preceded by "You'd never believe what I saw today..." Gyll held McWilms at arm's length, studying him and shaking his head. "Look at you, boy. When I saw you last, your face was a wreck, and this arm was gone. They did a fine job on you. Gods, that's good to see."

"And you, Ulthane. The standards haven't touched you. In fact, you look better than my memory of you. I'll bet you could still show me some tricks with the vibrofoil."

They grinned at each other, hugging once again. For a moment, there was some awkwardness. Gyll did not know what to say, or rather, there were too many topics from which to choose; McWilms seemed to revert to the shyness of his apprenticehood. Finally Gyll pointed at a tavern just down the street. "A drink, Jeriad?" Gyll shrugged away the remembrance of Mondom's warning—*stay away from the kin, Gyll*. He'd not sought out McWilms; it was simply chance. Dame Fate laughing. And if the Dame wanted them to meet, who was he to gainsay Her? Jeriad, for his part, seemed to be at ease. If Mondom didn't want Gyll consorting with his former kin, she evidently hadn't told the Hoorka. Jeriad nodded at Gyll's suggestion, and glanced up at the sunstar, just rising above the spires of Tri-Guild Church, a few blocks away.

"I've some time," he said. "Why not? A good cup of mulled wine would take the chill out of me."

The inn was one of the fancier ones in Sterka, holding an eternal twilight behind cut-glass doors and maroon curtains. They took a booth toward the back, both pretending to ignore the gawking of the patrons. Gyll eased himself behind a plastic table masquerading as malawood; Jeriad sat across from him. Gyll shook his head at the man. "I can't believe it, Jeriad. You look *good*, my friend. It must have been a rough few standards after the accident."

McWilms shrugged. He toyed with a napkin. "It took some time, yah. But it wasn't that difficult or painful. The kin could afford the treatments then, even if the Regent hadn't picked up the bills. It wouldn't be so lucky for an apprentice now." He looked up, and his smoky eyes were troubled.

Gyll frowned. "I've heard rumors to that effect, and Mondom hinted at it when I talked to her in Underasgard."

"That *was* you, then, that caused all the commotion. Mondom wouldn't talk about it afterward, but all the older kin said it had to be you, or the Thane wouldn't have been so upset. She really laid into the entrance guards." Jeriad smiled.

"Are things really that bad, Jeriad?"

McWilms's smile faded as quickly as it had come. His gaze dropped back to the napkin wrapped in his fingers. "I shouldn't complain, I suppose. But, yah, the contracts have gotten scarce, and most of them we do get are the Li-Gallant's. We haven't been offworld since Heritage. Our equipment suffers most of all. The flitters are old and eating into the treasury with repairs—we only have two that are at all reliable. The bodyshields"—Gyll saw a shadow of pain cross McWilms's face—"are in poor shape. I'm convinced they cost Ric's life on our last contract."

"I saw the smoke of the funeral. I didn't know who . . . D'Mannberg's gone to the Hag?" Gyll asked softly. "I'm very sorry to hear that."

"He was my kin-father. I guess you wouldn't have known that; my initiation came after you left. He gave me the rites, sponsored me." He'd dropped the mangled napkin. He rubbed at his right arm—the budded one—as if it pained him, as if some vestige of the former hurt lurked there.

"I'm sorry, Jeriad." Gyll reached out to touch McWilms's right hand, still on the table.

McWilms gave him a wan smile. "We all knew about the shields, Ulthane. It's no one's fault really; we knew their limitations, and Ric and I should have been more careful, neh? Thane Mondom would have had them repaired if she could. It's ironic; with the money from that contract, she *did* have two of them fixed." With a visible effort, McWilms shook off his mood. He pulled his hand back, sat back against the wall of the booth. "How about the drink, neh? On me."

"After that tale? I've got all of the Oldins' money to spend, Jeriad. I'll waste some of it here."

Gyll looked up—the innkeeper seemed to be engrossed in a conversation at the bar, but he was not looking at the woman with whom he talked. His attention wandered everywhere but in their direction. He would not look at Gyll. The woman placed money on the bar and left, following another couple out the ornate doors. Gyll noticed for the first time that most of the patrons seemed to have departed—the inn was nearly empty now. The innkeeper finally glanced their way, an unhappy look in his eyes. Gyll waggled a finger to attract his attention. "Two mulled wines, if you please, sirrah." The innkeeper nodded.

The wine arrived a few minutes later. The innkeeper was ill-at-ease, serving them. Sweat dappled his generous brow. He wiped meaty hands on his apron. "We don't often see Hoorka in here," he said. His smile slipped in and out, uncertain, a false sun behind quickly moving clouds. "Can we expect to see more of your excellent kin in here in the future, sirrah?" He glanced from Gyll to Jeriad.

McWilms stared at Gyll for a long moment, but Gyll could not read his expression. Then the Hoorka glanced up at the innkeeper. "I doubt it, sirrah," he said with the exaggerated politeness of guilded kin. "I simply happened to see my friend here on the street. Your fine establishment was convenient and attracted us."

"Ahh, that's sad news." It hadn't seemed to make him excessively unhappy. The tentative smile almost broke into a full grin, and there was relief in his voice. "I'm glad you chose us for a quick refreshment, though." There was perhaps too much emphasis on the word "quick." Gyll would have spoken, but a glance from McWilms made him sit silently.

"We just wished to warm ourselves for a few minutes."

"Well, enjoy it, sirrahs." The man sauntered back to the bar. Halfway there, he began whistling.

They didn't say anything for a moment, hands around the warmth of the mugs. Gyll was taken aback by the innkeeper's unsubtle hints; McWilms seemed simply bemused.

"That sort of thing happen often?" Gyll asked.

McWilms nodded. "It was always there, Ulthane. Even when you were on Neweden last."

"Call me Gyll. I'm not Ulthane anymore."

"Gyll, then. You remember it—that vague hostility from the guilded kin. It's gotten worse. A lot worse, sometimes. Nobody's particularly overt, because the Hoorka are still feared, but they all know that we can barely lay claim to being high kin with our finances so tight. We couldn't afford the tithing for the last election, so no rule-guild represents us on Council this session. Not that that matters; most kin look on us as allied with the Li-Gallant's rule-guild. They won't do anything to disturb Vingi, but they don't like us." McWilms sipped his wine. "Try it, Gyll. It's pretty good."

"You don't want to talk about this?"

"*None* of the Hoorka would want to talk about it." He sipped again. "Sometimes I feel like we're on the down side of our evolution, like the Hoorka are going to be the lassari we once were."

"Because of your Thane and the way she's handling the guild?"

That brought up McWilms's head. He started to speak, then shook his head and started again. "Is that what you'd like to think, Gyll?"

"I'm trying not to think anything."

"It's not her fault. It's Neweden, and the way it's changed."

"Then maybe Hoorka should change."

"That's not what you used to say, is it?" Then McWilms gave a short chuckle. "Can we change the subject?—it depresses me. Tell me about the Family Oldin, Gyll. How do they function, what are you doing there, and who are these Trader-Hoorka I keep seeing around the port?"

"Thane Mondom wouldn't want me to talk about them."

"She doesn't have to know." A pause. "Please, Gyll. I'm curious. It's been ages since I've heard from you, and you know about the kin. How about *you*?"

"All right," Gyll said. And he spoke.

"That was pretty good, Renard. Do you always burn down half a district to make your points? If so, remind me to stay out of the fire-insurance racket."

"How was I to know that the Li-Gallant'd respond so frigging slow? I know you, dwarf; you're not worried about all the innocent lives, are you?"

It was a squalid and dingy room hidden in a warren of dark streets and buildings deserted by all but the poorest. Of the two men, only Helgin could stand upright. The illumination was a candle set precariously on a rickety table. A mattress festooned with snarled bedsheets was in one corner. Helgin's bare feet scratched against the gritty dust of the floor. "Nice place you got here," the Motsognir said. "How much is the rent?"

"I'm only here for a few days—then we'll go back to the old place. I'd be interested to know how you found it, though."

"I followed my nose. That plant-pet of yours stinks, remember?"

Renard fondled the thick coil of the creature around his shoulders. He was sitting across the table from Helgin. Candlelight wavered across his face, glinting in his dark eyes. "Don't hide behind insults, Helgin. What's on your mind that you'd take the effort to find me? As I said, I doubt that you've been stricken with a conscience this late in your life."

Helgin shrugged. "You can't effect change without some harm. I just don't like seeing it done wholesale. You could have been more subtle, Renard."

"Is that you speaking, or FitzEvard Oldin?"

"Me." A throaty grumble.

"Then don't whine about my tactics, dwarf. I do what I feel I need to do. No more, no less, and *Oldin* pays me, not you."

"I'm FitzEvard's representative here."

"And that pet Sula of yours isn't, neh? Don't be upset; I know you have to show off for the Li-Gallant, don't you? You even got some of my people the other night—the ones I wanted you to get, of course, but enough to satisfy Vingi. I didn't mean for Dasta to burn, but I don't have a hell of a lot of control over a riot, do I?"

Helgin laughed. Renard continued to stroke his plant-pet, but slowly he smiled. "Oh, you deserve congratulations," Helgin said. "You've put the Sula in a good light. I just don't want you to overstep your bounds, to forget your role in this little drama. Don't get the feeling that you've got the leading part, Renard. Don't start thinking of yourself as powerful."

"You're too damned ugly for the star role yourself, Motsognir."

Helgin grinned. He got to his feet. "Don't make me angry, Renard. You *can* be replaced or eliminated altogether. It might even give me pleasure, if you goad me too much."

"I don't worry about your threats."

"I think you'd better." Helgin went to the door. Hand on the latch, he turned to look at Renard again. "Why is it we don't get along? It'd be a lot easier if we did. You could try being properly subservient."

"Get out of here, dwarf."

"No answer, then?"

"Out."

Helgin pulled the door open. Down a short corridor, sunlight gleamed through the uneven boards of another door. "Don't be too zealous, Renard. Oldin wants something left of Neweden."

"Don't trouble your tiny brain about it, Motsognir. Just get me the things I need."

"They're being prepared. You'll get them soon."

"See that I do. And if you're done giving me your shit, I'd appreciate the privacy."

Helgin looked about the room. "You could always raise mushrooms. They need a lot of shit, too." He laughed. Still chuckling, he went out.

"Well, Helgin? How did your meeting with that distributor go?"

They were back aboard *Goshawk*, in Gyll's cabin. Neweden wheeled below them, half-shadowed. Gyll cuddled his bumblewort in his lap, scratching its ear flaps gently. It hissed in contentment.

Helgin was staring at the dark world outside the port. "Well enough, I suppose," he said. "The man's a penurious sort, but I managed to get some business done. You want the details?"

"No," Gyll replied. "Just put them on the com-unit, and I'll go over it later." He glanced at the broad back of the Motsognir. "You seem distracted tonight, Helgin."

"Just tired. The gravity here pulls on me too much."

"You haven't insulted anyone in hours. You've been almost civil."

"Not funny, Gyll." Helgin turned. The dwarf, with the side-to-side walk of the Motsognir, came over to Gyll's chair. He reached out to pet the wort. It chirruped in ecstasy at the attention, rolling over heavily onto its back. Helgin kneaded the soft fur of its underbelly. "You took care of the tariffs for the last shipments?"

"Yah. And I met someone as well—Jeriad McWilms. You

remember him? One of the apprentices—the one that was almost killed on Heritage."

"Not really."

Gyll glanced at the dwarf. He'd been joking, but there was a moodiness to the Motsognir that he'd never seen before. Helgin was quiet, laconic. He looked up at Gyll, noticing his stare, and his eyes were almost angry, the walnut pupils dark almost to black. "Well, did you talk to him? Is that what you're waiting for me to ask? You want to brag because you were brave enough to ignore Mondom's warning? How can I show you how impressed I am?"

Helgin pulled his hand away from the wort angrily. The animal screeched in protest at the roughness of the motion and jumped from Gyll's lap. It went to a corner of the room and curled up, keening softly to itself.

"Hey, Motsognir. Easy."

Helgin glowered at Gyll for a moment, unrepentant; then the rage seemed to leave him. He sighed deeply, rumbling an apology. "Sorry. I really am tired, Gyll. That's all. Still not used to Neweden yet, neh?" He knuckled his eyes, yawned widely. "What'd McWilms have to say? Evidently it bothers you, or you wouldn't have brought it up."

"Are you just impressing me with your perception, or do you really want to hear it?"

Despite his mood, Helgin grinned. "That sounds like one of my lines. You've been working with me too long. Reverse the two clauses, though; it works better."

Gyll smiled. "Yah?"

"You have to polish your insults. They don't just happen. So... what did McWilms tell you?"

Gyll leaned back in his floater. He put his feet up on his desk, clasped his hands behind his head. "What caught my attention wasn't really anything he said, specifically. It was the whole tone behind his words, coupled with what I've seen and heard so far. I think I might hate the Hoorka, what they've become. It bothers me to see them regarded as Vingi's private assassins, to see them treated like low kin, to see how poor they've become."

"Does that mean you'll be able to convince them to go with us easily?"

Gyll frowned. "If it were just that, probably yes. But

Mondom . . . she doesn't want me to get close to them—or her—again. Today was just an accident, not a defiance. But maybe that's what I should be: defiant. I don't know, Helgin. I hate what I see."

"You can't do a damn thing about it," the dwarf grumbled. "You ain't Hoorka; not that kind, anyway."

"But I created them."

"And you feel responsible."

"I feel like I might want to destroy them."

"And who the hell are you, one of the gods? I think you're being a trifle melodramatic, Gyll. Besides, you're here to recruit the Hoorka. They might be a little irritated if you start undermining them, and then FitzEvard would be angry with *you*, and he can act like a god a damned sight better than you." Helgin shook his head. "Better just to be unemotional about it. Be silent and unmoved, like a rock. Like me."

Gyll laughed, and his laughter had an edge. "You're no rock, Motsognir. You just hide your sensitivity and pretend it doesn't exist. That rock of yours is only a stage prop."

Helgin snorted derision. The wort looked up, curious, from the corner. "I still wouldn't try kicking it, Gyll. You might break your foot."

6

The state dinner was held in an ornate hall near the main entrance of Diplo Center. The high walls displayed a shifting landscape of arid beauty, molding imperceptibly at the corners. Above, the ceiling was masked by blue-gray streaks of cloud behind which lurked an orange sun. The clouds moved with the wall landscape, entering and leaving the room left to right. The people in the room could well believe that they sat on a small plateau high up in new and jagged peaks. Boulders sat here and there; the floor was earthen and except where the long table stood, was not level. One could see to the horizon in every direction; there, a long finger of topaz ocean, or a scintillating line of river snaking across windblown plain, and to the left the line of majestic and austere mountains marched into the haze.

Gyll did not envy the people that had to clean this up afterward.

Helgin walked to where the plateau, at the juncture of wall and floor, seemed to drop in a sheer, knife-edged peak. He leaned carefully forward, looking down. "Shit," he said. He backed up a step and bent at the waist again, reaching out with a forefinger. He touched nothing, and—badly overbalanced—rocked back on his feet once more. He took a tentative step toward the cliff and repeated the process. This time his probing finger was halted by the invisible wall.

"Hah," he announced. "If anyone here has vertigo problems, their supper's going to be all over the floor. Good thing it's dirt."

Gyll held back a laugh. McClannan, standing beside d'Embry, looked annoyed. The Regent herself seemed politely amused while nearby waiters (actually some of the lower echelon Diplo staffers recruited for the evening) smiled but kept a discreet silence. Helgin moved to the door, which stood without visible support at one end of the plateau. He leaned as close to the wall as he could without touching it, peering around the back of the door.

"Good," he said. "You wrapped the diorama around the back as well. The thing even throws a shadow. Very good." He tapped the wall with a fingernail. It gave off a sound like crystal. "Too damned good for Neweden." The dwarf glanced from McClannan to d'Embry. "Who's supposed to be impressed?"

Gyll began to speak, but McClannan was quicker. "It obviously impressed *you*; did it not, though I can see where a much-traveled Trader might be jaded—"

"*Seneschal*," d'Embry interrupted. McClannan glanced at her; she smiled up at him too sweetly. "I'm afraid you've fallen into the Motsognir's trap. He deliberately goads you. Do you not, sirrah?" she asked, turning to Helgin.

The dwarf grinned at Gyll, who shook his head. Then he bowed deeply. "You render me transparent, Regent. It's a fault of mine, I'm afraid; I like to see people make asses of themselves."

McClannan scowled. D'Embry, the hump of the symbiote concealed in glittering cloth that flickered uneasily from azure to scarlet, nodded back to the dwarf. "You see, Seneschal," she said, "Traders are wonderful manipulators, and the Motsognir are most likely their teachers. FitzEvard, best of all, has learned his lessons."

Gyll cleared his throat. He was dressed in a close-fitting tunic and pants, white piped with blue. The color flattered him, the fit accentuated the lean hardness of his body. He spoke softly, pleasantly. "I've always found FitzEvard Oldin to be a man of his word, Regent."

"I don't doubt that he is, Sula. If, for instance, he said that he would never kill you, he'd send somebody else to do the job."

Gyll bridled at that. His eyes narrowed, and the polite smile he'd worn as part of his costume dissolved. "You play the same games as the Motsognir, Regent. At least *he* doesn't pretend to have the veneer of civility."

Gyll expected anger, expected d'Embry to turn cold and ask them—civilly—to leave. Certainly the expression on McClannan's face was that of unmasked venom. But d'Embry simply waved a hand (glinting silver) in dismissal. "Sula," she said, "the Motsognir insults simply because he enjoys getting the reactions; whether he says the truth or not doesn't matter to him. I was Regent when FitzEvard Oldin came to Printemps. There was another Trader on that world as well, of the Family Shannon. They argued, and I was forced to intervene. FitzEvard vowed to me that he would do nothing to harm this man. *He* didn't. In fact, FitzEvard was with me when an intruder killed the Trader Shannon. I could never prove anything, but both FitzEvard and I knew what had happened." She paused a moment, and her face took on an aspect of sternness. She seemed to stand straighter. "Up to that time, I thought I liked Oldin well enough myself. We'd even flirted, and I'd considered letting it go further. He was handsome enough then—he probably still is; his type seems to age gracefully. He was slick, and he looked straight at me and lied with a smile on his face and we both knew he was lying. It didn't bother him that I knew, as long as nothing could be proved."

She stopped and regarded Gyll. "I only tell you this to warn you about your employer, Sula."

"I think I know him well enough already. And I also think your bias shows, Regent."

The discussion went no further. The doorward chimed, and the Li-Gallant Vingi entered. He moved, as always, heavily, ponderously, each step deliberate and certain. Rolls of flesh jiggled under a wide and ornate belt; his multitude of rings flashed light. Behind him came the kin-lords of the other rule-guilds. Gyll searched the crowd for familiar faces as d'Embry nodded to the waiters to begin circulating with trays of hors d'oeuvres and wine. Gyll recognized only one of them: Sirrah d'Vegnes, who had been one of the underlings in Gunnar's rule-guild standards ago, once one of the challengers to Vingi's dictatorship. D'Vegnes wore the belt-holo of kin-lord now, and he was not at all the match of his slain predecessor. He fawned over the Li-Gallant, posturing. Gyll took a glass from one of the waiters, watching as d'Embry and McClannan moved among their guests. There were polite compliments on the setting of the room.

"You know what gives it away, Gyll?" Helgin startled Gyll out of his reverie. He looked down at the Motsognir. Helgin held two glasses of wine; as Gyll watched, the dwarf drained one and set it firmly upside down in the dirt.

"What gives what away?"

"The illusion of this room. The acoustics foul the pretense. This still sounds like a room, not outdoors. Too much presence, too much quick echo and reverberation. Once you notice it, you can't be taken in again."

Gyll made a face. "Thanks. I was rather enjoying it."

"Well, that's the trouble with illusions. They fall through too quickly."

"Some people simply can't appreciate beauty when they see it."

"Some people just like being fooled," Helgin retorted.

They stared at each other, half-smiling. Then Gyll shook his head. Helgin slapped him on the rump. They laughed.

"Well, it's good to see that Traders, unlike our two Alliance hosts, get along well." The voice was a low purr: the Li-Gallant approached them. Helgin nodded to Vingi, Gyll gave the low bow of kin. After a hesitation, the Li-Gallant

85

bowed in return—though less fully—to Gyll. "What gives the two of you so much amusement?"

"We were just discussing the room."

Vingi nodded massively, glancing slowly about. "It's rather effective, isn't it? It would be nice to have something on this scale in the keep. Could the Families do this?"

"We could do it easily enough," Gyll replied. "I've seen Oldin dens that had much the same, if not on quite so elaborate a scale—mainly, we simply project holos beyond false windows. But I'm certain it could be duplicated without trouble."

"Ah." Vingi twisted a ring around a finger. He plucked a meatrind from a passing tray. "Perhaps I should price your equipment in comparison with that of the Alliance." Daintily he placed the meatrind in his mouth.

"The Oldins will be cheaper," Helgin said.

The Li-Gallant rolled the meatrind around his tongue appreciatively. He swallowed. "Yah, but will it continue to work after the ship has gone?"

"Simply make certain that we stay, Li-Gallant."

"Perhaps I could. If it were worth my effort." Vingi looked from Helgin to Gyll.

"We've no doubts as to your abilities, Li-Gallant," Gyll said.

"Very polite of you to mention it, Sula." A bell chimed. "But I think we're being called to dinner. Maybe we can continue this conversation there."

They had no chance. Vingi was seated next to d'Embry, at the head of the table. Gyll and Helgin flanked McClannan at the other end. Only Helgin relished that arrangement. He picked up a fork, examined the silver critically. "Not bad, Seneschal," he said, polishing the tines on his sleeve. "It's even clean."

McClannan did not seem disposed to comment. He smiled, weakly, tiredly. He looked resigned to a trying evening.

The dinner was long and varied, a sampling of cuisine from many worlds of the Alliance. Portions were small but multitudinous. Gyll more than once found himself glancing quizzically at Helgin after a plate of unidentifiable something was set before him. Several others he recognized, though he'd tasted few of them before: cockatrice from Thule, spineballs,

unijells, Terran beef, and even a puffindle from Neweden's
cold seas. Gyll was sated well before the last course—a pastry
of questionable origin that tasted too sweet—but found that
he could not resist sampling. Helgin ate everything placed
before him, quickly, as if it might be taken away if he tarried.

McClannan talked with Gyll as they ate the pastry. "You
know, Sula, what strikes me as the worst fault of the Families
is their lack of a central government. We Diplos, for instance,
answer to Diplo Center on Niffleheim, which in turn is under
the leadership of the Legatus Primus and thence there the entire
Alliance structure. There is accountability for all our actions."

"Which doesn't prevent mistakes, but simply breeds
cautious, slow, and mediocre Diplos." Gyll toyed with his
pastry, not looking at the Seneschal; crumbs flaked delicately
away from his fork. "It's my feeling that the looseness of
Family society is its virtue, not the opposite."

"I can't agree." McClannan leaned forward, pushing his
plate away. His handsome face was eager. "It's been proved
time and time again that anarchy is no answer. Our entire
history tells us that: all the times of a strong central government are the times of expansion. When there is none, human
space is in shambles."

"Every time of strong government, from the Reduxtors
of the First Empire through Huard, has also ended in chaos.
Everyone grabs for the power—spread it out, and there's less
chance of losing everything."

"Still, you can't blame the Interregnums on anything but
Dame Fate. And it has always been a centralized government, one unified entity, that has brought us back out of
those times."

Gyll shrugged. "But in all that scrambling, we've yet to
match the technologies of the First Empire. . . ."

Gyll found that McClannan bothered him less as he
began to know the man. That facile, easy handsomeness must
have actually been a burden to him; Gyll suspected that
McClannan had always been expected to be successful and
had often fallen short of that mark. He was ambitious but not
overly gifted with talents to aid that ambition. Gyll would not
have wanted the Seneschal on his staff or anywhere in a
position of importance, but if the man ever managed to make
a friend, he would probably not be a bad companion: facile,

and not deep. The polar opposite of d'Embry.... Gyll made his disagreements in the discussion milder than he might have. "I might also point out, Seneschal," Gyll continued, "that it was only the Trading Families that kept any glimmer of civilization alive during those dark times. Could the Alliance have formed at all without our work having given them the chance?"

"You speak as a convert, Sula. All converts are more zealous and less objective."

"Then let a nonconvert speak, man," Helgin broke in. He dabbed at his plate with a forefinger, picking up stray crumbs. "The Motsognir have no allegiance to either the Families or the Alliance. For myself, having seen both, I far prefer the Families' society." He licked his finger.

McClannan made a poor attempt to mask his revulsion. "Without meaning offense, what do the dwarves know of human civilization? The Motsognir fled human space centuries ago after you stole the ship *Naglfar* from the Reduxtor Pieter III—you made your choice, then."

"The Motsognir are as human as you, McClannan—and a hell of a lot smarter. *We* had no choice about being reengineered—that was an experiment of one of your precious strong central governments," Helgin said darkly. His mouth twitched under the growth of beard. Gyll began to interrupt, hoping to head off the too-fragile temper of the dwarf, but the doorward chimed. Everyone at the table looked about. At the table's head, a puzzled d'Embry gestured to one of the waiters. The man began to move toward the door, but it burst open in a gout of sparks, wrecked. Amidst shouts, a group of several lassari entered the room, holding crowd-prods and stings. Gyll jerked to his feet as, around the table, people frantically tried to scramble from their seats. The foremost of the lassari lifted her sting and fired at the ceiling. There was a crystalline explosion; a shower of broken sky rained down on the table. Someone screamed.

"*Sit down, all of you!*" the woman shouted. "Sit *down!*"

Most of the guests did so. Gyll hesitated, glancing at Helgin. "After-dinner entertainment, I suppose," the Motsognir muttered, and shrugged. He sat, as did Gyll. McClannan had not moved; he stared at the lassari, stricken. Pieces of the ceiling littered the table in front of them.

"Better, better," the woman said. She lowered the sting and looked slowly around the room. The sun was flickering, the clouds had vanished, there was a hole in the sky that revealed piping and wooden beams. "Isn't this nice. Well, Li-Gallant, was it a good dinner? Was there enough food for that gross stomach of yours?"

D'Embry rose to her feet; Vingi remained silent. "I'm the Regent d'Embry," she said coldly. "Who are you?"

"Does that matter to you, Regent? Well, I am Micha, and those behind me are part of the Hag's Legion. Somehow, our invitations didn't arrive for the dinner tonight. We're sorry we're late, but your guards were rather unfriendly."

"I want all of you out of here."

There was laughter from the lassari. "That's not a request you can enforce, Regent. Your guards are all asleep in the corridor—try to call them."

"If you've hurt any of them . . ."

"Hurt *them* like the Li-Gallant and his pack of pet killers hurt *us*?" She paused, and then she smiled. "We're not barbarians, Regent, despite our image."

Listening, Gyll felt helpless. Weaponless, outnumbered, there was little he or Helgin could do. If he could reach one of them before he was shot, get a sting, if Helgin could get to one as well . . . No. He squirmed in his seat, restless, a little frightened. The movement caused Micha to glance at him.

"Ahh, Sula," she said. "How does it feel to know that your Hoorka are now nothing but the hired thugs of that pig down the table? Does it bother you? I hope so. And I hope it bothers you to have to sit there, helpless, wondering what we intend to do with you." She glanced around the table. "I hope it bothers all of you."

Gyll could see panic and shock in some of the guests now. The Li-Gallant, especially, seemed touched by fear. He was breathing too quickly, his bulk pressed back against his chair as if to be as far as possible from the threatening woman. His face was pale, his eyes wide. Gyll knew that the Li-Gallant did not expect to live. For himself, Gyll knew only that he would try to take someone to the Hag with him, should it come to that. Ransom for his soul.

"What do you want?" d'Embry asked. She alone had a voice; she, of all of them, was calm, had the shreds of her presence around her despite the situation.

"Perhaps we're going to cut the hump from your back and see how long it takes you to die, Regent." Micha grinned at d'Embry's sudden intake of breath. "Or maybe we'll give the Li-Gallant an immediate diet, remove some of that excess weight he carries. It would be simple, and even just, as well." She shrugged, one-shouldered. "Oh, that's lassari methods, isn't it?—without honor. Your gods must weep for us."

"You'd never get away with it," Vingi stuttered.

"Resorting to *clichés*, Li-Gallant? Words—especially old, worn-out ones—are a poor shield against a sting. Well, unfortunately, you're nearly right. Killing any of you in this way would only increase our difficulties. We're not ready yet to take full advantage of your absence, Li-Gallant. I'd fear for the existence of all lassari if someone worse than you were ruler. We simply want to make a point. We want to be heard."

Micha gestured harshly, scowling now, all pretense of her sarcastic good humor banished. Two lassari stepped from the mob behind her, carrying a long object wrapped in cloth. It was an awkward burden, for they staggered as they moved. Gyll recognized it—he'd seen it too many times. But before he could speak, the lassari cast it down on the floor, holding the ends of the cloth. A body rolled out onto the dirt—a thin, gaunt woman with sunken cheeks and a bloated belly. Her arms were empty bags of flesh, the muscles slack in a pouch of flesh. Those at the table were in an uproar, most standing now, their faces horrified.

"She died of starvation. We don't know her name—no one does," Micha said. "She's lassari, so no kin cared about her. Her death was lonely and long. That's what we wanted you to see." She stared at them with somber and furious eyes. "I hope all of you enjoyed your meal."

Again, she gestured. The lassari began to leave the room, Micha in their midst; the body, accusing, was left behind. Someone down the table was vomiting noisily. Gyll watched the lassari leave, the muscles in his stomach slowly unknotting. He glanced at d'Embry, her face reflecting a cool inner rage, and back to the departing intruders.

And he caught a glimpse of steel.

"*Down!*" he shouted, flinging himself to one side. A throwing knife hissed through the air. He heard the *tchunk* as the blade struck the wall, and he rolled to his feet, certain that the weapon had been intended for the Li-Gallant.

But it was Helgin who sat in his chair, head turned to contemplate the knife just centimeters from his head. The weapon seemed to hover, shorn of its point, motionless, in the landscape of mountains.

Helgin wrenched the knife from the wall. His bearded face unreadable, he examined the blade, then tossed it onto the table. China clattered and broke.

"Wasn't close enough to bother moving," he said.

The best that could be said for Felling's stew was that it was hot and took away some of the chill of Underasgard. It wasn't particularly Felling's fault that the Hoorka found it unappetizing: it was plain fare, but savory enough. He'd simply served the stew or something akin to it too often. But stew made use of meats and odd ends—it was the most economical way to cook, and Thane Mondom insisted on economy.

McWilms toyed with the conglomeration on his plate like the rest. The bread, at least, was newly baked, and the mead was satisfactory, if slightly diluted. McWilms broke off a piece from the loaf and chewed enthusiastically, trying to convince his palate that this was an amazingly subtle combination of tastes.

His palate was not fooled.

The Hoorka were gathered in the common room off the kitchens. Apprentices, who would eat later, stood waiting along the walls, which were studded with glittering nodules of calcite deposits. From the kitchen could be heard the noise of the jussar applicants, doing their drudge work under Felling's baleful eye.

McWilms sat at the Thane's table with most of the elder kin: Serita, Bachier, Kristagon, Sholla, and others. Mondom ate with them, and she seemed no happier than the rest with their menu. "Smile, Serita," she said. "I told Felling to buy some groceries tomorrow with part of the money from your contract. Supper should be much better." She stabbed at a piece of meat with her fork, and contemplated the gristle marbling it. "It should be better than this, certainly, with no offense to Felling, who's doing the best he can."

"Well, I'm glad to hear it," Serita said. Her face was mottled with a bruise on one cheek, a remnant of her fight with Meka Joh after their return from the contract. Joh, his arm in a sling and a wrapping around a leg, sat elsewhere. "I was beginning to think we needed to expand into the thieving business and hit the food stalls at Market Square." She mused on that for a moment. "Ric would have volunteered," she added, a sadness in her voice. D'Mannberg had been one of her lovers, and his appetite had been the source of many well-intentioned comments among the kin.

The mention of his kin-father blunted what little remained of McWilms's own hunger. He pushed the half-finished plate of stew away and laid down his bread. He glanced at the table: rough, gaps between some of the planks, scarred with gouges from idle knives, and stained with spilled food. It made him think of his apprentice days, when Felling would set them all to scrubbing down the tables. When Gyll had been Thane.

As if in counterpoint to his own thoughts, Bachier spoke wistfully from down the table. "Do you remember the feast we had when we first had a contract from the Diplos, under old Regent Vogel? Ulthane Gyll had Felling buy ice-steak for all the full kin. By She of the Five, *that* was a meal. I remember how the apprentices all looked forlorn when it was gone—no scraps left, just a few well-gnawed bones."

McWilms laughed. "I was one of those apprentices, Bachier. And if you think we didn't get to sample that dinner, you're wrong. Old Felling's eyes have never been fast enough to stop us from lifting a few choice pieces. Remember, Kris?—you were an apprentice then as well."

"Tender and incredibly rich—and of course we took only the choicest morsels," Kristagon elaborated. "We'd send the dregs out to the kin."

The laughter rippled around the table, but McWilms noticed that Mondom didn't seem to share the amusement. He wondered at that. "What do you think, Thane?" he asked. "Are good times like those still waiting for us?"

She smiled back at him, but the gesture touched only

her lips. Her eyes, with the fine time-wrinkles at the corners, seemed to be almost hurt. "You never know, Jeriad."

"The Ulthane loved his food as well as the rest of us," Bachier said. "Began to show on him a little toward the end, though—still, he always did well enough on the practice strips. Wonder how he looks now? Can't have lost his skills too much, considering how he snuck in here recently." Then, to Mondom's accusing stare: "We all know it had to be him, Thane. Who else would you have let leave peacefully after that?"

"The Ulthane looks very good," McWilms said without thinking. He could feel Mondom's gaze on him now, and he didn't dare look at her. He berated himself. *Fool, does such a little mead go to your head so quickly that you can't control your mouth?* "I saw him on a street in Sterka, going the other way," he added as casually as he could. He picked up his bread again, broke off another chunk.

"Did he speak to you?" Mondom asked sharply. Her voice was acid, stern.

"You told us to avoid the Traders," he answered. It seemed to satisfy her, though she still looked at McWilms appraisingly.

"If *I'd* been one of the kin the Ulthane met on his way in, it would have been different," Bachier said. "He wouldn't have put *me* on the floor."

Mondom's head snapped around to him. "Don't be so damned sure," she said. "You're strong enough, Bachier, but the *Sula*"—she used Gyll's new title with heavy emphasis—"has always been one quite able to counter strength with a move."

"Thane—"

"No," she interrupted. "I don't know why the Sula returned here just to sit in the back caverns, but my orders still stand. I want all of you to leave him alone, and to tell me if he trys to contact any of you. And I hate this subject," she added. "Let's find another."

"Thane," McWilms said. He kept his voice gentle, casual. "The Ulthane isn't Hoorka's enemy, after all. He *did* create the guild, made us kin. We shouldn't pretend that he doesn't exist. Some of us had great affection for him . . ." His voice trailed off as he glanced at her.

He knew he'd gone too far, said too much. He could see it in the way Mondom drew back, in the flush that crept up her neck, in the way her fingers curled around the arm of her chair. She hovered on the edge of anger, and he could see her fighting it. There was silence around the table. Slowly, Mondom relaxed, the creases in her face softening. McWilms regretted, far too many times at this supper, his words.

"Thane, I'm very sorry," he said. "Sometimes there's an idiot working my mouth."

She shook her head tightly. Her voice played with nonchalance and failed. "It's all right, Jeriad. What you say is true. We shouldn't forget our past or what the Sula has meant to us." She nodded to the kin. "If you'll excuse me, I need to get the money ready for Felling."

Deliberately, Mondom pushed her chair back from the table and rose. She bowed slightly to the kin and, walking a shade too quickly, left the room.

"Stuck your feet in it that time, didn't you?" Serita said to McWilms when she had gone.

He didn't answer. He stared into the darkness after the Thane.

The night was uneasy for Gyll. The dream at first was gentle and erotic. Kaethe was with him, as she had been the night he'd left with Helgin for Neweden. She was on top of him, moving, her eyes closed, lost in their passion. He reached up to touch her swaying breasts, and they were suddenly Mondom's; smaller, the texture of the skin rougher under his hands, and it was not Kaethe's face that loomed over him but some strange melding of Kaethe and Mondom— his two lovers, his two lives. In his dream, he did not care, but lunged with her as they sought release, and when they finally found it, he cried out as Kaethe/Mondom laughed.

He woke, sweat-drenched, and oddly frightened of the dream. He forced himself to stay awake long hours after that, watching Neweden move beneath his ship. In time, he could not keep his eyes open, his tired body forcing him to return to his bed.

When he dreamed again, it was of lassari and dead women and knives of bright, sharp steel.

7

The note had come to Gyll in a most roundabout fashion, handed to a Diplo guard at Sterka Port by an apprentice Hoorka, and then given to one of the Family Oldin crew on their shuttle. When the shuttle returned to *Goshawk*, it was placed on Fischer's desk, who gave it to Sula Hermond.

It said, simply: "Ten A.M., the river below the falls. Mondom."

The note did not seem to require an answer, and evidently Mondom did not expect him to miss the appointment; she knew him that well. Gyll took the next shuttle down, wondering, memories of his odd dream and the fiasco of d'Embry's dinner occupying his thoughts.

The falls spread cold mist over the morning. The wind shifted, and curtains of water spread across the river. The falls were pretty but unspectacular—some worlds were blessed with a hundred better scenes. The cascade clambered down the worn steps of the bluffs well outside Sterka. There was the normal amount of litter scattered about, remnants of old rendezvous. Gyll shrugged his jacket tighter around him. The mists beaded his hair. He ran a hand through the wetness, shook his head. He reached down and picked up a flat rock. He skimmed it across the roiling water.

"Hello, Gyll."

He'd not heard her approach in the clamor of the falls. She wore the Hoorka nightcloak, the hood up. "Chilly out here," he said.

"Sorry."

"Your note didn't give a reason for this..." He didn't know what to call it.

"You talked to McWilms."

There was a flat and curiously dispassionate accusation in her voice. Gyll could sense her body under the cover of the nightcloak; muscles flexed, ready to move at need, as if the confrontation would of necessity be physical. All he could see of her were her eyes and a strand of hair curling down over her forehead.

He didn't bother to deny her charge—he didn't lie easily; Helgin had told him many times how transparent he was when he tried. "Did Jeriad tell you?"

"He didn't have to."

"Don't blame him," Gyll said. "We really didn't seek each other out. It was just a chance meeting on the street, and I invited him to have a drink. I know you asked me to stay away from the kin, but I don't find anything horrible in talking to Jeriad. Have some compassion, Mondom. He's an old friend."

The wind blew mist back into their faces. Mondom turned away before he could see if there was a reaction to his words in her eyes. When she finally looked back, there was a troubled hardness to her stare. "I've as much compassion as any of the kin, Gyll," she said. "At least that's what I tell myself. But the Thane sometimes isn't allowed to show it or respond to it. She has to be a bitch." Now she swept the hood back, turned down the collar. Mist swept down eagerly. "I don't like it, but it's necessary. You should know that." Slowly, faintly, she smiled. "I *do* understand, Gyll. I don't really mind."

Gyll smiled tentatively back. "Good. I'd hate to have you angry with me. We've done that to each other too often in the past."

"I'm not angry."

"Then can we move out of this damned mist?"

She laughed, her face sheened with water. "Certainly."

Down the riverbank, they found a sheltering wall of cliff. There was a small hollow where the wind could not find them. Narrow, it brought them close together of necessity, and each of them pressed their back to stone to lessen the intimacy. Gyll stared out at the river, not at her face, suddenly too near his own. "I assume you had some other purpose with the note than just giving me a shower?"

"I want to know more. I want to know why you've come back, what you intend to do."

"I thought I'd told you."

"Maybe. I'm not sure *you* know. From what I gathered

from Jeriad, he seems to think that you're rather perturbed by Hoorka, by what you've seen since you got here." She said it carefully, neutral. Her gaze sought his, but she seemed only attentive, waiting for his answer.

"Yah. I don't like it. I especially don't like what people keep telling me." Her eyes would not let him go.

"What is that?"

"That the Hoorka belong to Vingi."

Lines creased her forehead, her lips tightened into a scowl. "You've been listening to the wrong sources, then. Give me some credit, Gyll. I've followed your code, strictly. If that gives Hoorka the appearance of being Vingi's, then it's the code's fault, not mine." The timbre of her voice changed, tinged with spite. "*You* weren't around to see how that might come about."

Gyll reached out a hand, touched her shoulder through the nightcloak, amazed at the texture of the material—he'd remembered it as softer. Mondom flinched away from his touch, and he let his hand drop back. "No, I wasn't around," he said softly. "And I've learned quite a bit since then—about myself, mostly. For one, I've learned that you shouldn't let pride speak before necessity. I know I would never have said this before, but maybe the code needs to be changed."

The mildness of his answer only seemed to feed her ire. She made a sound of disgust deep in her throat, taking a step out of the hollow and back. She glared at him. "Gods, the Family Oldin's done wonders for you, hasn't it? The bitch Kaethe feeds you her dreams, and FitzEvard substitutes his own vision for yours. What's happened to you, Gyll? You're not the person I made love with, the proud Hoorka-Thane. Do the Oldins unman all their employees?"

Fury raced through Gyll, a blind, white heat. But he did not move, didn't instinctively reach for the sheathed blade at his side as he once would have done. He willed himself into some semblance of control—the same rules he'd imposed on his Trader-Hoorka. *Think before action. There's usually more time than you believe, and deeds aren't easily undone.* He tore his gaze away from Mondom's challenging eyes. He breathed deeply, listening to the rushing dance of the river. "I don't understand this, Mondom," he said at last. "I don't understand why we insist on making each other angry."

Bleak, he turned to face her. "And, by the Dame, you succeed in it. You succeed admirably. But I don't kill anymore, and I only fight when there's no other recourse. If you're trying to goad me to that extent, it won't work. I won't let it."

She didn't believe him; he could see it. Her stance mocked him, her face scoffed. "You're Sula, head of a military force. You tell me that you don't fight, don't kill?"

"I teach."

"You send others to do your dirty work, then, like the Li-Gallant."

He visibly recoiled from that accusation, sagging against the rock of the cliff as if wounded. A jagged finger of stone dug into his back. Wearily he shook his head. "I still believe much of what Neweden taught me, Mondom. The blame for any death rests with the person that ordered that killing, no matter who held the weapon. But I avoid such a final decision if I can avoid it, and the Oldins seem to prefer that approach."

"It's more devious."

"It's more effective."

"Then why in the hell do you want my Hoorka? What good can we do you? We kill, Gyll. That's what you set us up to do, trained us to be—assassins. Nothing more."

"I'd like to retrain you, use your skills in other ways. . . ." He shrugged, thrusting away from the wall with his shoulders. They were very close. He could smell the spice of Mondom's breath. "And, in any case, killing is still a needed skill."

Her gaze searched his face, curiously soft. He began to wonder if her anger had merely been a sham devised to destroy the vestiges of their old affection. "Gyll . . ." she began; then her lashes came down to shield those eyes, drawing deep lines at the corners. "Just what is it that you're offering?"

"Comfort, challenge, a new meaning to our kinship." He paused, wondering how to phrase what he wanted to say. "Maybe even to see if we can be friends—or more—again."

"Those are just words, Gyll. They don't mean anything."

He smiled. "You're right. You want specifics: the Hoorka here would be the nucleus of a special-forces division within my current group, for use when one or two people are needed—for subversive work, perhaps even assassinations, though I would prefer not. We'd move you from Neweden to a planet near OldinHome that I've made my base. You'd be in charge of the kin, Mondom."

"But subject to your orders."

"To FitzEvard Oldin, through me."

"Or just you, if you decide something needs to be done. The Oldins would back you, wouldn't they?"

"I suppose that's possible," he admitted.

"And we'd be back to where we were eight standards ago."

"Was it so bad?"

She sighed, and he knew that she was finally beyond the reflexive Neweden anger. A melancholy smile drifted over her face and she cocked her head, listening to the distant thunder of the falls. "I've changed a lot too, Gyll, if not in the same ways you have. For me to do this would be the same as admitting I've ruined Hoorka, and I simply don't believe that. We've had bad times recently—I'd admit that to anyone— hell, *Neweden's* had bad times, but the kin are still together. I've talked with d'Embry about new offworld contracts and I'm hopeful that she'll consider them. We've had two contracts in the last half-standard that weren't Vingi's. I'm not going to admit defeat, Gyll, and that's what you're asking." She passed her hand through her hair, raining droplets on the ground. "No, it wasn't all bad between us, Gyll. I enjoyed being with you, learning from you, being your lover. It was a good time. But we also had our differences; they drove us apart then. I figure the same thing would happen now, and I'm getting too old to want to take that kind of chance."

"You sound like I did," he said. "Eight standards ago."

She grinned. "Maybe."

"And I've found that I was wrong in that thinking. Mondom, the Oldins are what Hoorka needs to grow. The Alliance is only a dead end, Neweden is just a blind alley. We suit the Families, they suit us. From everything I've seen and heard here, the Hoorka will be lassari shit in another few standards, dead like the ippicators. Let me at least make my offer to the kin, let them decide."

The grin had fallen from her face. "No," she answered; then again, softer: "No."

"Why?"

"Because I don't trust the Family Oldin."

"Then you don't trust me. Gods, you sound like d'Embry."

"Maybe she's right."

Gyll scuffed a heel against rock. He sighed, a long exhalation. Mondom waited as he looked upward at the mist-driven sky. Then she did something that surprised him. She took a step, pressing against him, her arms around him in a firm hug. A moment, and then he responded, clasping her against him. The sudden affection brought back a flooding of memory. He bent his head down to kiss her, but she had moved back again. "Why did you do that?" he asked.

"I wanted to do it while I still could," she answered. Gyll didn't know what to say to that. He stood there, shifting his weight uncertainly until she spoke again. "You were a fine lover, Gyll, but you never were very easy with affection. You'd always say nothing, or the wrong thing."

"You could give me another chance at it. You could let me talk with the kin."

"With *my* kin," she emphasized. "It's not their decision to make, Gyll. I'm Thane, and I've said no."

"Mondom, I don't like what Hoorka has become. It makes me sick to think of the guilded kin reviling my creation. I want that to end, one way or the other."

Her anger was back before he'd finished speaking. A minute ago, he'd thought there was a chance. But all that vanished, riven, with the rage that twisted her face. She clambered away from the hollow, into the wind and mist, her hair tousled, the heavy fabric of the nightcloak swirling. "*Damn* you, Hermond. You've no more sensitivity than a frigging stone. All you can think about is how things affect you."

"And what are you doing?" he asked mildly.

"You believe I'm just as selfish, neh?" She put her hood up against the wind. "Maybe I am. Maybe I can't stand the thought of losing my little tithing of power. If it is, so be it. No, Gyll. That's going to remain my answer to you. No. If I find that you're trying to go around me, I'll take actions. We were friends and more—I'd hate to see us become enemies."

"Mondom," he persisted. "Everything I see of Hoorka here makes me angry."

"And what bothers you most is that you have no power over it. Well, you gave that up voluntarily, Gyll. You understood Neweden and Hoorka fit it very well, but you went looking for power elsewhere. It's a shame, because I don't think you understand the Families and the Alliance much at all, and I'm afraid they're going to swallow you whole."

"Then come with me and help me understand."

"Stay away from us, Gyll."

"Hoorka was my creation."

"And we're past you now. Sula Hermond is not kin, and he has nothing to do with us."

He ignored her tone, her use of the impersonal mode. "I'm not certain of that."

"Stay away, Sula." Her lips narrowed. She spat out the words as if they burned her tongue. "Or I'll kill you. I swear it, Gyll, I'll use my knife."

She turned in the middle of his reply, the nightcloak moving around her with finality. He made no effort to go after her. He listened to the sound of her boots against rock, his head leaning back against the cold stone. Finally, he could hear nothing but the soughing of the river; still, he did not move. It was only when the sunstar, climbing, found him that he kicked himself away from the cliff and began the walk back to Sterka.

"Li-Gallant, I want to apologize." The words tasted like gall. D'Embry didn't care for Vingi's office, didn't like the discomfort in her chest and the headache with which she'd awakened, didn't enjoy the half-smirk on the Li-Gallant's face. "I don't know how that disturbance happened last night, but I'm damned well going to find out."

"There is an old adage on Neweden about closing the cage after the moonwailer has gotten out."

D'Embry watched as the Li-Gallant laced thick fingers together. All of his face frowned except for the eyes: they openly laughed at her. She tried to find a comfortable position in her floater; the movement threatened to split her head. A hammer thudded behind her skull. *Damn it, symbiote, do something.* "Li-Gallant, we thought that the security arrangements we had were more than sufficient, and we were on the Center grounds, as well. That's Alliance territory."

"Evidently your captains were wrong about the security, and lassari don't care for territorial semantics."

Fine, be difficult about this, you bastard. You're enjoying it. Gods, symbiote, aren't you going to ease this throbbing? "What can I say, Li-Gallant? From what we've reconstructed so far, the lassari knew the layout and location of the guards perfectly. We've made the assumption that one of the guards— or one of the guests—was sympathetic to the Hag's Legion or was bribed. All of the Diplo staff are undergoing psych evaluation—we'll get our subversive and punish him to the full extent of Alliance law. They couldn't have gotten in and out without help."

"That fact worries me more than the rest, Regent." His slow regard moved down to the sea-wash illumination of his desk terminal. Green light swirled the lines of his face. Then he looked at her again. "You look pale this morning. I trust that the excitement and apprehension haven't been too much for your, ahh, condition." He arrayed himself in comic concern.

Bastard. She forced herself to ignore the ache in her head, the catch in her breathing. "I'm not that delicate an individual," she said, unsmiling. "I never have been. I don't allow infirmities to rule me."

"Ahh, but sometimes we have to realize that they limit us."

You're so obvious with your baiting, fat man. Stuff your limitations. She forced a smile that was as false as his solicitations. "It's the mind that matters, not the body, as you must know, Li-Gallant." *There, mull on that for a bit.*

He did. He didn't seem to enjoy it. He peered back into the terminal, idly touching a contact. "I understand the symbiote puts its own natural drugs into your bloodstream. It must dull the pain considerably, Regent."

And the mind; right, Li-Gallant? "Not as much as the available treatments would. You misunderstand the purpose of the symbiote. It's a regulator, not something to debilitate me. A regent, a li-gallant, *anyone* in a position of power, can't afford to have a fogged mind."

"In Neweden culture, one is supposed to submit to the inevitable. I'm afraid your symbiote is useless for me, should

I ever be in a position to need such a thing. I would lose all respect from guilded kin for my avoidance of the commands of Dame Fate. I would be ousted, and the parasite taken from me. One should not hide from Hag Death, Regent."

"Are you telling me that you fail to respect *me*, Li-Gallant?"

He smiled. "I'm a product of my culture, inescapably, Regent. But I *do* understand that your mores are not Neweden's, that different rules apply to you. Perhaps other guilded kin cannot make that distinction, but I can."

D'Embry's brows tightened with pain; she hoped it resembled concentration. The headache was making her sick to her stomach, as well. She promised herself an hour's nap—*later this afternoon. Just let me get through this. Damn, if Niffleheim would have sent me someone competent for seneschal . . .* "Li-Gallant, I can only offer my apologies again for the dinner, and my assurance that we will do everything we can to apprehend those responsible. It won't happen again."

Vingi nodded. "Your apology is accepted, Regent." Again, he stared down at the terminal, lips pursed. "But you must admit that a question might cross the minds of the guilded kin here: if the Regent can't protect us, maybe her Seneschal could have. Or, if there's nothing at all the Alliance could have changed, then possibly the Family Oldin would be more effective."

His smile was that of a predator. "An interesting speculation, isn't it?" he said.

Helgin threw the knife down on the floor before Renard. It stuck there, quivering. Micha, flanking the larger man, stared down at the blade. Renard raised an eyebrow quizzically. His left hand slowly stroked the plant-pet around his shoulders.

"You seem angry, Motsognir," he commented.

"You'd *damned* well better believe it," Helgin roared. His fury contorted his bearded face. Legs widespread, hands on hips, he glared up at Renard, eyes flaring under thick brows. "I got Micha and her bunch of goons in, and it was perfect—until someone decided to throw *that*." He pointed at the knife. "Renard, we'd agreed that an entirely peaceful demonstration was what we needed to impress them. What the hell did you have in mind with that damned knife, and who was supposed to be hit?"

"An accident, Motsognir," Renard purred, his deep voice resonant. "A mistake."

"Then I want the man that threw it. I want to know why he aimed at me, and I want to see how he'll look with that knife sticking up his ass."

"Micha's already talked with him. He threw at the Li-Gallant."

"Then he's as blind as a cave-fish. The fat man's a big target, and he was halfway down the table." Helgin spat on the floor; Renard looked from spittle to dwarf. "Don't play me for a fool, Renard," Helgin growled. "Let me talk to this myopic knife-flinger."

"He's dead," Micha said. She could not keep her gaze from the knife-hilt protruding from the floorboards. It seemed to fascinate her. "An argument with someone in Dasta. Yesterday."

"Awfully convenient."

She shrugged. "True."

Helgin rumbled disgust. A bare foot stamped the floor.

Renard smiled over to Micha. "I don't think our little co-conspirator believes us, Micha."

"Your little co-conspirator is wondering whether he should beat the truth out of the two of you," Helgin answered.

Renard's eyes went hard. His hand ceased caressing the plant-pet and went to his side. He drew in a long breath, filling his chest. "I wouldn't make a threat you can't keep, dwarf."

"Oh, I never do." Helgin smiled into Renard's stare. He flexed powerful arms, folding them across his chest. "Never."

For a moment, the confrontation held on edge, caught by tension. Micha held her breath, waiting. Then Renard's stiff posture relaxed. He bellowed a rich laugh, and his hand sought the beast around his neck once more. "Maybe next time I'll ask you to prove that boast, Motsognir."

"Why delay my pleasure? I haven't had a good fight in days."

"As you've pointed out to me before, FitzEvard has his own interests, and he doesn't care to see his agents at each other's throats."

"Then remember who's in charge here."

"On *Goshawk* and with the Alliance, you rule, Motsognir. Here, on Neweden territory, *I* have the final say. Oldin has given me his orders, and, curious as I might find them, I carry them out."

"The same way your people end a simple demonstration? With a thrown knife—treachery?"

Micha started to speak again, but Renard's upraised hand stopped her. "Dwarf, you begin to sound like that Sula of yours—everything words with no action. Are you afraid of blades, like your pet Hoorka? Does the stench of blood bother you, as it bothers Hermond?"

The smile seemed cemented beneath the cover of Helgin's beard. His feet rasped against floor, and he crouched lower, tensing. "One more word, Renard, that's all it will take. Leave Gyll out of this—he's an honest and admirable man, better than either one of us."

Renard spread his hands wide. He shook his head. "So you keep telling me."

"Believe it, or I'll teach you to say it—ungently."

"FitzEvard wouldn't like your tone."

"Then let's talk about something he would like."

Renard nodded agreement. In slow stages, Helgin relaxed. He strode over to the knife in the floor and pulled it loose from the boards. He touched the tip to his forefinger; flesh cratered around it. Looking at the weapon, he spoke to Renard. "A pity we're both so loyal. I'd enjoy being your enemy."

"Maybe later." Renard smiled back. "You might yet get your chance, neh? But until then, let me tell you what else we have planned. . . ."

8

There were twenty-three of them, and they were the Dead, a group of lassari who, hopeless, had given themselves entirely to the vagaries of Dame Fate and the claws of Hag

Death. They were walking in their endless march to nowhere, far from any of the cities of Neweden. Sterka was
three hundred kilometers to the south—they were moving
vaguely in its direction. The rolling hills of the Preada Valley
spread around them; a river coursed to their right, swelling
with more speed and purpose toward the distant city. In a
few days more, the small towns that clustered around Sterka
like anxious children around a parent would appear. For now,
they could be striding through the long grass of Neweden's
primal past. The landscape was gently soothing and, except
for themselves (who were, by their own reckoning, already
outside the ken of the living), barren of the intruder humanity.

They did not care. The Dead care only for the Hag.
They chanted the sibilant phrases of the eternal mantra; they
tolled their bells and swung their censers.

The carcass lay in their path—a fairly large animal. It
had been dead a few days. The stench of decay hung around
it like a foul cloak, and some local carrion-eaters had torn at
it. The vanguard of the Dead chanted their way around it,
perhaps with an involuntary wrinkling of noses and rolling of
eyes. Perhaps some of them even noticed that it was not any
beast with which they were familiar; it was not until the
midpoint of the line that an older man dressed in the tatters
of a cloak stumbled to a halt, eyes wide. Those behind him
stopped as well, bumping him. He stared at the dead animal,
his filthy head shaking slowly from side to side. The censer he
held dropped unheeded to the ground with a soft thud, coals
smoldering in the grass.

He breathed a word which rustled like a paean through
the ranks of the Dead, spoken louder and louder until it
became a shout.

The beast of fable, the long-extinct god-creature of
Neweden. Omen, pet of the gods. Symbol, whose very bones
meant power.

Ippicator.

"Well, Thane. Did you meet with him?"
"Yah, Jeriad. I did."
"And?"
"No. I'm sorry, Jeriad, but I told him no."

9

He'd been sullenly quiet during the flight to the village of Malcala. She endured his sullenness, his monosyllabic replies to questions until the flitter landed and they clambered out. They could both see the apprentice waiting for them at the edge of the park in which they'd set down, but she held him back.

"What is it, Jeriad?" she demanded.

"What, Thane?" Under the hood of his nightcloak, McWilms looked back at her. His voice was heavy with some emotion, short and clipped.

Mondom dropped her voice to match his. Her fingers gripped his shoulder tightly. "Listen, Jeriad. I won't take that tone from you. Not in private, and most certainly not on a contract. Spit it out, kin-brother, if something's troubling you. I don't want to play the nasty kin-lord, but I'll do it if I have to." She paused. "Well?"

She thought for a moment that McWilms wasn't going to answer, that she'd have to send him back to Underasgard and finish the contract with the apprentices, for she wasn't about to go further with his unspilled rancor fouling their teamwork. Too many kin lost their lives that way.

But his mouth worked, though his steady regard remained a challenge. His cerulean eyes watched her. "It's another contract for the Li-Gallant, isn't it?"

So that's it. He's guessed it, like the rest. She did not deny or acknowledge the charge. "Remember the code, Jeriad. We're just weapons. It doesn't matter to us who signed the contracts."

He shook himself away from her grasp. In the darkness, she heard more than saw his movement. Behind her, the flitter's engines moaned into silence—she knew that the apprentice piloting it would be watching them, curious; the tale would get back to Underasgard, no doubt well-embroidered.

107

"It didn't really matter, once," McWilms said. "I think you know that sometimes, who we're working for *does* make a difference—when it's always the Li-Gallant's signature. It bothers all the Hoorka, especially the older kin."

"What do you want me to do, Jeriad? The Hoorka would starve without those contracts. And I notice that you're willing to eat the food we get from those same contracts."

McWilms rubbed at his right hand, as if a memory of pain troubled him. "Thane, I'm sorry if what I say bothers you, but surely you realize how this troubles all the kin. None of us like the whispered gossip we hear every time you go to Vingi's keep to collect our money. I do what I have to do, but it leaves a bitter taste."

"If it's making you act the way you do now, Jeriad, then I don't feel safe. If the rest of the kin are the same, then I'm surprised we haven't lost more kin than d'Mannberg recently."

McWilms's face took on a strange aspect between sorrow and anger. "Thane, I hope you don't place the blame of my kin-father's death on me. If you do, then we have more to settle than just a few contracts."

Mondom could hear the pain in his voice. She softened her words. "No, Jeriad, I don't. That was Dame Fate's whim and a cowardly ambush from that Hag-kin Vasella. Still, we have to hunt tonight, and I don't want you slow to react because it's the Li-Gallant's enemy we look for."

"Then it is Vingi's contract?"

She shrugged. "Does it matter?"

"I suppose not." The answer was a second too slow.

"Then let's go meet the apprentices, or the dawnrock will call us too early."

They moved away from the flitter into a fragrant night. Boots shushed against sandy grass. Malcala was a collection of a few houses and buildings on the eastern edge of the Sterkian continent. They could smell the tang of salt water and rotting fish, hear the boom of surf. The sea was Malcala's life. Everyone here was tied to its moods, its tides. A quiet place with homes where people retired early and woke with the sunstar.

Usually.

The long, gangly form of the apprentice Ritti waited for them at the edge of the village. A crowd stood behind him at a short distance. The lights of Malcala threw their shadows at the Hoorka. Mondom glanced from the onlookers to Ritti. "Trouble?" she asked.

The boy's voice wavered between tenor and baritone. "Not yet, Thane, Sirrah McWilms. But the Shipmaster would like to speak with you." Ritti sounded uncertain, vacillating between hilarity and fear as his voice did between child and man.

One of the spectators stepped forward. Even in the dimness, the Hoorka could see his weathered skin, the thick muscles of his shoulders and chest. The scent of salt was on his clothes. "I'm Shipmaster Le Plath," he said. The voice matched the frame: thick, ponderous.

Mondom bowed, kin to kin. Beside her, McWilms did the same. "Shipmaster, I can't wait here. Forgive my abruptness, which is not worthy of you as kin-lord, but what is your reason for delaying us on our contract?" Mondom's words were polite but laden with the Hoorka aloofness. Le Plath didn't quail, as she had seen others do. He simply planted his large feet in the sand and scratched at his armpit through his tunic.

"We have a problem," he said.

"We?"

"The Hoorka and Malcala," he answered. His hands plunged into his pockets; at her side, she felt McWilms suddenly tense at the gesture, his hand going for his vibro hilt. Le Plath noticed, as well. His thick eyebrows knotted over his splayed nose. "You got to tell the Li-Gallant he can't have Pauli."

"Pauli Shroyer? Shipmaster, he's our victim, and the Hag will have him or not as Dame Fate and She of the Five will. It's not up to you or me."

"Ain't talking about you or me. I'm talking about the Li-Gallant; I want you to tell him."

"You misunderstand the Hoorka, Shipmaster," McWilms broke in. He shot a strange glance at Mondom. "We've no communications with the Li-Gallant other than any contract we might have, nor, in any case, do we reveal the signer of a contract until after the hunt."

"That ain't what people say," Le Plath continued doggedly.

"Then people are wrong," Mondom declared harshly, all

attempts at kin-politeness gone. "And you're delaying us too much, Shipmaster."

Le Plath did not move, did not react. The Hoorka began to see the crowd as something more than just a passive irritation. If these onlookers chose to resist, neither McWilms nor Mondom nor the apprentices could really stop them, not without better weapons and more kin—the apprentice's report had told them that Shroyer had armed himself only with vibrofoil, and the Hoorka had given themselves the same weapons. Enough determination from these people and they would go down; with an entourage to parade before the Hag, but they would die. Mondom wondered whether they shouldn't retreat to the flitter and call Underasgard.

Le Plath sniffed and swallowed.

"Pauli Shroyer has a mouth that speaks the truth too much," he said. Stolid, slow, plodding, the words came. "Pauli knows that the Li-Gallant taxes us too much. He said that to the wrong people. That's his crime, Hoorka. Would you kill him for that, leave all his kin weeping? He's a good man. I need him."

"You may still have him—if the Dame wishes."

Le Plath's smile was as slow as his speech. "The Dame is like the sea, always changing. I don't trust Her."

"It's your only way, Shipmaster." Mondom glanced at McWilms. His face told her nothing. He seemed impatient, yet at the same time almost gleeful, as if this reception vindicated his feelings about the contract. "If you try to stop us," she continued, "more than Shroyer might die. The Hoorka don't want that; we've no interest in killing anyone but our victim. Come between us and him, and you endanger yourself. How valuable can one man be, set against the potential loss of many others?"

Le Plath mulled that over, one large hand stroking a thick-stubbled chin. "I understand what you say, Hoorka, but we had wanted the Li-Gallant to know that we would have paid the fine for Pauli's insolence."

"The victim was offered that alternative," McWilms said. "That's our code."

"Then Pauli never spoke of it to me. He's that way." His gaze rolled back and forth between them. "What's the price of Pauli's life?"

McWilms looked at Mondom. "Two thousand," she said.

"A small cost for a life, isn't it? It would seem that the Li-Gallant only wanted a lesson taught."

Mondom shrugged. "*Whoever* signed the contract set the price, not Hoorka," she said. "And only he knows his reasons."

"Well, let me see." Le Plath turned. Hands on hips, he faced the ranks of spectators. "You heard the Hoorka-kin. We need two thousand to save Pauli. He's done things for most of you; now you do something for him. I've a hundred here myself—what about the rest of you?"

They dug into pockets. Others went to nearby houses to return with their offerings. Le Plath counted it all in his deliberate, methodical manner; cajoling, pleading, threatening until, by small increments, the entire amount was collected. He handed the thick wad of scrip to Mondom. "Two thousand," he said, simply. "Do you wish to count it?"

Mondom took the money silently. She held it a moment, then thrust it into a pocket of her nightcloak. "Ritti," she said.

The apprentice jerked into alertness. "Thane?" His voice broke on the word.

"Is Steban watching Sirrah Shroyer?"

"Yah, Thane."

"Then go find him. Both of you will tell Sirrah Shroyer that the contract can be voided due to Shipmaster Le Plath's intercession. See if that is acceptable to him." Turning to the Shipmaster, she bowed. She spoke with unaltered, uncaring aloofness. "We'll wait for our apprentices in our flitter, Shipmaster, then return to Underasgard. Good night, Sirrah."

His smile was wry and twisted. "The Li-Gallant bleeds us dry whether Pauli lives or not, it would appear. We're poor here, m'Dame, and that two thousand is more than the taxes we might have paid—that we'll have to pay anyway. Either way, you've hurt us."

"You've given the man back his life. That's what you wanted, that's what you've accomplished. If that doesn't please you, Shipmaster, then there's nothing the Hoorka can do for you." Distant, always distant, as the Hoorka must be.

"We just continue to feed the Li-Gallant's hunger."

Mondom allowed a hint of anger to color her voice. Her eyes danced warningly, her hand near her weapon's hilt. "Do not mistake the Hoorka for the Li-Gallant's guild, Shipmaster. The *Hoorka* will keep your money, and return the signer's fee. And remember that this signer is always unknown unless the victim is killed. You may make what assumptions you will, but keep them to yourself. If you have a grievance with the Li-Gallant Vingi, then declare bloodfeud against the man."

"I'm not so foolish, m'Dame."

"Then listen to your lack of foolishness and be quiet." She turned to McWilms. "Let's go back to the flitter, kinbrother."

They moved back into the sibilant grasses, toward the flitter in its circle of harsh light. They walked in silence for several strides; then McWilms spoke, a whisper that Mondom almost did not hear.

"Two thousand?"

Mondom's mind was still on Le Plath's stubborn insistence on lecturing the Hoorka. She snapped back at McWilms carelessly. "Yah, two thousand," she spat.

"Awfully little money, isn't it?"

"You take what you can get. It puts food on the table."

"The Li-Gallant's food. A mere scrap from his larder."

Mondom whirled about. Sand scattered beneath her boots. "That's *it*, Jeriad," she hissed. "Say anything more and I'll have you working with the apprentices tomorrow."

"Thane—"

"I mean it, man."

McWilms nodded. He was suddenly very formal, as if talking to guilded kin outside the Hoorka. "I apologize, Thane. I didn't intend to insult you or your leadership. I will admit that I wish you'd decided to let Sula Hermond talk to the kin, but I haven't said so in front of the others. And I won't. I'll keep our disagreements private."

She did not say what she thought: *You'd damned well better, too*. She simply nodded to him in return. "Thank you for that," she said, as stiffly as McWilms.

The wait for the apprentices was long, freighted with a smothering, charged silence.

Gulltopp had slipped below the horizon. Sleipnir was yet to rise. The night was as dark as Neweden ever was under open sky. There were only the distant, aloof stars.

It pleased him. It was necessary.

He could see Vingi's keep just ahead, white stone stark under the glare of floodlamps. The building cast a reflected glow into the surrounding gardens, and he liked that very little. He wished now that he'd used some of the money they'd given him to purchase a light-shunter. *Greed gets me every time—by She of the Five, the scrip's half-gone already.* But no, he rationalized. Vingi's guards will swarm all over Neweden after this, looking for suspicious purchases. There wasn't time to do it right, and he was better off this way.

And if he could do this, his name would be remembered in the annals of Neweden forever. Fame *and* wealth: the ultimate combination. Enil d'Favre, set alongside the greatest names in history. Enil d'Favre, liberator of the lassari (that had a nice alliterative ring to it), hero of the social restructuring, destroyer of the tyrant.

Assassin of Vingi, the last Li-Gallant.

D'Favre moved from shadow to shadow, crouching, his eyes keen for a sign of the guards, his ears preternaturally alert. His sting thumped at his waist, its heavy presence a comforting reassurance. So far it had been easy, slipping over the wall into the garden and avoiding the sleepy guards. He'd seen nothing to worry him, nothing—no sudden flaring of lights, no wail of alarm, no increase in activity around the grounds. Easy. D'Favre wondered how Vingi had managed to live this long, if his security was so lax. He visualized the moment when he'd pull the trigger. That obese body would be torn by the slugs. He'd aim for the head, watch the brains splatter... *No, hit him lower, in the stomach. Let him see you, let him feel the pain, then give him the coup de grace.* In his vision, there was very little gore. It was almost sterile and clean—d'Favre had never seen a body struck by the violence of a sting.

Fifty meters, and he would be at the keep's left wall, in shadows between the floodlights. He hunkered down behind a prickly shrub, studying the ground between himself and the wall. No cover at all, just open grass. Still, all the windows there were polarized black or were unlit. Nobody was watching.

Easy.

He thought he heard a noise to his right, a rustling of wind or a footfall. D'Favre went rigid, suddenly frightened, the fear twisting his stomach until he thought he might moan from the pain. He bit his lower lip, trying to breathe softly and slowly, straining to hear more.

Nothing. He relaxed again, the muscles unclenching, his bowels loosening. He smiled to himself. *Fool.* You're *the one creeping in the night. They should be afraid of you. Enil d'Favre, the night-monster.* He shifted his feet, balancing on his toes, his weight leaning forward for the run.

And then sudden harsh light pinned him. His head came up, he gaped in terror, almost falling. *"Don't move!"* someone shouted at him, too loud, too near. Even as his sphincter relaxed involuntarily and he soiled himself, he fumbled for the sting at his side. He fired wildly in the direction of the voice, his eyes squinting against the revealing glare. The noise of his weapon pounded at him, the recoil bucking the muzzle upward; a voice cursed in darkness.

A blow hammered at him, throwing him to the right, then back to stunned equilibrium as another blast slammed into his chest. He was vaguely aware that two concussions had accompanied the pain. His head lolled down and he saw the ruins of his chest and body. It was not clean, and there was too much gore. He vomited blood as he fell.

It became very dark, the light narrowing into a globe, then a pinpoint like a star. He reached to grasp the tiny sun, but it eluded him and winked out.

Enil d'Favre was lost in night.

"What was his name, Domoraj?"

Vingi did not like being summarily awakened in the middle of the night. He'd thrown on a robe and then grudgingly trudged out to his office, where the Domoraj Kile, head of his security force, waited for him with news of the attempted assassination.

"Enil d'Favre, Li-Gallant. A lassari from Dasta. No previous record of him in the Magistrate's files except for the normal minor lassari offenses. He had a press release—handwritten—in one pocket, taking credit for your death in the name of the Hag's Legion." The Domoraj held up a paper from a pile of oddments on a cloth draped over Vingi's desk.

114

Vingi frowned at the note in disgust—there were ugly stains on the paper. He made no move to touch it.

"Did you need to bring all this in here?" he asked.

The Domoraj looked visibly disturbed. A tall and too thin man, when under stress, his Adam's apple bobbed restlessly, and his jaws twitched. The Domoraj ground on a molar before replying. "I'm sorry, Li-Gallant. I thought you might need to see the lassari's effects, and I thought . . ." He stopped abruptly, realizing that Vingi's sleepy stare was fixed on him. He swallowed; the bulge of his throat danced.

"Please don't think, Domoraj. It's too late at night for that. You've done your job splendidly, I'm sure, though a live prisoner might have been a trifle more useful than this collection of artifacts." Vingi paused to ascertain that his criticism had the proper effect on the Domoraj; the Li-Gallant was willing to trade a certain amount of effectiveness for servility in his guards. The Domoraj was the essence of fear when in the presence of his kin-lord, and Vingi knew that the man passed down his shame at being thus treated by employing strict and harsh measures with his own subordinates. The chain of dominance gave Vingi moments of pleasant contemplation.

"He fired on us, Li-Gallant. For the protection of our kin I couldn't afford gentleness." The Domoraj spoke forcefully enough, but his face was woebegone.

At another time, Vingi might have enjoyed playing out the scene, toying with the Domoraj, seeing how the man balanced between fright and confidence; tonight, he was tired. Vingi wanted only his bed and the kin-sister who was warming it. He tugged at the expanse of his robe. "I'm not doubting your judgment, Domoraj, just commenting on the whims of Dame Fate. I assume you've something else to show me in this pile?"

The Domoraj's face took on a feral expression. He slid over to the cloth and stood behind it, like a merchant displaying his wares. "D'Favre had quite a bit of money in his possession, Li-Gallant. Quite a lot."

Vingi glanced wearily at the pouch the Domoraj held. "So he was paid. That's hardly surprising."

The Domoraj's eyes gleamed. He seemed to pounce on the Li-Gallant's words. "Ah, yes. But the money is not

Neweden currency, Li-Gallant. It's all new Alliance scrip."
His bony chin came up in triumph; he dumped the contents
of the pouch on the desk—brightly colored paper fell.

Then Vingi laughed, a full-throated roar that demolished
the Domoraj's triumph and set his throat back to quivering.
"By all the gods, that's really clumsy. Domoraj, you must see
that this ploy's far too obvious. I doubt that the Hag's Legion,
if they sent poor d'Favre, expected me to truly believe that
they were privy to Alliance scrip, in d'Embry's employ. I
don't doubt that they *stole* it somewhere, but to have us think
that d'Embry..." He roared again. "That *is* good. Well,
Domoraj, I'll play the game a bit and see what it get me.
Alliance scrip..."

The Domoraj grinned uncertainly into Vingi's hilarity. If
the Li-Gallant was happy, he was happy. Or at least he hoped
so. The Domoraj ground his incisors softly.

Being a Neweden native and once a kin-lord had its
advantages. Gyll heard the news—perhaps—before the Li-
Gallant or the Regent d'Embry. Certainly the word came to
him before the kin and lassari of Neweden, who awoke to the
startling news in the morning.

A newly dead ippicator had been found.

Gyll didn't know what thoughts might run through the
minds of those on the ball of mud below *Goshawk*, whether
Neweden might turn to piety or destruction. A dark and
disquieting suspicion grew in his own head, causing him to
push the bumblewort from its comfortable seat on his lap and
pace his room. The wort howled thinly at him for the neglect,
but Gyll ignored the creature. He stopped before his viewport
and glared down at Neweden.

He'd seen an ippicator once before—alive: in a nutrient
tank aboard *Peregrine*, Kaethe Oldin's craft. She had told him
then that the ippicator, cloned from ancient tissue samples in
the Oldin Archives, had been destroyed. Gyll had insisted on
that, knowing what the creatures meant to both economy and
theology on Neweden. She had promised, and he had witnessed
what he'd thought had been the beast's end.

She had promised. Now he wasn't certain that Kaethe's
promise had meant anything beyond the bare words. He
didn't like the feeling that he might have been duped, that he

might not be in control of everything that happened aboard his ship. A slow fury began to build in him; the bumblewort, perhaps sensing this, left off its useless protest and sulked underneath the desk.

"*Damn!*" Gyll slammed his open hand against the port—a smudge obscured Neweden. Gyll stormed from his cabin, following the tortuous corridors of the ship to the biological section.

"Camden!" Gyll shouted as he entered the small lab. His sharp tone caused the woman there to start and lift puzzled eyes from a com-unit.

"Sula, what can I do for you?" she asked. She wiped her hands on her smock; the Sula made her nervous. She found his presence intimidating. He was always polite but never friendly; the crew whispered that he'd been an assassin for standards, that—though they'd never seen him in a fight—he enjoyed killing. The smell of blood, a bitter tang, always seemed to be about him, although she knew it must be only her imagination. She smoothed her smock over her chunky figure, trying to smile.

Gyll was in no mood for amenities. He was far less polite to Camden than he had been. "Call up your inventory," he said sharply. He strode over to the com-unit, swiveled the terminal so that it faced him. "Get this junk off the screen."

Camden stared at him, then reached out for the keyboard with a stubby finger. The screen flashed emerald and went blank. "What are you looking for, Sula? Maybe I can help."

Gyll brushed her offer aside with a wave of his hand. "I'm not sure. Just get me the inventory files."

He busied himself with the lists for the next hour, occasionally asking Camden to explain an obscure entry to him. She gave him the answers with a growing curiosity. Finally, he rubbed weary eyes and leaned back from the terminal. He slapped at the powering contact, and the unit sank into the desk.

"You look tired, Sula. Tea? Mocha?"

His fury had been dulled by frustration. He'd seen nothing in the inventories to indicate that the ippicator might have been manufactured on *Goshawk*, but he wasn't going to fool himself—if someone had wanted to hide the equipment

and supplies in the com files, it could have been done easily
enough under another access. Hell, it might not have been
entered at all. Gyll wasn't going to find it. "I *am* tired," he
said to Camden. "Tea would be nice."

Camden, with a strange glance at him that he couldn't
decipher, went to a small plate set on a counter. In a few
minutes, water was boiling. "I could help you more if I knew
what it was you're looking for, Sula," she said, her back to
him. "This *is* my bay, and I know everything that's here."

"I know," he replied. "But I don't want to tell anyone at
this point—I don't need gossip." He realized how that must
sound to her and tried to apologize. "I'm sorry. It has nothing
to do with not trusting you. The only trust I'm worried about
is my own, I suppose."

Camden brought back cups. Stains were set in the china,
blotches of discoloration. She saw him glance at them. "Don't
worry," she said. "They're sterile. You won't get poisoned."

Gyll smiled. He sipped at the tea noisily. "Hot." He set
the cup down. "Camden, have you or anyone else used the
nutrient tanks lately?"

She thought a moment, the cup steaming in her thick
hands. "Just me, and not too recently. Last time was a week
or so ago, when that clumsy dockhand—what's his name?...
ahh, Dani, I think—lost three fingers forgetting to fasten a
shield. Before that..." She shrugged. Gyll was scowling, and
she kept the questions she wanted to ask him inside—the
Sula didn't seem to be able to tolerate an interrogation.

"Damn," Gyll muttered. "By the Hag..." He glanced at
Camden, caught her staring at him. She glanced away hur-
riedly. "Where else on *Goshawk* could someone clone a large
animal, say, three meters long or more?"

Camden shrugged again. "Nowhere. You'd need too
much equipment that's only available here. I'd know about
it."

Gyll sighed. He tapped fingers on the desk, then
abruptly swung to his feet, startling Camden with the
motion. Tea sloshed over the rim of her cup. Gyll didn't
notice her discomfiture. He nodded to the woman and
stalked out of the lab without another word. Openmouthed,
she gazed after him. "Thanks for the tea," she said under
her breath.

She brushed dampness from her smock. "That damn frigging killer's too spooky for me," she said.

10

"Regent, the Li-Gallant is furious. I've never seen him so angry."

"Santos, the Li-Gallant wanted you to *think* he's furious. The man can be a half-decent actor when he wants to make the attempt. I wonder if he's ever been on the stage."

D'Embry leaned back in her floater with her eyes closed, half-turned on her side so that her full weight wasn't on the hump of the symbiote. She'd had a bad, restless night; her chest had ached, her breath had been shallow and gasping, and nothing the symbiote pumped into her seemed to have much effect. She'd almost thought she could sense the parasite's fear that she might die. Yet she hadn't called the Center's physician. Instead, she sat in her bed, fighting the pain. Eventually, in the early hours of the morning, it had passed. She'd been able to sleep, if not for long, before the almost-simultaneous reports of the finding of the ippicator and the attempt on the Li-Gallant's life.

She knew who had to be responsible for both events. When she found the energy, she was going to be very angry herself.

D'Embry listened to McClannan pacing the room in front of her desk. "Let me guess, Santos," she said. "He made the accusation that someone at Diplo Center—his implication is, of course, that it's me—sent this lassari d'Favre after him. He was righteously indignant, threatening to sever his ties with the Alliance government." Gods, she thought, I'd love a few more hours' sleep. "He's done it before, Seneschal. It's not a new stunt."

"Regent, if you read the report, you know that d'Favre was carrying Alliance scrip. I can see where that might make the Li-Gallant suspicious."

"The Li-Gallant probably finds that as obvious as I do."
She did not open her eyes. "Alliance currency isn't *that* hard
to obtain on Neweden."

"In those denominations, Regent? This is a poor world—
who'd have that kind of resources?"

She knew, but she said nothing, knowing that if he'd
bother to puzzle it out, he'd know as well.

"The Li-Gallant had other questions, as well," McClannan
continued. "He was asking if we've made any progress finding the ones responsible for wrecking the dinner party."

"Hinting that we're dragging our heels on it because it's
someone here, yah?" Sighing, she sat up, opening her eyes.
McClannan was staring at her. He glanced away. "It's raining
out," she said.

McClannan's gaze went from d'Embry to the window. An
eyebrow raised quizzically. "Yah, it is," he said abstractedly.
"Regent, what we're discussing is a trifle more important than
the weather. I want to send a full report to Niffleheim
Center."

"No!" D'Embry's vehemence widened McClannan's eyes
and sent the Regent into a fit of coughing. She reached for a
tissue, wiped at her mouth. "No," she repeated, more softly
this time. "It's not worth the trouble and expense, Santos.
We should deal with it here, unless you want Niffleheim to
think we're incompetent." The tension in her chest eased
slowly as the symbiote wriggled against her.

"Regent, with all due respect, there's the possibility we
may have someone high up in the staff who's deliberately
sabotaging us. I think that's worth reporting. Niffleheim
could check backgrounds to which we haven't access." His
handsome face was intent and serious.

"You believe the Li-Gallant, then?"

"We can't disregard that possibility."

"Do you also suspect me?"

He waited a breath too long before replying. "I didn't say
that."

"That's good."

"Then let me send the report, Regent. If nothing else, it
will ease the Li-Gallant's suspicions, show him we're actually
making an effort to help him."

Once more, d'Embry leaned back gingerly. She looked

at her hands—she'd neglected to put on her usual bodytint this morning. Her hands were pale, withered, cracked-skin claws. They mocked her with age and stiffness. She glanced up at McClannan so she would no longer see them.

"No," she said.

He started to stalk away, disgust radiating from him. She let him get nearly to the door before speaking.

"Santos."

He turned, his hand on the door's contact. "Regent?"

"Be reasonable. If *you* wanted the Alliance off Neweden, how would you go about it? You'd do just what is now happening: try to make us seem culpable, try to place the blame for everything on the Diplos. You'd finance the Hag's Legion. You might even fake an ippicator just for the chaos it could create in this society."

"You think the ippicator's faked? The report I saw—"

"Wait until you have more information before you commit yourself to an opinion, Santos. That's what I intend to do, and that's why I don't want you to send a report. All you'll do is cause unnecessary concern and trouble for us here."

"You're just concerned with your own reputation," he said harshly. Then his face smoothed into blandness once more. "I probably shouldn't have said that, Regent, but you'll have to admit that it's one appearance your refusal gives. Either that or you have something to hide."

His accusation stunned her. *Am I really doing that, at the bottom of it all? Is he right?* She shook her head in denial, not trusting words. "Seneschal," she said finally, "Neweden had very little trouble until the Oldins arrived. Now that they're back, it's beginning again."

"It's never stopped, Regent. Neweden's been in upheaval for standards. Things seem to be finally reaching a head, that's all. The Family Oldin is a convenient scapegoat for you."

"If you believe *that*, Seneschal, then you're more a danger to us than anyone." Her voice was dangerously quiet.

He didn't answer her. He slapped at the contact and the door irised open. He went out.

D'Embry closed her eyes again. *Come on, symbiote. Do something so that I don't care what the fool thinks.* But she

121

knew the parasite had no drugs for that. Worry burned at her stomach like acid.

Helgin had been fairly sure that the ploy wouldn't work. He was surprised—Mondom *would* accept the invitation to dinner aboard *Goshawk*. It nearly forced him out of his composure. "No business will be discussed at all, Thane. That's what Gyll told me to tell you. It's simply a dinner, conversation; a pleasant time."

"Simply being there at all allows you to 'impress' me without speaking a word, doesn't it? It's a little more subtle that way, Sirrah Motsognir, but that's still business," she'd replied, but her tone was soft. Helgin had found that he liked her voice, her wry unwillingness to let him twist words. "Why does Gyll really want to see me?"

"I don't know." He could answer that truthfully. He didn't know, because Gyll had never requested that Mondom dine with him. Helgin wasn't even sure why he'd decided to fool with such a deception, except that Gyll was increasingly gloomy about his failure to convince Mondom to tie the Hoorka with the Family Oldin. Helgin suspected that Gyll's moodiness went deeper than that; the Motsognir was certain that Gyll missed Mondom the lover as well as Mondom the Thane. Gyll had bedded his share of partners in the standards he'd been gone from Neweden—if nothing else, he'd seemed to be the rising new star in the Oldin firmament, and there were those who threw themselves at him only for that—but Gyll had formed no permanent relationships. He seemed to avoid them, in fact.

Helgin could understand that. The dwarves tended toward solitude as well. But seeing Mondom again had altered that in Gyll; therefore, Gyll should be given all the opportunities he needed or wanted. That was simple enough. Gyll was a friend, as much of a friend as Helgin had ever had. A bit of deception in personal matters didn't bother him: what was another small lie in the midst of much larger ones?

Mondom had accepted his statement; Gyll, after all, had been known for his closemouthed secrecy concerning his feelings. "I'll come," she'd said. "But no business, remember. No Family Oldin propaganda."

No business, no propaganda. Helgin had hurried to tell

Gyll what "Gyll" had just done. The Sula tried to scold Helgin halfheartedly, but his delight kept breaking out in a smile. "You little bastard," Gyll had said at last, laughing. Helgin had bowed, grinning. "Someone's gotta run your life for you, Gyll. You do such a lousy job by yourself."

Now Helgin wasn't so sure the idea had been that brilliant. He'd been trying to keep the conversation going for what seemed to be a century. It was tiring work; he'd already drunk half a liter of brandy, and his throat ached. He reached for the decanter again. "Don't let *Goshawk* intimidate you," he said to Mondom, who sat solemn-faced at one end of the table. "It's just a big hunk of metal that's been made to look confusing to the casual eye—that's just a way to dazzle the visitors."

Mondom sat stiffly in her nightcloak, the holo clasp of the Hoorka glinting in shiplight. Her gaze kept drifting to Gyll, uncertain; whenever they happened to meet eyes, they'd both look away. "It doesn't intimidate me," she said. "The reaction's quite the opposite. The ship makes me feel claustrophobic, confined."

"But living in a cave doesn't?"

She made a sound that might have been a laugh. "That sounds silly, doesn't it? But Underasgard feels comfortable, natural."

There were uncomfortable moments of silence. Helgin pleaded silently with Gyll to say something. He didn't. The Sula toyed with his food. "Did you ever have that problem, Gyll?" Helgin asked finally, desperate.

"Hmm?" Gyll glanced up at Helgin, who frowned at him. Belatedly, he shrugged. "No, I didn't, I suppose."

Helgin waited for elaboration. There was none. Mondom had lapsed back into silence as well. Helgin sighed deep in his chest. He inhaled, filling his lungs.

"*Hell!*" he roared suddenly, slapping the table with an open hand. Liquid sloshed, china clattered; Mondom's hand, unbidden, went to the hilt of her dagger. Gyll started, half-rising and suddenly alert. "I've *had* it!" the dwarf shouted, standing on the seat of his floater. "I've tried to make this miserable dinner work, but it's no good. You two can sit and converse with your spoons if you want, but *I'm* going to find someone with more conversational skills than your average stone. Enjoy yourselves." He stormed out in the middle of a stunned silence, with a glare at each of them in turn. The door slid shut behind him.

Mondom looked at Gyll. "Does he always do that?"

"He's . . . volatile." Gyll settled back into the cushions of his floater. "And, yah, he's like that a lot."

"It almost seemed that this hadn't turned out the way he'd expected, as if he'd been trying to arrange things."

"He likes to think he's in charge of destiny, not Dame Fate." Gyll hedged his answer. *Damn the dwarf for his intrigues, and especially for leaving me with the shambles of them.*

"Was this really your idea, Gyll?"

He would have lied, had she appeared angry or upset. But she merely gazed at him, head propped on chin, elbows on the table, a half-smile flitting at the corners of her mouth. He smiled back at her. "I never could lie to you," he said.

"No, you couldn't. Are you going to try doing it now?"

"No. Helgin planned it all."

Her expression didn't change. That cheered him. "Well, Gyll, *he* lies awfully well. How do you manage to trust him?"

"I don't know always," Gyll admitted, "but I do."

Mondom nodded. She turned her attention to her food again. Silence settled around them as she took a forkful of meat. Gyll cut his portion into small pieces but made no move to eat.

"You can go ahead," Mondom said. "You're skinny enough."

That brought back his smile. "Thanks. That wasn't the case eight standards ago, was it?"

"You were out of shape," she said matter-of-factly. "You look much better now."

Mondom took another bite, Gyll shoved the pieces across his plate. "Is what you said true, Mondom—*Goshawk* makes you uncomfortable?"

"That sounds like an overture to business, Gyll."

"I'm just curious."

She sighed, glancing at him as if to be certain of his intentions, pushing her floater away from the table. He watched her. "Yah, it makes me uneasy," she said. "That's a better word, I think. I don't like the sense of enclosure. Underasgard never gives me that feeling—and somewhere there's a psychologist waiting to explain all the arcane symbolism behind that. I like knowing that the floor is just earth, not some metal deck with gravity conductors running underneath. I'm sorry, Gyll." She shrugged at him. "I'm sure it's a big, beautiful, wonderful ship you command, but I don't like it."

"You always were candid."

"When I should have been diplomatic?" She smiled. "We were both that way. Maybe things would have been different if we weren't."

"You make it sound so final." He could not keep the wistfulness out of his voice. *You're too damned honest, Gyll. Anyone can read you.* Helgin's words.

Her eyes narrowed, the lips thinned. "It's a little too late for reconciliations, Gyll. Eight standards too late. I thought we both knew that already."

"I don't want to believe that."

"You're joking." Her voice was flat with disbelief. "You can't possibly mean that, Gyll. With all the problems between us, you think we could still be lovers or even friends?"

"Yes."

"It won't work. It can't work."

"You don't want it to work, that's all."

She shook her head, her short hair moving. It was not so much denial as bewilderment. Gyll didn't press her. He waited. He looked for a sign of optimism in her face, her hands, her posture. There was nothing. She sat rigid in her floater, fingertips touching on the table. He remembered those hands—they were rougher, more calloused than before, thick with work. Practical, deadly. They had been loving as well; it was easy to forget that they also killed.

"Don't say any more, Gyll. It'll only make this worse."

"I'm not trying to pressure you, Mondom," he said gently. He raised one shoulder in a desultory half-shrug. "Just trying to understand."

"It's damned obvious, I'd think." Her voice began to rise a little; whether from anger or some other emotion, he couldn't tell. Her eyes had a curious sheen. "Gyll, you left Neweden, you left your kin, and you left me. You can't expect to come back and regain all or any of that simply because that's the way you wish things would happen—there's too much time and too much damage between us. Oh, damn it, I've told you all this before. Didn't you *listen?*" She bowed her head, hand over eyes. "Please drop it, Gyll," she said, her voice almost a whisper. "You made your choice."

"I don't regret my choice," he said slowly, after a long pause. "That's where you're wrong, Mondom. I find that I prefer most of my present life to my past one. I feel like I've gotten younger, not older. Gods, I used to brood about my age all the time. But there are still parts that I miss: you, the rest of the kin. And I'd like for you to have the opportunities I've had."

Her head came up. "You're back to business."

He waved the objection aside. "On this topic, it's not something I can entirely avoid."

"Then change the subject."

"To what? The finding of the ippicator, Alliance music, Trader fashion, what?"

"Anything at all. I don't care."

"If we could avoid tender subjects, would you think about staying here tonight?"

He didn't really understand what compelled him to ask that; a whim, a sudden boldness. It sounded lame and melodramatically passionate to his ears, like a line in a bad play. In the play, the woman would turn in her seat, tears would brim in her eyes, and a shy smile would touch her lips. "I've been wanting you to say that for so long," she would say.

Mondom frowned, and her eyes were dry.

"Gods, no," she said.

Then she closed her eyes for a long moment. "I guess you deserve more explanation than that, though. Gyll, part of me would like to stay, the part that remembers Thane Gyll. But I don't know that I love you anymore. I don't even know if I *like* you, because I don't know Sula Hermond at all. And going to bed with him won't tell me much that's important about him."

Gyll felt foolish under her steady regard. He regretted his impulse. *Think before actions, old man. That's what you tell your people.* "I'm sorry, Mondom," he said at last. "I suppose I was trying to presume upon the past. Too much."

She was becoming aloof again, slipping into the role of Hoorka-Thane. It distressed him. Her back straightened, her gaze became remote. "No apology's necessary, Gyll. I understand."

He knew that any chance for intimacy was gone, destroyed. He knew that she would be Hoorka-Thane and he Sula for the remainder of the evening. He felt sadness for that, and he masked it with a false smile. "Would you like to see the rest of *Goshawk* while you're here?" he asked. "I promise you; no business, just a tour."

Her face told him nothing. Her features might have been a carving. "Just a tour," she said flatly.

11

Gyll did not sleep well that night. His thoughts and dreams mingled, contentious. When the bell of his com-unit chimed, he was awake but tired. He knuckled his eyes, yawned. "Yah, Fischer?" he said to the darkness of the bedroom.

"Sula, the Regent d'Embry is calling for you. Line fourteen."

"Tell her I'll call her back in ten minutes."

"She was quite adamant, Sula."

Gyll closed his eyes, opened them again. He brushed hair back from his forehead. "Stall her for a few minutes, then. Off."

He lurched from the bedfield, yawning again. He turned on the lights and dressed. Grimacing at the image in the mirror, he combed his hair perfunctorily. Then he sat at his desk and touched a contact; the screen pulsed into life. "I'm ready now, Fischer."

"Here she is, then. Enjoy yourself, Sula."

The screen flickered with interference and settled into the figure of d'Embry. Immediately, Gyll's mood darkened— her face was skewed with anger. "I thought you to be more subtle and honest, Sula," she said without preface.

"And I thought you more clear, Regent. What *are* you talking about?"

He could see the hump of the symbiote as she shifted in her seat. "Don't be obtuse, Sula. I know you have your contacts on this world. You're well aware of what occurs here: I'm speaking specifically of the attempted assassination of the Li-Gallant, and of the finding of a certain creature thought holy by Neweden—and that may well be more important than the other. There are already reports of small-scale disturbances in some of the cities here."

Gyll punched up a side screen, scanned it. "In Irast, Sterka, and Remeale—a few deaths, a few injuries, some property damaged, mostly in the lassari sectors," he said. "And the attempted assassin was named Enil d'Favre, killed by Vingi's security people." He glanced back at d'Embry. "It seems he had a goodly amount of Alliance scrip."

D'Embry smiled without amusement. "There, you see. I knew you weren't as innocent of the facts as you pretended."

"Helgin gave me most of the news last night, among other items more important to our trading mission here. It didn't mean that much to me, I'm afraid. The man never got close to the Li-Gallant, Regent. It's a cowardly and dishonorable act, but unfortunately that's become less and less important to Neweden. The Alliance's influence, I fear. As for the ippicator, I'll wait until the carcass has been examined before I venture an opinion there."

His tone bordered on the jocular. It soured d'Embry's face further. "Don't go playing games with me, Sula," she said sharply. "You know damned well that someone set us up to be blamed for d'Favre. That leads me to an obvious conclusion."

"Let me tell you how I think on the matter, Regent. I have only your word that this assassin wasn't one of your people. That's all. And it leads me to make no conclusions at all, except that you're upsetting yourself unnecessarily." He said it forcefully enough, but inside the doubts arose to nag at him—the mission to Neweden was beginning to stink in his nostrils, a vague uneasiness that events were proceeding around him over which he had no control.

D'Embry's cheeks flushed. She sat silent for a second, then struck the top of her desk—Gyll saw the motion, heard the slap of her hand below the edge of the screen. "Sula, I'm going to order *Goshawk* out of Neweden space. I know the damned pact, too: you can expect to have notice of a formal hearing before the arbitrators before four local days, as soon as I can get them here. I want you gone."

"Regent, I think you're moving too fast with too little evidence." He spoke quickly, trying to sound calm while wondering why her words disturbed him so much. *What makes you so afraid of that, old man? Are you unwilling to admit that you've failed in your task, or are you frightened that the arbitrators might find that you've been duped?*

"Evidence, man? Dame Fate would laugh at you. Funny how the Hag's Legion springs full-fledged into open defiance just as you arrive; strange how assassins prowl the Li-Gallant's grounds with Alliance scrip in their pockets, or that lassari burst into private gatherings on Alliance territory. Odd that an ippicator appears at a critical moment in the crisis. And the Family Oldin just happens to be there."

"There is such a thing in this universe as coincidence." He did not believe it, not really. He knew she wouldn't, either. It sounded pompous and lame.

She laughed harshly, a syllable of derision. "I don't believe you expect me to credit that."

"It's still true," he persisted. "Consider how the arbitrators might choose. You've no evidence beyond the coincidence of timing. The Hag's Legion call this Renard their leader. Who is he? And would I have aided the Li-Gallant after Vasella's funeral if I intended to kill him a few weeks later? If my sources are as good as you claim them to be, then they've told me correctly that the Li-Gallant has as much as made a formal accusation against the Alliance for the assassination attempt."

That struck her; he could see her go suddenly cold and distant. That was more frightening than her anger, for it was more the d'Embry that he remembered. "As for the ippicators," he continued, "they are the pets of the gods, Regent, and the Family Oldin doesn't claim godhood. Ippicators aren't in our province."

"I've heard rumors that say otherwise, Sula."

Gyll wondered at that, whether she knew more than he thought concerning the samples in the Oldin Archives, or whether she was simply playing with words. He'd told Mondom of the episode with Kaethe, eight standards ago. If Mondom had told others of the embryonic ippicator he'd seen, or mentioned it to the Regent herself, then the charade was over—he had implicated himself, a lie of omission. He hated lies, but they seemed to be all around, and untruths were sometimes the easy path.

But he knew he was safe when she spoke. "Sula, you've gained yourself time, but don't fall into delusions. You're right; I haven't enough evidence, and I thought I could frighten you into leaving on your own." She paused. "I *will* get that evidence, Sula, and if you've violated the pact, I'll have you and all the Oldins prosecuted. I'll hound you with legalities and fines and whatever else I can find. Are you certain you don't want to leave now?"

"I haven't finished my work here." *But if last night was an indication, you have.*

D'Embry shook her head. A hand came up to cup her chin; the fingers were tinted aquamarine. "Sula, you puzzle me. You're either totally ignorant of what your people are doing, or you know and don't care."

"I know my ship *and* my people," Gyll said stiffly. "I'll take responsibility for them."

"And you still haven't lost that prickly Neweden pride."

"It offends me to be unjustly accused, yah."

She said nothing to that. He saw her reach out as if to sever the contact, but then her hand drew back. "I wasn't bluffing, Sula. I'm going to dig for that evidence."

"I never thought you were bluffing, Regent. That idea never even occurred to me. You won't find anything."

"You can't believe that."

"I do."

He could tell that she didn't believe *that*, either. The Regent mused for a moment, clearing her throat noisily, as if she suddenly found it difficult to breathe. "As you wish, Sula. I understand that the Li-Gallant intends to display the ippicator in Sterka Square a few days from now."

"Yah, and he's employed me to be in charge of security. It seems he doesn't trust the Diplos. Helgin is already on-planet, making arrangements for the viewing."

"You know that it's simply a political maneuver on his part. It has nothing to do with your expertise."

"You're entitled to that opinion."

She nodded, her face stony. "Then I'll leave you to your tasks, Sula." She peered at him strangely for a moment. "You know, Sula, there are times I can almost believe you."

"I'm glad to hear that," Gyll replied, his voice without inflection.

"And because of that, I feel very sorry for you. FitzEvard doesn't care what happens to those he uses, so long as he gets the results he's after."

"I've often heard the same about you, Regent—with no offense intended."

He had hoped that she would show some reaction to that, show hurt or anger. But she did nothing beyond a slow nod. "Yes, I'm sure you have," she said firmly. He thought that she was finished and began to make his leave, but she continued. "I meant what I said about feeling sorry for you, Sula, and that bothers me. It's not good to have sympathy for your enemy."

"I don't consider us enemies."

"Then that's even worse, Sula."

"You know, Gyll, I've never had anything that could be construed as a religious experience."

"Well, dwarf, all of Neweden gets one of those today."

They were inside the circle of Trader-Hoorka surrounding the body of the ippicator. Behind them, a shield sparked at the four corners of the large hover-plate on which the beast reposed. The ippicator stank; Gyll was glad that the breeze blew in his face and that the day was overcast and cool.

"Did you know that Vingi wanted to restrict the viewing to the guilded kin—the fool. No low kin, even, and certainly not the lassari and jussar."

"I'm glad you talked him out of that notion."

"I'd've *beat* him out of it before I'd have let you put our people out—this place would have been absolute chaos. He would have had a running battle for us to deal with. He'd gotten his private viewing, and that was all he cared about."

Tri-Guild Square was a static ocean of humanity. In convoluted paths defined by glowing beacon-lines, they trudged slowly up to gaze at the dead beast. Trader-Hoorka moved them along, not letting anyone gaze overlong. "Do we have lights, Helgin? We're going to be here all night."

The dwarf laughed. "All night, and the next day and the next: Vingi now wants it kept out here for three days. The scientists are screaming to get their hands on it, the revelates are spouting contradicting prophecies and doing their own screaming for 'relics.' Gods, I hope the refrigeration units in the plate hold up—if that thing gets any riper, no one will be able to get within fifty meters of it. You could have reminded me that Neweden law forbids the use of preservatives."

"One gives to Hag Death all She wants—or She comes after you."

"She wants the ippicator badly, then."

Gyll laughed. "Has there been any trouble yet?"

"Neh. Your setup is working fine. We've vendors all along the lines, as you suggested, and guards are circulating prominently. There's been a few skirmishes and more than one bloody nose, but not much else. It's strange; I expected worse, especially after the violence just finding the thing caused."

"I did, too. One would think a Parousia would have a strong impact. You'd think the Hag's Legion would have thought of it."

"Maybe they have—we shouldn't get smug yet."

Gyll turned to look at the beast again, the myth made real. It was ugly—the skin left by the carrion eaters was a sickly, splotched orange with a dull sheen. The five legs were stumpy and ungraceful; he could see the probe in the fifth leg where the animal sensed burrowing insects and animals—its food. The snout was well-formed for digging; a hard, thin proboscis complemented the long claws of the forefeet. It looked dumb, stupid; the eyes were porcine and small, the braincase narrow. Not an imposing sight, really. And it was small, no longer than a man, much smaller than the skeleton that lay in the caverns of Underasgard.

A young specimen, or one just out of the nutrient tank.

The presence still filled Gyll with foreboding. He didn't like looking at it. He studied instead the faces of those who stared at the creature. If he was looking for signs there, he fared no better. He saw shock, awe, fear; a hundred variations on each. The ippicator might be a portent, yes, but Neweden seemed unsure exactly what it heralded.

Gyll glanced back at Helgin, who, hands on hips, was glaring at the crowds. "When I first heard about this ippicator, I scoured *Goshawk*, looking for proof it had been made there."

Helgin did not turn. He still watched faces: an old woman weeping, a jussar with a defiant gaze and an open mouth that belied the angry eyes. "You did, eh? Find anything?"

"No. But then, I didn't expect to."

A revelate shuffled forward, ecstatic, his lips moving in silent prayer, followed by a guilded kin in his finery, his stare contemplative. "Decided you could trust me, then. Is that it?"

"I decided that if you or anyone else had wanted to hide it, FitzEvard could have arranged that easily enough."

Helgin made as if to spit on the pavement, scowling, then seemed to recollect where he was. He swallowed loudly. "Gyll, that sounds oddly like you're making an accusation."

"Don't be angry, Helgin." Gyll put a hand on the dwarf's shoulder. He could feel muscles bunching underneath. "I'm simply letting you know what I'm thinking—trusting you with my paranoias. I'm sure you're willing to share such things with me, as well."

"Hmm," the dwarf grumped, sniffing. "Why don't you just ask me outright: 'Helgin, did you have anything to do with that ugly bag of bones in back of us?' Or shouldn't friends be that direct?"

Gyll ignored the jibe. "D'Embry's sure that it's our doing, somehow. And she's reason to be concerned. There are the riots, and religious zealots left and right proclaiming the end, lassari who look on the ippicators as a sign."

"Sterka's been quiet."

"You sound disappointed, Motsognir, and you're changing the subject."

"I thought you'd gotten your answer."

"I suppose I have. I'm sorry, Helgin. It's just that the creature back there bothers me."

"I thought you were over the god-madness of Neweden. Damn, Gyll, next you'll be getting a revelate to shrive you." The Motsognir kicked at the pavement. He set his hands on his hips again. "Don't give me this crap, Gyll. That thing's just an animal, and a very dead one. It doesn't *mean* a damned thing. If I thought it'd taste good, I'd carve it up for steak."

Gyll's mouth was compressed tightly; his brow was carved with lines. He tried to smile; the effort was a failure. "Most of the people here would say you blaspheme, Helgin. I'd keep my voice soft."

"I don't believe in signs or gods."

"It doesn't matter what *you* believe. What matters is that Neweden does."

"Well, fine, maybe we'll have some excitement. This is damned boring."

"We'll have more than you want, I'd wager."

Gyll's prophecy seemed in error by night. There were skirmishes and scuffles, the usual results of having too many people in a confined space, but no real difficulties. As the sunstar slid behind the spires of Tri-Guild Church, hoverlamps were lit, transforming the square. The crowds had not eased; there were always more to replace those who had left. Floodlamps cast their blue-white glare on the ippicator. Near midnight, Gyll sent Helgin back to *Goshawk*. Gyll stayed, still uneasy, and—though he would not have admitted it to the Motsognir—unwilling to leave the presence of the five-legged beast. He was surprised that he saw none of the Neweden Hoorka among the crowds. She of the Five, goddess of the ippicators, was the patron of the guild, his own choice. The ippicator should have aroused great interest in the devout among the Hoorka, even if Mondom had been noncommittal about it. He wondered if perhaps, for some reasons of her own, she had ordered the Hoorka to stay away.

Gulltopp was riding at zenith, Sleipnir was hauling itself up toward its brother moon. Everything was double-shadowed outside the blaze of light around the ippicator. The night chill had caused Gyll to put on a jacket—light but warm, with the emblem of the Oldins blazoned at the chest: a stylized bird of prey clutching at a world with its claw. The crowds, hours into the viewing, showed no signs of declining. Around the square they shuffled, following the beacon-lines, waiting for their few seconds of closeness.

"Sula?" She was a woman in the white tunic and pants of the Trader-Hoorka. She held her crowd-prod nervously, twisting it in her hand. Gyll thought he remembered her name.

"You're Alden Hessia?"

"Hestia," she corrected. "Sula, I've been making the perimeter check. We're missing one of the sniffers."

Gyll was immediately concerned; the sniffers were Trader-Hoorka equipped with explosive-detection devices. The equipment was not capable of sensing anything particularly sophisticated, but Gyll had not expected sophistication of Neweden. Certainly, as Thane, well-versed in Neweden's offensive weaponry, he had known nothing that would elude a good sniffer. That one of them was missing filled him with foreboding—he could see the fear in Hestia's eyes, as well.

"What's the name of the sniffer?" He searched the crowd near him as if the man might suddenly appear there. The faces suddenly had an ominous cast. They no longer pleased or entertained him.

"Culdoon."

"Culdoon... Damn, he's been no trouble beforehand. You know him better, though. He couldn't have gone off by himself, taken a rest while his officer was somewhere else?"

"He's not that type, Sula. I know him pretty well." Hestia was confident of her evaluation. Her round face was taut with earnestness. "I'd have looked more if I'd thought that. I came here right away."

"How long could he be missing?"

"I'm to check every hour—no longer than that."

Gyll pursed his lips in concentration. "Yah. Hestia... get another sniffer to cover Culdoon's post. Tell Lutana Creption to get her squad and sweep that sector: see if she can find Culdoon. And tell the Lutana to get her squad's sniffer moving in the lines—they aren't moving too fast, so our intruder can't be too far in; no more than a quarter of the way. Neh..." Gyll abandoned that thought. "He might be paying to get closer—best to check all the way from the beast out. I'll get the people here to slow the lines down—that'll buy us time, since we can't clear the crowds without starting a riot." He was thinking out loud, realized it. Adrenaline made his voice tense and quick. "Move, Hestia—let me make arrangements. Go!"

The woman saluted and moved off at a run. Gyll went to the com-net and called *Goshawk*. Quickly he advised Helgin of the situation. "It may just be someone sleeping on duty, but I've a bad feeling, Helgin."

"I'll be down as soon as I can, Gyll, but it won't be soon enough, if you're right."

"Then let's not waste time talking. You contact the Li-Gallant, tell him to be ready to provide medical assistance and additional guards if we need 'em. Hurry, Motsognir." Gyll cut the contact and touched the code for Lutana Creption. She answered his call gruffly.

"Creption here."

"Lutana, this is Sula Hermond. Any news?"

Her voice immediately became less irritable. "I've begun the sweeps, Sula. I'll let you know immediately if we find Culdoon. If he's asleep or having fun with some local, he'll wish he *had* been ambushed."

"You have a sniffer in the lines?"

"Yes."

"Our intruder will be halfway in or better—they'll have known how long they had before the sniffer was missed. Get another sniffer off the perimeter and into the lines. Let me know if anything's spotted. And make sure everyone's using a shield."

There was very little he could do beyond that. He could watch the faces that came up to stare at the ippicator and wonder if one of them harbored something other than reverent curiosity. He could worry. What was the intruder—if there was one—planning? Did he take out the sniffer because he had explosives, and if so, what type, where would they be placed or thrown? Could it be a red herring, a diversion to lead them away from the real focus of trouble? Could it, please Dame Fate, be nothing at all?

Gyll felt impotent, helpless. It had been different with the Neweden Hoorka. Then you knew what you were expected to do, knew what your victim might attempt. Everything was open, everything was one-on-one, personal. You and someone else. He hated crowd actions because they were impersonal and confusing. Lutana Creption was probably a better tactician with this situation. *I hate it. Give me the chase, the contract, the hunt.*

The Trader-Hoorka nearest to him knew that something was awry. Gyll could sense it in the covert glances back at him, and he suddenly realized that he was pacing, hands behind his back, near the com-net. He forced himself to stand still, to wait. That was the hardest part of his present job—to delegate the authority and then just await results.

The com-net chimed. "Sula here."

It was Lutana Creption. "We've found Culdoon. He's just about alive; someone used an altered prod on him. He was behind a stack of crates in an alley a few streets away from the square."

She said nothing else, waiting. Gyll knew that her thoughts were running parallel to his own. "Then they've got someone in the crowd," he said. "Shit."

"I'm sorry, Sula. And since they bothered to go after a sniffer, I'd worry about explosives first."

"The two sniffers we have checking the lines aren't enough, then. Send in all the perimeter crews and seal off the square to anyone trying to enter the lines. If they want *out*, fine, let 'em go, but let's not get anyone else in danger."

A brief silence spoke her uncertainty. "We're going to have problems with that—these people keep coming to see the beast. They won't like being turned back."

"They'll have to wait."

"We'll have trouble."

"Then we'll have to handle it," Gyll snapped. "Seal off the square and send the sniffers in. If we need more bodies, use Vingi's guards until Helgin can get here with more Hoorka."

"Yes, Sula." She did not sound pleased.

"Lutana, I know these people. I'm one of them. Be firm, but be very polite. Make sure your people frame everything with respect—they're touchy about honor and you might find yourself in a fight by accidentally insulting the wrong person. But they do understand authority; they'll obey if it's handled correctly."

He heard her sigh. "Polite but firm. Yes, Sula."

"And gently, Lutana. I don't want any innocents hurt because our people were clumsy."

"As you say."

Gyll cut the switch. The Hoorka nearby were looking at

him again. He ignored them, pretending calm. He beckoned to one. "I'm taking a net patch. You stay by the com and relay any calls for me."

"Yes, Sula."

Gyll stuck the patch—a small, sticky pad—in place just behind his ear. He touched the vibro on his belt, made sure that it slipped easily in its sheath. Then he moved into the crowd, sprinkling apologies before him, though all but the high kin moved back from him without asking, recognizing the uniform as belonging to those running the spectacle. Though he had no clear idea of what he intended, it felt better to be moving, to be closer to any potential action.

Rising on his toes to peer above the crowd, he saw one of the sniffers two lines over. Excusing himself to those around him, he made his way over to the man. "Anything yet, Benoit?"

Benoit didn't look up from the display screen of the bulky equipment strapped to his chest. "There's a slight reading, Sula—I'm trying to vector it now." He swiveled in place, his hands moving over knobs. He shook his head, grimacing. "I can't get it isolated—wait! There it is. A hundred-twenty, hundred-thirty meters southeast. Crude stuff, but there's got to be a lot of it if I'm picking it up this far off. Stuff's leaking into the air like homemade. It'll be volatile junk, Sula. Want to move closer?" He was speaking in a whisper now. Gyll had to lean forward to hear him above the crowd's noise.

"Hold a moment." Gyll touched the patch. "Lutana?" he said, subvocalizing. The patch's reception was tinny but clear. Her voice seemed to reverberate in his head.

"Here, Sula."

"Benoit's got the intruder." Gyll leaned over the screen and read coordinates to her. "Got that? I want you to start closing in on that area: shield up. Get as close as you can without alarming him. Benoit and I will start working our way in, and I'll have him work with the other sniffers to get a more precise location. Don't close or let him see you. And we could use a volunteer to take off shield and uniform, get close enough to give a visual description."

"Should we still be polite?" He could hear inflection

through the patch that annoyed him—he would have to speak with her after this, and not mildly.

"You'd damned well better be if you don't want a riot. Let me know immediately when your volunteer has that description."

"He" turned out to be a woman. The description was relayed to Gyll: "Dark hair, close-cropped, not too clean. She's wearing a loose leather coat, tan-colored, and she looks to be pregnant—that'll be the bomb, I'm sure. Light blue pants, brown boots. She's in line, looks a little nervous, keeps glancing around."

Lutana Creption broke in. "I've got someone with a nightscope in a building along the square, Sula. He says it's a bad shot; she's packed in with the rest. Getting her out isn't going to be easy, and the people around her aren't wearing bodyshields. If she gets too nervous, we're going to lose a hell of a lot of locals."

"Let me think a second, Lutana." The people around Gyll stared at the sniffer, at the white-haired Trader-Hoorka beside him. Gyll could feel their sublimated hostility—they were the Li-Gallant's hirelings. "We're the only safe ones out here—if we can surround her with shields, it'll confine the damage."

"Nobody's safe if the blast throws us into something—the shields aren't going to help with that, or the concussion."

"It'll take five or six of us, more if we're not close. I'm one. How about you, Lutana?"

A pause, static-filled. "That's two."

"You got a few more daredevils in the squad?"

After a minute, she replied. "I'm stocked with fools."

Gyll chuckled despite himself, wondering why he suddenly felt good again. "Fine. Is your spotter still there?"

"Yah, Sula," came the voice.

"Your task is to fake a collapse—heart attack, anything that'll give us an excuse to be hurrying in your direction. With that pretext, we should be able to move people aside, out of the way, and maybe even get to her before she does anything stupid. I doubt that she's suicidal; if she can't place the bomb and get away, we should be able to take her safely."

"And if she decides to become a martyr?" Lutana Creption.

"Then we'll hope the shields work. Gods, I wish we had

139

the ship's stores close; a paralyzer, stun-gas—there's a dozen alternatives on the ship."

"You couldn't anticipate all the needs, Sula." Creption's voice was oddly respectful. It made Gyll smile quickly. "If we'd brought an arsenal, there'd still be problems. Your plan's as good as the next."

"That doesn't make me feel better. Well, let's see if it works. Make certain the shields are up and the ears are protected."

The collapse was well-performed; the spotter was a decent actor. From his vantage point, Gyll could see little, but he heard the welling of loud voices, the sudden heightening of crowd-awareness as heads craned to see what had caused the commotion. "Let me through, please!" Gyll shouted as he began pushing toward the woman. Each person behind him was one less likely to be injured—the Oldin bodyshields were far superior to those Gyll had known on Neweden. They did not hinder a person much at all. For any explosive he could conceive of this woman having, they would shelter the fragile body from the initial burst and any shrapnel as well; though they well might be flung away like sticks, perhaps scorched from the blast, they would in all likelihood survive. Not the kin and lassari around the woman—they would be fragile dolls in a hurricane; broken, torn, and bloody.

Gyll could not get that red-imbued vision from his head. He struggled forward against the crowd's resistance. Shadows from the hoverlamps threw crazy, erratic shadows over them; the buildings around the square loomed against moonlight.

Suddenly, he could see her. She clutched at the expanse of her belly, wide-eyed, her gaze skittering like that of a trapped animal. She was pretty in a disheveled way, not at all the hard, stoic woman he'd expected to see, but a woman-child, frightened. To his right, a knot of Trader-Hoorka were bending over a prone figure. Others came in, moving Newedeners aside, crowd-prods out. The woman was becoming more isolated, and he could sense her desperation, could see that she now knew that she was discovered and trapped. More of Gyll's people arrived, shouldering aside those nearest the woman. He took a step toward her as the ring began to close.

"No!" she shouted, startling him. She whirled to flee,

only to find Lutana Creption standing there. She swung about again, arms swinging, her coat flapping open—Gyll could see something strapped there. He lunged for her—his hand caught her sleeve, but she wrenched it away, cloth tearing. "Renard!" she cried, as if to the air. "You promised—" She said nothing more.

A flash of orange-white, a deafening "thu-*whump*." Gyll's shield went rigid in that instant—he felt himself being tossed, striking something, bouncing. The world whirled about him, dancing, tumbling; the echo of the explosion dinned in his ears through the plugs; his vision was lost in a welter of glaring afterimages. He hit something hard—even through the constriction of the shield his head snapped back.

Amidst a roaring, sight faded.

Someone had used his head for an anvil. He could taste the iron-tang of blood in his mouth, and his legs didn't seem to want to work. Either he couldn't open his eyes or he couldn't see. He could hear vague noises, garbled speech. He hawked, spat up phlegm.

"Shit!" someone said. "I might've known you'd aim for me."

"Helgin?" His throat rasped the word.

"No, your friggin' mother. Who the hell do you think it is?"

"I can't see." Each word was a breath, an agony.

"Your eyes are bandaged, fool. Here, feel."

Gyll felt someone take his hand, move it to his face. His fingertips touched soft cloth. Gyll sighed and tried to flex his legs—pain shot through him, but they moved.

"You certainly like to cause yourself unnecessary pain," Helgin commented, "but you probably won't settle down until I give you the details, right?—No, don't answer; I know you. The medics say you'll be fine, no thanks to your little attempt at heroism. Didn't you ever hear about delegating authority? Staying in one piece is one of the advantages of doing that."

"Couldn't ask without . . ." His mouth was dry. He swallowed. ". . . going myself."

"Damned nice of you. That's gotten you flashburns on the face and hands, a small concussion even through your thick skull, assorted bumps and bruises, but nothing broken. You'll have a hearing loss for the next several days—I'm damn near shouting at you now. They want you in the medi-doc overnight, but after that you're on your own again."

"The others?" He wanted water, anything.

"All our people are fine—all in much better shape than you. The blast killed nine bystanders and the woman, of course. There's about thirty others in for various injuries; all of them should make it. It could have been a lot worse, Gyll. A lot worse. The Li-Gallant has managed to praise you and condemn you all at the same time."

"Water?"

"Here."

Something nudged Gyll in the lips—a straw. He sucked on it greedily, feeling the coolness soothe his throat. Helgin pulled it away before he finished. "That's the whole glass, Gyll—you want more?"

"In a moment." He could speak again. "She didn't set it off, Helgin." He licked dry lips, found them cracked and torn. "I saw her hands the whole time. I think she was using a transmitter—she called Renard—the Hag's Legion. Then it went off."

"We found some of the pieces. It was triggered by a remote switch."

"Renard."

Gyll could hear the Motsognir's shrug, a rustling of cloth. "Most likely."

"I want him."

"Thought we weren't going to interfere in Neweden politics?"

Gyll tried to sit up, couldn't. He felt dizzy, and lay back, panting, until the spell passed. "This isn't politics," he said at last. "It's filthy murder. Killing without the redemption of honor. I want that bastard."

"D'Embry might have something to say about it. So might Vingi."

"I want him. I don't give a damn about the rest, Motsognir."

"I don't blame you. I want him too." The dwarf sounded strangely fierce. "He was watching, you can bet. Watching, and waiting for the right moment." He paused. Gyll stared at the darkness before his eyes until the Motsognir spoke again. "I think I can find him, as well. A week, Gyll, then we'll go together, when you're well. I'll find him."

"A week." Gyll repeated the words.

He heard Helgin rise and walk away. More footsteps approached. A hand touched him on the shoulder. "Sula?" It was a gentle voice; a woman. "We're going to move you back to *Goshawk* now." There was a cold swabbing; something pricked his arm. A cold numbness began to spread over his chest. "I've given you a sedative for the trip—just let yourself sleep, Sula. You'll be back on the ship when you wake."

He felt himself being lifted. He swayed. The motion was curiously restful. He was moving—he could feel the breeze on his face.

And somewhere, he slowly drifted into dreamless sleep.

12

It was the first time they'd made love.

Afterward, he kissed her and rolled from the bedfield. He came back with a hot washcloth and a soft towel. Gently he cleaned her. She hadn't expected such tenderness from him— it surprised her, touched her. She stroked his face as he used the towel.

"Thank you," she said. "That was nice."

"Good." His voice was husky, a bedroom whisper.

"Part of your code?" she teased.

"A personal part."

"And a good Thane always follows his own rules."

"Rules are made to be obeyed."

She brought his head down, kissed him long and thoroughly. His hands moved on her body, arousing her again. She brought her arms around his shoulders, rolled him on top of her. "Don't ever change that code."

"You don't change what works."

Mondom sat before the headless skeleton of the ippicator

and watched the light of her hoverlamp shift colors along the bars of the ribcage. The cavern walls flickered gold and green. Thoughts raced, directionless, in her mind. She did not resist. She drifted helplessly with them.

Damn Gyll. Damn him for coming back, damn him for leaving. And, most especially, damn him for making her realize that she still cared about him. She thought she'd exorcised that ghost. She missed the intimacy which she hadn't been able to find with any others among the kin, and she wished him gone so that the old pain would settle into dormancy again.

Go away, Gyll. You hurt me too much.

Drifting . . .

An ippicator—not long extinct, but newly dead. She of the Five, what is that supposed to mean? Why do You send Your pet back to this world—in the lore, it says that the world will dissolve into chaos. Is that what You intend?

Drifting . . .

You don't change what works. And if it doesn't work? The code would kill them, a long and slow strangulation as the society on which it was based changed around it. You have to do something, woman; you even know what it must be, but you don't want to take the step, do you? You're afraid.

You're damned right I'm afraid. But I'll do it.

"I'll do it." The sound of her voice brought her from her reverie. She was surprised so much time had passed since she'd come here; she was surprised to find that, unknowingly, she'd been crying. Mondom sniffed, obliterating the wetness on her cheeks with the sleeve of her nightcloak.

She flicked the tether of the hoverlamp and the light obediently bobbed toward her. Letting it ride above her head, she began walking back toward the outer sections of Underasgard. Her contemplation had helped, though the strangely moving events of Neweden still puzzled her. At least it seemed clear to her what Hoorka must at last do.

Abandon the code of Gyll. Ally the guild with Vingi. Only that way would they survive. The Regent would be no help to them, and she did not trust the Oldins. She didn't like the taste of her decision, but she could think of no other solutions.

She was very afraid that there were none.

13

Helgin had not wanted Gyll to come with them. He cited the lingering effects of Gyll's injuries: a slight limp, a ruddiness to the skin. Gyll told him curtly that the doctors had released him and he *was* going. They'd glared at each other for a moment, then Helgin had given in to the inevitable. Gyll was Sula, and could halt the entire operation with a word. Helgin bowed to that fact with a Motsognir's normal ill grace, but he bowed.

It just made his intentions much harder to realize.

It was night. Dasta Burrough crawled with life. The five of them, in the dingy, tattered clothing of lassari, moved through the shadowy streets—Gyll, Helgin, and three of the Trader-Hoorka. Despite their guise, there were still stares and whispered comments—there was no disguising the Motsognir build. Dasta was worse than Gyll had remembered. Parts of it were now scarred, blackened rubble from what the populace called Vasella's Fire; the rest was cluttered and filthy. Garbage piled uncollected against the buildings and in the central gutter of the street. Occasionally they would come across a wirehead sprawled unconscious in the pathway, oblivious of his surroundings. Jussar—youths caught between kinship and lassari—prowled in gangs, rowdy and noisy; the lassari and low kin walked the streets with an air of paranoid caution, weapons (for the kin) placed visibly on their belts. Prostitutes of both and indeterminate sexes cajoled and insulted from doorways and windows.

"Gods, I hate this place," Gyll muttered.

"I don't know; in some ways, I rather like it," Helgin replied.

"You would."

"Hey, it has a certain energy, a vivid, crude life."

"Next you'll be talking about the ambience."

Helgin grinned. "I mean it, Gyll. Just because it's dirty

145

and squalid—which it is—doesn't mean that it's not a 'good' place. It has a feeling of secrecy, of adventure."

"It's squalid, yah, and the only things that lurk here are hatred and despair."

"Both are honest emotions."

"They're not ones I care to experience."

"Right," Helgin said. "And which one of us wanted Renard's ass?"

"It's an honest emotion, dwarf."

They turned where a narrow alleyway held darkness between two tall buildings. There, hidden behind a stack of broken crates, they checked their weapons: tanglefeet bombs, crowd-prods, two stun-grenades, vibros. Helgin had an ancient projectile weapon holstered to his side. Gyll frowned at the sight of it. "You'll only kill someone with that, Helgin. I'd rather have him alive."

Helgin put his hands on his hips, belligerent. "I want something that'll stop someone quick, if I need to. None of this junk'll do that."

Gyll stood, unmoving, for a moment, then shrugged. "Then be damned careful with it. I don't trust revolvers, and they're frigging noisy. They're also not honorable weapons."

"Neither's a bomb."

Gyll nodded. "Your point's taken. Just be careful with it."

"Don't worry—just stay out of my way."

Helgin did not say what he really thought—if all went well tonight, Renard would not be alive to tell his tale of treachery. He would be forever silent, and Gyll would never know of Helgin's involvement in the Hag's Legion. The Motsognir wanted Renard removed from Neweden; if this was the only way, so be it. The relative morality of the situation didn't bother him. He'd long been pragmatic about such things.

Gyll gestured for silence. His hand moved in familiar patterns: the Hoorka assassin's hand-code, the code he'd taught to the Trader-Hoorka as well. *Quiet. Helgin . . . lead.*

They'd traded their lassari disguises for dark, form-fitting clothing. Their faces were darkened as necessary, and the blackened handles of their weapons hung within easy reach. They slipped from shadow to shadow like wraiths: down the alley, across the next street quickly and unnoticed, then into a warren of claustrophobic lanes. Helgin stopped them again just inside the mouth of another alley. *There*. He gestured to a doorway across the street and to their left.

Gyll signaled to one of the others to check the area. The man unslung a snooper, swinging it in an arc—all the monitors remained green. He shook his head.

? Gyll queried Helgin, who frowned. *Something wrong*, the dwarf replied.

Pull back?

No. Helgin glanced out at the street once more. No one moved down its short length. Few of the windows of the buildings were lit, and there were no streetlamps. *Traps?* he gestured to the Hoorka with the snooper, who swung it about again. Green. *No*.

Trap? Helgin asked again. The Hoorka, with a grimace of irritation, held out the snooper to the Motsognir. Helgin hesitated, but took the device. He tested all functions, then surveyed the street once more. All LEDs remained emerald. The dwarf's shoulders slumped visibly; he handed the snooper back. The man took it urgently.

Gyll leaned out, glancing left and right himself. The snooper would have detected most alarms or suspicious concentrations of metal, but that left a hundred possibilities. He didn't like the feel of the situation, and he knew that the others felt that unease as well. There was a subtle sense of something being awry: the street was too deserted, the task looking too easy. Gyll hesitated, half-tempted to call off the operation rather than walk into an ambush the snooper had missed. He'd expected *something* in the way of guards for Renard.

Weapons out, he gestured at last. *You*—to Liana, the fastest of them—*go across*. *Quickly*. The woman nodded; she crouched, leaning, then ran, her footsteps loud in the stillness. Gyll watched the street, the windows, the rooftops. Lightly panting, Liana had flattened herself against a wall. She examined the buildings across from her, then gave a wave of her arm. *Clear*.

Gyll glanced back at Helgin, received a shrug. He signaled to the others. *Let's move*.

The Motsognir, surprising Gyll with his speed, hit the

door first—the wood splintered under his foot. Another kick, and it swung crazily open. Helgin was inside with the motion, rolling a hand-flare into the room as he ducked right. The others entered behind him in a rush, ready, but Helgin had already slid his weapon into its holster. The room was neat, shabby furniture set in place, the desk scarred but clean. There was no dust. It looked as if someone had set the room in order before leaving. Helgin kicked at a chair; it clattered to the floor.

The Motsognir turned to Gyll. His dark eyes glinted under thick eyebrows; he pulled at his beard.

"The bastard's gone," he said.

It began as a routine visit to the Li-Gallant's offices. Vingi's signature was needed on a release form for those being treated at the Diplo hospital after the explosion in Tri-Guild Square. Afterward, McClannan and Vingi were to appear at a press conference. But the Li-Gallant steered the Seneschal aside into Vingi's private office, and he had startled McClannan with his first words.

"You strike me as the ambitious sort, Seneschal. Why don't you get rid of d'Embry?"

McClannan found himself momentarily speechless. The Li-Gallant grinned corpulently at him, fingers steepled under his trebled chin. Animo paintings swirled dizzily on the walls. McClannan decided to try for righteous anger. He put the expression on his face like a mask.

"That's not the way the Alliance works, Li-Gallant. And she *is* my superior."

The order of excuses did not escape the Li-Gallant, nor did McClannan's attempt at judicious irritation fool him. He laughed under his breath, a snort of amusement. "Seneschal, please don't assume that because I'm fat I'm also stupid. I've seen the Alliance work for decades now, and I know that you work much the same as Neweden, once you dig under the surface of your laws. I also know that d'Embry isn't exactly in favor back on Niffleheim—she's offended too many of *her* superiors, neh?" Vingi sat back in his floater; he fiddled with one of his many rings. "You should take a lesson from that, Seneschal. She's achieved her reputation by defying those in power when she felt they were wrong. One must be selfish to achieve either reputation or power, and one must know when to go against those above you."

McClannan did not disagree. He drew himself up to his full height and let his eyes narrow slightly as he smiled. It was one of his favorite poses. "It's a dangerous course of action, as well."

"One never gets anywhere without taking risks. That's one of my axioms, Seneschal, as true here as in the Alliance. The danger may be physical or not, but it's always there. Do you gamble?"

"I've been known to do so."

"Then you must know that to win you always choose with an eye to the odds and to your luck. Do you feel lucky?"

McClannan allowed himself a small laugh. He shifted his position slightly, a model's turn. Long, well-manicured fingers tapped at his belt. "I've done well enough. I've been lucky."

Vingi nodded. "You know that there's been continuous pressure from Niffleheim for d'Embry to resign, especially after that Hoorka contract on Heritage."

A nod. Vingi studied McClannan—he didn't like the man, found him to be as superficially intelligent as he was superficially handsome, but he knew that the man was pliable. His ambition was his weakness, and Vingi prided himself on his ability to exploit weaknesses. "Bring her down and *you* become Regent—you're already being primed for that job. A word to the right ear, and the title is yours."

Vingi watched McClannan lean forward as he said the words. The man could not keep the eagerness from that face; it made the handsomeness ugly, feral. "And what do I whisper to that ear, Li-Gallant? What more can I tell them? They've already heard all the rumors and have done nothing. They know what she does."

The man's vapid willingness to engage in treachery repelled Vingi. *Gods, the bastard doesn't even bother to disguise it. He doesn't worry about recordings or countertreachery or blackmail. He either discounts that possibility or chooses to ignore it. Either way he's a fool, an easy fool. No wonder d'Embry despises him. Can he really be this gullible, or is he a trap within a trap? No . . . that's not d'Embry's way.* Vingi made no attempt to conceal his disgust. He looked up at

McClannan with distaste in his eyes. "Are you always so ready to stab someone in the back, Seneschal? I'm looking for allies, not new enemies."

McClannan looked confused now—why had the Li-Gallant suddenly retreated? "I'm not your enemy, Li-Gallant. Nor is the Alliance."

"D'Embry's help has always come grudgingly to me."

"That will change when I'm Regent, I assure you." There, McClannan thought; back to the subject.

"I get the same assurances from the Family Oldin—if I'm willing to rescind the treaty Neweden has with Niffleheim." He'd expected that statement to have an effect. He was not disappointed. The studied posturing of McClannan gave way to incredulity. "You wouldn't do that."

"I would. All it takes is a vote of the Neweden Assembly. I own that particular institution."

"But that's never . . . Gods, the reputations of the Diplos of a world that left—"

Vingi pounced on the phrase. "*Your* reputation, Seneschal? That's your alternative, man. Enhance your reputation or ruin it—it's your choice."

"You're bluffing." McClannan didn't sound convinced. "The Alliance has much more to offer than the Family Oldin."

"You're just spouting the party line, McClannan." Vingi's voice was suddenly harsh and strident. He spoke quickly, as if delivering a lecture to an errant student. "You, like most of the Diplos, know very little about the Trading Families, the Oldins in particular. Your d'Embry is an exception to that, and that's why she fears FitzEvard so much. As for *me*, Seneschal, I'm a pragmatist and an opportunist—I pretend to be nothing else. I plan, and I take what's offered to me. An example: I spoke with Thane Mondom of the Hoorka yesterday. She's going to ally the assassins with my guild, and I intend to take them. The Hoorka will give me fear, and I can use that fear to enhance my own standing. So if you think I'm bluffing, Seneschal, simply turn around prettily and walk out of this office and I'll see you at the press conference in ten minutes. What I'll have to say to the reporters isn't in the script you've been given."

Vingi waited, staring at the man before him, unsmiling. McClannan grimaced. His eyes squinted, then relaxed. His gaze could not stay with Vingi's steady regard. He studied his hands, turning them over and curling the fingers. But he did not move toward the door.

"I can tell Niffleheim that the only alternative to losing Neweden to the Family Oldin is to replace d'Embry?"

Got him. Vingi nodded slowly. "One should always tell the truth to one's superiors—if it serves him to do so."

Tight-lipped, McClannan nodded in return. "I'll do it," he said, simply.

Vingi smiled. With a groan of effort, he hoisted himself from his floater and arranged the expanse of his clothing. "Then let's go to the damned conference and pretend to be signing papers." A pause. "Regent McClannan."

The day was windy and cool, with spatters of rain from scattered clusters of cloud. Few people braved the weather this afternoon. Tri-Guild Square was nearly empty. Even the Mason's Guild, which had been repairing the jagged hole in the pavement, had retreated before the elements. McWilms walked past a temporary barrier of ropes, ignoring the sign warning him back. He gazed at the last mute remnants of the ippicator's visit—the beast was now under study in a government lab.

McWilms didn't know what he was looking for here—a sign, perhaps, a symbol, something to give him direction.

The last several days had been nothing but arguments in Underasgard. It had begun with the display of the ippicator. Many of the kin had wanted to see the mythical beast, the visible sign of She of the Five. But Mondom had refused them permission to go. Too many people, she'd said. A potential hazard. Their presence might spark a confrontation. Her arguments had fallen with dull precision, and she had ignored all discussion on the subject.

Hands in the pockets of his nightcloak, McWilms stared down at the hole. Rain had pooled there, and not much work had been done thus far. He tried to imagine the violence of the explosion, how it must have been, bodies flung, blood everywhere. He could not visualize it well—his experience of death had always been closer, with a knife or a hand weapon, individual. As a Newedener, he didn't truly understand this distanced, random killing that the Hag's Legion had employed.

It was foreign, alien. No honor was there; they didn't even know who might be sent to the Hag. Who had they been after?

The argument about the ippicator had not been the last. A few days later, she had told the kin that she intended to alter the code—Hoorka would align itself with Vingi's rule-guild. They would still accept contracts on the same terms from anyone, but the Li-Gallant would have the approval of them. A roar of protest had followed—they were. then no better than the Li-Gallant's personal assassins, and how soon after this would they no longer give Dame Fate Her chance, but agree to kill anyone contracted, without the victim's chance of escape being given. Mondom had been cool, logical; she'd opened the guild's books to all of them, shown them how badly Hoorka fared. It would not get better; Neweden was changing. Ulthane Gyll had said you don't change what works, but his code no longer worked here.

Neweden was changing. Had changed.

His ignorance bothered him more and more. Neweden society, after centuries of only slow evolution, had altered drastically. He could feel it. Neweden was more and more an alien place with alien mores, and none of the guilded kin had experience of that. Ulthane Gyll had become one of the outsiders, but *he* knew, McWilms was convinced. Mondom wanted the Hoorka to remain ignorant; that, to McWilms, led to the death of the guild as certainly as the Thane's alliance with Vingi, as Neweden's contact with the Alliance had dealt a fatal blow to its society.

As the ippicators had died, unable to cope with evolution. But now an ippicator had returned, god-sent. What did it portend? If the gods of Neweden had any control, it meant something. It must.

McWilms couldn't read meanings from shattered tiles and broken ground. The square had been washed clean—nothing except the mute hole remained to show the violence that had erupted there. McWilms scuffed a piece of tile over the crumbling edge—it splashed in the muddy pool.

It began to rain again, cold and hard, beading on the cloth of his nightcloak. McWilms pulled the hood over his head, moving back over the barrier once more. His head down against the wind-driven shower, he went to the center of the square, where the ippicator had been displayed. Blinking water from his eyes, he looked around the square. Tri-Guild Church was lopped off at mid-spire by low clouds. A few uncomfortable-looking kin hurried diagonally across a corner, cloaks flying. Incongruously, a break in the clouds let the sunstar touch a cluster of tall buildings a few blocks away, light sliding quickly up the sides. The gap closed as McWilms watched; Sterka became dreary again.

Suddenly McWilms laughed, loud and long. His amusement echoed from the buildings around the square. "Gods," he said, "I'm looking for signs in the weather, omens in the dirt. Jeriad, you're quite an ass."

14

"I want to see that frigging son of a bitch McClannan. Now!"

D'Embry slapped the com-unit's contact without waiting for her secretary's answer. She could feel the hot flush of anger on her cheeks. She leaned back, breathing hard and loud. The symbiote squirmed on her back, and slowly she felt her breathing ease again, her face cool. When she felt somewhat normal, she bent forward with a groan and picked up the flimsy on her desk. Her hands trembled as she glared at it, the paper rustling so that she could hardly read the words. She didn't need to see them; they had burned their image into her mind the first time they'd been read.

EFFECTIVE IMMEDIATELY: IN APPRECIATION OF YOUR LONG SERVICE TO THE ALLIANCE AND THE DIPLOMATIC RESOURCES TEAM, AND CONSIDERING YOUR UNCERTAIN HEALTH, YOUR RESIGNATION HAS BEEN ACCEPTED. ALL BENEFITS ACCRUED TO YOU ARE NOW RELEASED PENDING YOUR ARRIVAL AT NIFFLEHEIM CENTER. YOU ARE TO GIVE REGENT MCCLANNAN ACCESS TO ALL DIPLO CODES AND RECORDS, AND FACILITATE THE QUICKEST TRANSFER OF POWER TO HIM. REPORT TO NIFFLEHEIM CENTER ON 6:22:225. PASSAGE ABOARD THE CRUISER MENGELO HAS

BEEN ARRANGED, DUE IN NEWEDEN ORBIT 3:5:225. DEAR LADY,
SOMETIMES EVEN THE ELDEST HAVE TO GIVE WAY.

It was signed "A. Pettengill, Director," over the stamp of
the Legatis Primus de Matraup. The last sentence was
Pettengill's, she knew, telling her that this time there was no
way around the forced resignation—it had been Arthol who
was at the end of many of the strings she'd pulled to keep the
Regency after the Heritage fiasco. All debts have been paid,
he was saying.

She had a sinking feeling that he might be right.

D'Embry stared at the flimsy as if the intensity of her
gaze could alter the words. The symbiote fed her cooling
balms that did little to quench her fury.

Santos McClannan entered her office without knocking.
He strode over and extruded a chair from the floor before her
desk. He sat, watching her. She let the flimsy fall to the desk.
A thin forefinger tinted bright orange skidded it across the
slick surface toward McClannan. "I assume you've seen this,"
she said dryly.

Something between smile and frown tugged at his mouth.
He picked up the paper with a strange gingerness. One hand
ruffled through his hair as he scanned it—as she had somehow known it would, his hair fell back perfectly in place. "I
was aware of the decision," he said at last. He was not sure
how she was going to respond, and he was also a little
frightened—d'Embry could see that in the way he sat, in his
fiddling with the edges of the flimsy, in the fact that he could
not look at her directly for more than a few seconds. *Damned
frigging coward. I wonder where he got the courage to go
over my head?*

"I'm not going to make any pretense, McClannan," she
said. "You're responsible for this, aren't you?"

His face shifted to shocked innocence an instant too late.
"M'Dame, I—"

She shook her head. The motion stopped his protest. "I
could still fight this, McClannan. I don't have to accept this
forced resignation." She said it merely to see how he would
react—she was not disappointed. He sat back, dumbfounded,
hands clenched into fists on her desk. "That would be a waste
of time, m'Dame." The fact that he neglected her title didn't
escape her. "Surely you know that," he said in his darkest

tones, full of gentle sympathy whose falseness burned at her.
"You'd simply compound the difficulties here, maybe wreck
all that you've worked to gain on Neweden. Simply for spite?
I don't believe you're that selfish, m'Dame. I won't believe
it."

She didn't answer for long seconds. McClannan looked
more and more uncomfortable with her silence. When she
did speak, it was to say one word.

"Bullshit."

She closed her eyes and felt dizziness. *Make it stop,
symbiote. Come on, you damned Trader slug.* And with that
came an unbidden afterthought: *Maybe they're right. When
you must divide your attention between crises and your
health . . .*

McClannan's soft voice interrupted her reverie.
"M'Dame—"

"It used to be 'Regent.'" She did not open her eyes.

"M'Dame," he persisted, "all that you'll gain by fighting
this decision is dissension, both within the Neweden government and our staff here."

"*Our* staff?" Her eyes opened, blue-gray eyes blinking.
"You mean *your* staff, don't you, *Regent* McClannan?"

"I'd hoped you wouldn't be bitter, m'Dame."

"Just what the hell did you expect me to be, McClannan?"
She shouted as loudly as she dared, feeling the raggedness in
her throat. She forced down a fit of coughing. *Not now,
symbiote. Punish me later.* "Did you think I'd sidle up to you,
all sweetness, and kiss your cheeks proudly? Did you want
me to tell you how glad I am that you stabbed me in the
back?"

"I did nothing."

"Gods, spare me your protestations. I *know* what you
did, McClannan, at least some of it—my com-unit logs all
calls from this Center, and I know you contacted Niffleheim
two days ago. Don't tell me that's coincidence."

This time, at least, he didn't deny the allegation. "M'Dame,
didn't you defy those in power when you felt they were
wrong?" He seemed to be mouthing someone else's words.
She wondered whose they were—Sula Hermond's, the Li-
Gallant's, or some other traitor within her staff. "Who told
you that trash?" she snapped.

He did not lie well. He almost stuttered his reply. "M'Dame, your reputation . . . in the classes at Diplo Center, they talked about you, about some of your, ahh, old confrontations with authority. And the teachers, the Diplos who'd known you . . ."

D'Embry waved a hand as if brushing aside a troublesome insect. Multihued flesh broke off McClannan's sentence. "It's not important, I suppose. You've done it, McClannan. You're now the Regent. I hope that Dame Fate sees that you receive what you deserve for it."

He looked relieved, knowing that she would not fight the resignation. "M'Dame, I think you'll be surprised to find that I'm quite competent."

"You're right, McClannan, I will be. Let me tell you what I think will happen." She leaned forward, elbows on the desk. Her thin, much-lined face was intent with the force of her emotions. "You're a conceited, ineffectual fool—a good toady because you frighten easily. You'd make someone a fine assistant as long as they didn't give you too much responsibility."

He stiffened in his chair. His voice was suddenly formal and distant. "M'Dame, I don't have to sit here and be insulted. As Regent, I have much work facing me. Neweden—*your* old regency—is a mess." He began to rise.

"Sit down," she said. "If you think I'm a toothless old beast, you're wrong. None of the staff knows about your appointment yet. I could have you incarcerated on some trumped-up charge, and how do you think Niffleheim Center would react to that? They'd still replace me, but they'd send someone to replace *you* as well, just to be safe. So sit down and listen, if you really want this job."

"I don't believe you," he said. He did not sit, but neither did he move toward the door.

"Then walk," she replied. Her finger poised over a contact on her desk. "I'll have Karl put you under house arrest as soon as you touch the door. Embezzlement should be a good charge—easy to fix, hard to disprove."

Still he hesitated. Then, fists clenched at his side, his mouth a hard line, he sat again.

"You see, McClannan, that's one of your problems. You can't judge the risks properly. If you knew me at all, you'd know that I've given my life to the Diplos, the Alliance. I wouldn't do anything to hurt them because I believe in what we're doing, if not always in how we go about it. And if you knew that, you'd have known that I also realize when I'm beaten. It was a bluff, McClannan, but you took it, so you might as well stay and listen to the rest." She paused, winded. The shortness of breath was returning, and with it the paroxysms of coughing, the bile she would spit up from her ravaged lungs. *A while longer, symbiote. A few minutes more. Please.*

McClannan looked more angry than before. As Vingi had seen, he was not handsome in his rage. "Get on with your speech, then."

"It'll be short," she said, and the first of the deep coughs struck her. She reached for a tissue as she hacked, hunched over in her floater. When it passed, she spat; folding the tissue, she wiped savagely at her mouth. "You've much to learn, McClannan, and now you've ensured that I won't be here to give the lessons. Let me tell you what I see happening if you don't learn quickly. You'll lose Neweden—violently, most likely—because you'll be the dupe of the Li-Gallant, and for all his subterfuge and wiles, he's no match for FitzEvard Oldin. I'd give you no more than a standard, maybe two, before that happens."

"That's your own paranoia speaking," he said. "You're obsessed with the Family Oldin. You invent plots when there are none."

"I assure you, it's not paranoia. FitzEvard and I go back decades. We've skirmished many times on many worlds."

"I can't agree, m'Dame," he replied, still distant with anger.

"Then there's very little I can teach you in the few months I'll still be here. I don't have the patience to coddle an unwilling student."

"In that case, what good's your proud altruism for the Alliance?" he answered. The words stung her, and she sat in silence, unsure how to reply. McClannan rose again, going to the door this time. "You may keep this room as your office until the *Mengelo* arrives, m'Dame. I'll use my own office for the Regent's business. I expect you to

157

disclose the contents of the letter to your staff this afternoon. Good day, m'Dame."

He left. D'Embry waited, knowing that the punishment would come now. She was amazed at how little she cared. "Maybe you're right, McClannan," she whispered. "But I still only give you six months." Then the attack struck her and she could speak no more.

Mondom thought that she could gladly kill Gyll at that moment.

Not that it was his fault. Probably not. If anyone should be blamed, it should be Dame Fate. The note's seal had been addressed to Thane Mondom only—who could have anticipated that a clumsy courier would have knocked off the seal in his pouch and, rather than reattaching it, have stuffed it inside the envelope. And the apprentice who received the note at the entrance to Underasgard gave it to McWilms first, because the Thane was busy on the practice strip. McWilms had read it to see if he should interrupt the Thane at her exercise.

The words were Gyll's typical blend of arrogance and innocent disbelief that anyone could see the world in a manner different from the way he viewed it.

Goshawk *will be leaving soon, I'm afraid. With her will go our last opportunity to get the Hoorka off this dead-end world. I don't mean to be so unforgiving of my homeworld, but I've been outside it now for some time, and so can view it in a more dispassionate light. It is a dead end for Hoorka—in that, old Aldhelm was right. I'm asking you again to let the guild come with me. We'll share the leadership, Mondom, work it out whatever way we have to. Maybe we can do more than just settle our differences (or so I can hope). Let me know when I can talk with the kin and make an offer. Please, make it soon.*

Mondom crumpled the paper in a sweaty fist. McWilms, standing before her in the practice room, said nothing. She went to one of the benches set around the cavern (greenish light from the fungi-strips moving over her wet-dark clothing) and angrily pulled a towel from a stack set there. She began drying her short hair furiously, facing the rough stone wall. *By She of the Five, now I need another workout to get*

158

rid of this anger. Her shirt clung to her—down the back, under the arms and breasts, sweat-cold in the chill of Underasgard. She heard McWilms come up behind her, and she could also hear the sound of paper being unfolded— he'd picked up Gyll's message from where she'd dropped it. The cavern echoed with the clash of steel on steel: other Hoorka-kin fencing.

"If you want to keep this a secret from the kin, Thane, you shouldn't leave it lying around."

Mondom whirled about. McWilms's face was a study in neutrality. "Don't give me that sarcasm, Jeriad. I'm not exactly in the mood for it."

"You'll never be in the mood for this, will you?"

He said it quietly, matter-of-fact. Mondom, hands on hips, stared at him for long seconds. He stared back. Then she took a step away. She stretched, bending over at the waist to touch the ground. "I'll ignore that, Jeriad," she said, grunting with effort. "I've asked you once, now I'm telling you. Drop the subject."

"Thane—"

She came up. Her dark eyes flashed. "I mean it."

"I know you do," McWilms persisted. "I know, too, that Ulthane Gyll's offer would tempt quite a few of us. Is that why you don't bring the matter up before all kin? Are you letting your personal feelings get in the way of what's best for Hoorka?"

Mondom's eyes narrowed, her head reared back as if slapped. She glanced right and left, surveying the room. When she spoke, her voice was a harsh whisper; only McWilms could hear it in the noise of practicing kin. "You listen to me, Jeriad. If anyone else had said that to me, I'd have him on the floor now for first blood. Don't you *dare*"—the cords of her neck went taut with the half-shout of the word—"give me that kind of crap as an excuse. You don't deserve an explanation, but let me give it to you again. Sula Gyll made his choice against the Hoorka eight standards ago. If he's sorry for it—and he isn't—then let him apologize to the kin and see if they'll let him rejoin the guild. Maybe then I'll consider the offer."

"You want him to apologize to you, as well."

"Yah, damn it. I deserve it more than any of the rest of the kin, if it comes to that."

"And until you get it, you'll ignore whatever he has to say."

She glanced at him, then sat on the bench, leaning back against the rough wall. "Are you deliberately trying to provoke me, or are you no longer in control of your tongue?" Her voice was as cold as the stone at her spine.

McWilms breathed once; again. He was not looking at Mondom, but at the rest of the room—pairs of fencers, a knot of laughing kin, a huddle of apprentices around one of the kin-masters, a torn-down vibro in front of them.

"Jeriad, listen," Mondom said behind him, her voice suddenly gentle. "It's more complicated than simply my relationship with Gyll. It's the Traders, for one: I don't know that we can trust them."

"Gyll trusts them." He spoke without turning to her. Across the cavern, the kin-master adjusted the vibro for the apprentices, the click of the control ring loud and metallic.

"Gyll can be duped. That's one of his weaknesses—he's very trusting. He tends to believe what people tell him until a lie is obvious."

"Many people call that a virtue."

"It's only a virtue in a saint, and Gyll doesn't come close to that status." She waited, but McWilms didn't reply. "It's not just the Traders, either," she continued. "There's a whole pile of objections involved, with the Li-Gallant, with our arrangements with the Alliance, with our holdings on Neweden."

"You don't think those can be worked out?"

"If they can, is it worth the effort, or are we just throwing everything away for a false dream?"

"I think you're wrong," he said. He watched the kin-master snap the haft into the proper slot, reel in the vibro wire.

"You're not the Thane." Mondom's voice had lost its friendliness again; it walked on the edge of fury. McWilms could hear it.

"Gyll will wish that you weren't when he hears that you've allied us with Vingi."

McWilms heard the movement even as he began to turn to Mondom: a sharp intake of breath, a half-grunt of effort, the scratch of boots on stone. Instincts took hold. He sidestepped to the left and back, his left hand slipping the vibro from its sheath, his weaker arm up as a shield. Mondom was on her feet, crouching, ready to attack or defend. Her eyes were on his vibro. She was peripherally aware of the sudden silence in the cavern—they were being watched, and that deepened her anger. "Is this what you want, Jeriad? Fine, let me get my own vibro and I'll give you the satisfaction you're after. First blood, kin-brother? Fine."

McWilms shook his head. "That won't prove a thing. We both know that." But he did not sheath the weapon.

"Is Serita an acceptable choice for referee?"

"Thane—"

"*Answer me!*" she shouted. "Or is Jeriad McWilms afraid?"

Heat flushed his cheeks as she slipped into the impersonal mode, insulting him. His hand, reflexive, tightened around the vibro's hilt. "She's fine," he said tensely.

Mondom nodded. She straightened, wiped her hands on her pants. "Arioch!" she called. The kin-master looked up from the midst of his apprentices.

"Thane?"

"Send one of the youngsters to get Serita Iduna."

"Thane," McWilms broke in. The anger had left him. "I won't fight, not like this. I'll stand there holding my vibro if you insist, but I won't move, won't defend myself. First blood will be yours."

She stared at him. The tableau held for a second, Mondom stern, McWilms strangely sad. Then, with a sound of disgust, Mondom strode away from him, moving toward the entrance of the cavern.

McWilms watched her leave, feeling the stares of his kin.

The connection was damned expensive and not of particularly good quality.

Gyll would never have initiated the call himself. The fact that FitzEvard did so was well in character for Grandsire Oldin, who was well-known for costly extravagances—at the same time, Gyll knew him well enough not to expect the normal social amenities. He and Helgin, sitting before the flat-screen viewer, didn't get them.

FitzEvard had a voice of sandpaper, roughened further by the transmission difficulties. "You've made money, at least," he said without preamble. "I didn't expect you to get the Hoorka, Sula, not with the troubles Neweden is having. I was right, it seems."

Flares of interference gamboled through the face of FitzEvard. The family resemblance was stamped into him as it was in all the Oldins: wide, round faces; large and dark eyes under gilt eyebrows; bodies stocky and a bit too heavy by Alliance standards.

"I've not given up on that yet, sirrah," Gyll answered. He didn't enjoy talking with FitzEvard, never had—the man's gruff curtness made him uncomfortable.

"We'll see, Sula. I'll wager you a month's wages you won't get them."

"And if I fail to take that bet?"

"Then I'll know you're lying about not having given up."

"In that case, I'll take the bet, sirrah."

FitzEvard grinned. It reminded Gyll of Helgin's grin: dark, somehow devoid of much humor, interior. FitzEvard, it was gossiped, smiled only when shown a potential profit. Gyll knew that to be as true as any adage—he'd heard the Neweden saying that the Hoorka smiled only at death. A grain of truth, nothing more. Yet FitzEvard was a driven man and the parameters of his success could be outlined in wealth. "Good, Sula. You'll save me money on the payroll."

Helgin, feet up on the desk next to Gyll, snorted. "He'll make more than that back in the bonus—*Goshawk*'s stores are damned near empty."

"Trinkets for a small world," FitzEvard observed. His gaze stayed with Gyll as his image on the screen wavered and split. "Next time, Sula, we'll give you a wealthy world where the captain's bonus will be worth taking."

"Promises, promises," Helgin muttered.

FitzEvard's words came through a spluttering of static. "I didn't hear that, dwarf, but I assume it was an insult."

"You assume correctly."

"How do you like being back on Neweden, Helgin— away from me?"

Helgin grimaced. "I never thought I'd say this of you, but your ugly face looks better all the time. OldinHome will be welcomed."

"We've had some problems with a lassari named Renard," Gyll elaborated for the Motsognir.

"Ahh?" FitzEvard seemed to sit a bit higher in his seat, as if that comment had piqued his interest. "And how does this Renard trouble you?" he asked, glancing from Gyll to Helgin.

Gyll gave FitzEvard an account of the ippicator's display— he half-hoped that mentioning the beast would cause some display from FitzEvard, but the man disappointed him, seeming to be genuinely surprised. Gyll then spoke of the attempt to capture Renard. During the telling, he noticed that FitzEvard looked more to the Motsognir than to Gyll, and he wondered at that. He found himself glancing frequently at the Motsognir, who glumly endured the account. Puzzled, aware that some hidden exchange was occurring, he made his tale brief. "We intend to find him," he concluded.

"You do, eh," FitzEvard said heavily. Again, he was looking at Helgin, not at Gyll. Bands of jagged color scarred his face. "I doubt that it's worth the effort, Sula. Wouldn't you agree, Helgin?"

"Not when he interferes with us," Helgin replied.

"Maybe you're just standing in his way—and in any case, it's an internal Neweden matter; you and the Sula will be leaving soon."

Gyll felt increasingly irritated. He shifted in his seat, starting to say something about the side-conversation that seemed to exclude him, but then FitzEvard turned back to him. "Be careful, Sula. We wouldn't care to see you hurt." Again, that smile, marred and distorted by the transmission— tachyon relays were rarely good; this one seemed to be getting worse. FitzEvard's body swayed, distorted. "Kaethe asks after you, too. She's planning to bring *Peregrine* to OldinHome about the same time you'll be arriving—though what she sees in you, I don't know. You're too skinny."

Normally, that news would have cheered Gyll. He smiled weakly. "That's good news, sirrah."

"It had better be—it's not every whim of Kaethe's that I'll let her indulge." He leaned forward, as if peering through a fog. "This relay is terrible. It's not worth the money I'm spending on it. I'll see you both soon, then."

He gestured to someone offscreen and the relay ended in a blizzard of hues. The static-ridden hiss of the speakers cut off, leaving them in a sudden, aching silence. "What was going on, Helgin?" Gyll stared at the blank flat-screen.

"I'm getting ready to get some mocha. I need it." The dwarf grumbled to his feet, but Gyll, moving quickly, grasped Helgin's arm. He held the dwarf tightly, fingers whitening under the pressure.

"FitzEvard was talking to you, not me, Helgin. Something I didn't understand." His voice was harsh; deliberately, he softened his tone. His grip on Helgin's arm loosened. "I think of you as my friend. Tell me what I'm missing here."

"I don't know what you're talking about."

"You found Renard rather easily."

"I have contacts, just like you. And he wasn't there, was he?" The dwarf pulled away, rubbing at his bicep. "Damn it, Gyll—you do that again and I'll break that hand." It didn't sound to Gyll like the normal surliness of the Motsognir. The words had an edge.

"Would you lie to me?"

"What do you think?"

"I'd like to think you wouldn't."

"Good."

"Then what was going on?"

The Motsognir hesitated. Gyll thought he would speak at length. Then the dwarf grinned and shook his head. "Nothing," he said. "You want some mocha or not?"

"Then all I'm going to get from you is flippancy."

"Mocha, too." Then Helgin shook his head. "Gyll, I can't give you a conspiracy that doesn't exist, can I? Not unless you simply want some false collaboration for your paranoias. You should be glad we're leaving Neweden, my friend. It's making you see things."

15

Helgin came to see Gyll the next morning. "You checked with Camden in the bio section about the ippicator," he declared without preamble. His feet set well apart, he stood in front of Gyll's desk like an accusatory statue. Outside the port, Neweden threw the sunstar's light at *Goshawk*; the glare slashed across the room between Gyll and Helgin.

"Of course I did." Gyll had been standing behind the desk, reading a cargo manifest. He let the list fall to the desk. "What would you have done in my place? I was damned curious, having seen an ippicator on Kaethe's ship. Helgin, I told you that I looked aboard the ship. I wasn't hiding anything."

"You were paranoid, you mean. You don't trust me."

"It never occurred to me that you might have something to do with it, Helgin; I thought it might be someone else aboard the ship. So who's paranoid: me, or someone who'd sneak around to see if I'd been checking up on him?" Gyll paused, then tried to change the subject without segue. "We're damned low on the power chips we've been selling the southern continent. Can we divert some from anywhere else? I've an order from the Irastian Coalition."

"You don't want to talk about it."

"An astute observation, Helgin. We've a business to run."

"I think you're still looking for a conspiracy."

"I think you're the one that's paranoid."

With a growl, Helgin snatched the manifest from the desk, the white cloth of his tunic flaring as it entered Neweden's reflected light. He scanned it quickly. "We could divert some of the shipments to Remeale—"

The com-unit chimed. Gyll held up his hand. "Just a moment, Helgin." He touched a contact. "Yah, Fischer, what is it?"

165

"A call for Helgin from on-planet. The caller's rather insistent, so I thought I'd track him down. Is he there?"

Gyll glanced at the Motsognir, who shrugged his shoulders. "He's here, and he'll take the call from this extension." He activated the wall flat-screen. "I'll leave you to your call, Helgin. We can work with the manifest when you're done."

"You don't have to leave, Gyll. I'm not so paranoid that I worry about you hearing my private calls."

Gyll laughed at the overdone hurt in the dwarf's voice. "Fine. Whenever you're ready, Fischer."

The screen swelled with light, obliterating the planet's illumination. A man stared at them—tall, dark, with the coil of a spiked plant-pet wrapped about his shoulders. The room behind him was nondescript; wooden walls barren of decoration. "Good morning, Helgin, Sula."

Gyll saw Helgin's stance go wide again, defensive, and he wondered at that. "Sirrah d'Vomiis, is it not?" the Motsognir said. His voice was unusually deep and soft. "What do you want?"

The man smiled, slowly. One large hand stroked the plant-pet; it quivered, the thin spikes moving. "I've not seen you for some time, sirrah. I thought perhaps we had further business we could conduct."

The dwarf harrumphed. One foot scuffed the carpeted deck. "I'm afraid I'd written you off as an unreliable source, d'Vomiis."

"I know I missed our last, ahh, meeting," d'Vomiis replied pleasantly. His gaze flickered from the Motsognir to Gyll. "I apologize for that—it might have been mutually productive, in the right circumstances. I was wondering if I could make another appointment with you."

Something about the man's oily good manners bothered Gyll; it seemed to touch the Motsognir as well. The dwarf acted almost angry, as if the call irritated Helgin's already evil mood. For Gyll's part, this d'Vomiis was someone to whom he took an instant dislike, a gut reaction. There was nothing friendly about his smile—it was simply a uniform he put on to conduct business, and the plant-pet seemed a malevolent thing to wear—perhaps that was it.

"Is the meeting to be with the Sula Hermond as well?"

"I'd hate to waste the Sula's time for business that the

two of us are quite capable of handling, sirrah. I'm sure his time is quite important, and, in any case, what I have to say is only speculation." The hand slid along the barbed length of the plant-pet, the smile remained fixed in place.

"Where?" Helgin queried, curt and gruff.

"The Street of Singers in Sterka, near Oldman Church. There's a small market square there that I've made my center of trade."

"When?"

"Would eight tonight be convenient, Sterka time? I regret it can't be sooner—I've another meeting."

"I'll be there, but this had better be worth my time, d'Vomiis." He spoke in a growl. Gyll began to speak, swallowed the words.

"I think it will settle all the questions we've had, sirrah." D'Vomiis nodded to the Motsognir, then to Gyll; the half-bow of kin to kin, a Neweden politeness. "My thanks, sirrah. I'll leave you to your tasks. Until eight, then." His hand left the coil of the plant-pet and stabbed at something below the screen. He faded.

Neweden-light asserted dominance again, aquamarine.

"The Street of Singers isn't in the best area of Sterka. Mostly low kin." Gyll spoke to Helgin's back; the Motsognir still stared at the screen.

"I know the city well enough."

"He's one of our brokers? I don't recall his name on the lists."

"He wants to set up an arrangement. I've kept putting him off." Helgin turned, and his bearded face was fiercely jovial. "The man doesn't know when he's been bilked. I sold him a lot of faked T'Raith trinkets to see how he'd do. He had to fight to break even on the deal, but he's still interested."

"I'm surprised, after all that."

Helgin grinned. He spread his hands wide. "He thinks he can turn the tables on me, that's all. I'll teach him another lesson entirely. What do you think, Gyll? Am I the teacher type or not?"

"You've taught me a few things."

"Hah, you see."

"And you've always made sure that you still know more than me."

Helgin chuckled. "That keeps me in a job. It's the most important lesson of all."

The Street of Singers might once have been aptly named. That was no longer the case. Helgin heard no songs, and the only images the street would have evoked would have made sad and dreary verses. "Shabby" was the best word for the place; not barren and wrecked like Dasta Burrough, but the melancholy ugliness of riches gone to seed, of beauty neglected until it turned plain and old. The area had been wealthy enough once—he could see it in the lines of the ill-kept houses, in the spaciousness of trash-filled yards. A few houses here and there still reflected the pride of their owners, but those were increasingly rare as he approached Oldman Church. That name, at least, seemed apropos: the old ones sat on porches or stared from windows as he passed: empty, sagging faces.

The street was dark, as well. Many of the hoverlamps lay in shards, vandalized. Others were simply not functioning. The few that were still lit only seemed to accentuate the night, to deepen the shadows.

More and more Helgin was filled with foreboding, more and more Renard's arrangements had the smell of a trap.

He didn't care. An expected trap was not as dangerous as the one tripped unknowingly. He was prepared. It was seven, not eight; early enough to catch them off-guard. He swaggered down the middle of the street. He whistled, off-key, pursing his thick lips, a sound muffled in the tangle of his beard. He nodded to the wrinkled visage of an elderly woman in a window to his left, almost cheerful.

Oldman Church sat at the end of the Street of Singers, blocking the lane. Old, gray-wood, two-storied; it was as dreary as an old matron's face, half its windows gone, though a battered glow-sign proclaimed the times of service. Approaching the building, Helgin moved to the right side of the street, slowing, taking to the cover of the houses nearby. He slid the battered revolver from underneath his tunic, checked the cylinder. He chuckled. From the shadows, he bellowed, "Renard!"

The street seemed startled into silence. From the next

block over, a dog barked at the noise, but there was no reply. Helgin waited a few minutes, then called again.

Nothing.

He grunted as he shoved away from the sheltering wall with his shoulders. He eased out into the street, cautious, his ancient weapon ready. He did not expect the trap to be sprung, not yet. The street was deserted, but too public. Inside, that's where Renard would be, waiting. Helgin wondered what it would be—something mechanical, or an ambush, a person waiting with a sting. One, two, or a multilayer of tricks? The man had all day to prepare the place. Or would there be nothing, just Renard, maybe that woman of his?

You'll find out, won't you, Motsognir?

He examined the door and its frame carefully, using the thin beam of a pocket flash. Rotten wood, mostly, and a rough job of carpentry at that—Oldman Church must have been built later than the rest of the neighborhood. Low on the right there was a strip of wood that had a different grain than the rest. Helgin stood to one side, pushing at the door with the barrel of his gun. It swung open easily, and there was a quiet hiss and a soft *tchunk* as two small darts imbedded themselves in the wood to the left of the door. Compressed air, triggered by the opening of the door. Damned clumsy— only a fool would have walked straight in and been caught by that. Helgin knew that if he examined the tips of the tiny slivers of metal, he'd find them poisoned. Renard was outlining the rules of the game. Go back now, and there'd be no further contact between them, and Helgin would be telling Renard that he'd won. Go further, and there would come a final confrontation.

Helgin hesitated. There were a thousand ways to kill a man with traps, and there was no possibility that, armed and defended as he was, he could find them all. If Oldman Church was a maze of such things, the Motsognir would die. But that wasn't Renard's way, if he knew the man at all. He liked to see his killings, even if he didn't do them himself. He'd be here, to watch, maybe to take a hand.

No, not traps. An ambush.

And it was not a Motsognir trait to be subtle. There is a certain power to a straight overhand thrust when your opponent expects a feint and a jab. Standing to the side of the door, he called into the black interior. "Awfully clumsy, Renard. I want you, my friend, but if you think I'm going to walk into this pit, you're wrong. I'll find you some other time."

Silence; then the sound of someone moving in the darkness beyond the door. "Why wait, dwarf? I'm here now, and you'll be leaving soon. I could hide where you'd never find me in the time you have left. This may be your only chance."

"What, to meet you with all your friends?"

A low, quick laugh was his answer.

Not going in, that's for certain. Now to back out with a whole skin.

A scraping of wood above alerted him. He was almost too late, despite that. He whirled, moving aside, the revolver up. He heard the cough of the silenced sting before he saw the man leaning from the window. He felt a searing pain in his side as the ground next to him erupted in pouts of dust. He fired; the noise was deafening. The man screamed, dropping the sting and falling back inside the building. Helgin wasted no time wondering whether he'd hit the man or simply scared him with the noise. He grabbed the sting from the ground and ran, limping, feeling the wound in his side tear further. His tunic was wet, torn, dark with blood. He dodged between two houses, halted there a moment. He tore the tunic away, shivering in the cold air, probed the wound with tentative fingers—deep, but essentially superficial, he told himself, hoping he could believe it. The loss of blood worried him the most. He wrapped the shreds of the tunic around the worst of it, knotting the fabric viciously. *Best you can do, old son.* He checked the clip of the sting: five shells left. He thrust the revolver into his belt. The sting was a better weapon for this, a bit more comprehensive in its coverage: it didn't require much aiming, as the pellets spread.

He could hear them. Running footsteps, a panting breath. *So much for your damned appraisals, Motsognir. Public or not, he'll kill you here and blame it on the Hag's Legion. You shouldn't have come, shouldn't have come.* The thought thundered in his head.

He turned, began to run again. His side ached, already tightening, making him slow. He ignored the pain. Coming out from between the houses, he checked the next street. The dog he'd heard before was barking furiously now—he could see the animal in a front yard two doors down. It was facing back, between the houses. He decided to risk the street. Groaning, he bolted across the pavement and back between two buildings. He was halfway down the narrow space before he really saw the fence—board, both high and well-constructed. He made an attempt to scale it from a running start, his fingers scrabbling for the top. He did not make it, didn't come that close, and he felt a stabbing of pain from his wound, a gushing flow of blood. He collapsed, his back to the fence, sting across his knees. He squinted against the pain, fighting the onslaught of unconsciousness and shock. *Superficial, was it? Fool, fool!* When his vision cleared again, he struggled to his feet, blessing the low Motsognir center of balance and cursing the heavy Neweden gravity. He went back toward the street, one hand on the nearest building for support.

The dog was still barking. Suddenly, it went silent. He peered around the corner of the building. Lights were on now in several of the windows, but the residents stayed judiciously inside and hidden. Bloodfeud was a sacred custom on Neweden—you learned not to interfere in others' quarrels lest they become your own. They might watch, but they would not help. Helgin couldn't see the dog; he could only assume that its owner had taken it inside, or that Renard had rendered it permanently quiet. Helgin watched the street. Someone crossed it a hundred meters to his left, running in a crouch—too far for the sting, and the noise of the handgun would point to him like a finger. *Damn, they'll be coming at me from the back as well.* He felt the beginnings of despair and found he did not like the emotion. *Go out in the street again and they'll take you; stay here and you're trapped. A hell of a choice, dwarf.* He backed down the way he'd come, toward the fence.

There were windows. He tried them, one by one; all were locked. If Renard didn't know where he was, the shattering of glass would tell him, and a house was as much of a trap as this place—perhaps worse, for he'd have to deal with those inside. *Better to wait, at least for the moment.* He went to the fence and huddled into a corner of it, both weapons ready now, watching the opening to the street and listening for a sound.

It was the latter. Someone began climbing the fence from the far side. Helgin held his breath, not moving except to bring up the sting. Head tilted backward, he watched the city-glow of the sky. The silhouette of a head and shoulders appeared, with a hand holding a weapon to the right. Helgin aimed, pressed the trigger. The sting bucked, jamming hard into his shoulder, there was a dry cough from the silencer. The head was gone; there was the sound of a body falling to earth.

Amateurs, and a damned good thing—it might keep you alive. He struggled to his feet once again, using the sting as a crutch. *Now the windows; that body'll tell them exactly where I am. Move!*

He didn't have time.

A figure appeared at the street end of his cul-de-sac, hesitating a second and then whirling back. Helgin whipped the sting up and fired; the pellets scored paint, sent chips of masonry flying. He let himself fall to the left as the figure glanced around the corner—a line of brilliance arced across the alley; Helgin could smell paint blistering, the tang of scorched wood. *Oh, fine, he's got a hand-laser, and you came with a frigging handgun that can't hit much beyond thirty meters. Good choice, Motsognir, and I hope you live to regret it.* Helgin fired once more from his prone position. He had not thought of hitting the man—he could only hope to keep him back.

Someone was at the fence again: Helgin turned in time to see a head disappear. He aimed at the fence where the climber might have been, groaning as the sting jolted his shoulder once more. He was breathing heavily now, his side was soaked with blood. He could not even feel fear—the certainty that he was going to die was simply there, a cold realization. All he could do was delay the inevitable. He lifted the sting, thinking that it suddenly felt heavier, that the night was dimmer. He aimed for the corner once more, fired, then pointed the muzzle at the fence—this time there was only the click of the trigger striking an empty chamber. *Hell, you can't even count anymore, can you?* He let the sting drop, pulled the revolver from his waistband. *Keep them*

*down; that's all you can do. It won't help you. You're going to
find DwarfHome before you expected, Motsognir.*

He lurched along the wall, staggering, his hand against
the bricks, making his way to a window. Without aiming, he
fired at the street end of the space. *Keep them down.* He
thought he heard a sound behind him, and shot at the top of
the fence, splintering wood. He continued his slow progress
toward the window.

He didn't see the sting, just heard the scrape of a
footstep. Kicking against the wall, he flung himself backward—
the sting spoke; pellets struck him in mid-leap. He rolled,
helpless, the shock of impact knocking the handgun from his
grasp. Through pain-fogged eyes he could see a man standing
near him, bringing up the sting again. Helgin tried to lever
himself to his feet; his legs would not cooperate. He could
only stare at the death awaiting him.

But the man was suddenly down himself, as Helgin
heard the characteristic whine of a vibrofoil. Helgin blinked,
unbelieving. *By the great god Skafidur, not dead! Not dead
yet!*

"Gyll!" he tried to shout. His voice sounded like a
cracked whisper. "The fence..." He thought he was going to
go under. He fought the darkness.

Gyll stepped forward between the houses. He had a
vibro in one hand, a hand-laser in the other. He wore the
night-clothing of the Trader-Hoorka. A black cap covered his
grayed hair, and his hair and face were grimy with soot. "It's
taken care of," Gyll said. "Fischer's back there." Gyll whistled—
there was an answering call from the far side of the fence.
Gyll went to Helgin, switching off the vibro, holstering the
laser. He went to one knee. Helgin grinned up at Gyll
through a face twisted with pain.

"You took your damned time," he said. He tried to
laugh, found that he had to grit his teeth against the pain.

"You went there early." Gyll's hand probed Helgin's side,
his face grim. "How can I have you followed when you don't
follow the only schedule I knew—d'Vomiis had said eight."

"I was being smart."

"It looks like it was a real good idea, too."

"No thanks to you, I almost died."

"Next time, ask me to come along." He looked up from

his examination of Helgin. "You'll live, I suppose, though that's a nasty side wound, my friend. You've lost a lot of blood, and that last shot chewed up your right leg pretty well."

"Don't look at me with that long face, then, or are you lying to me?"

"None of the lies today came from me. You'll live." A groundcar screeched to a halt on the street. Trader-Hoorka leapt out.

"Then why so solemn, Gyll?"

"I killed that man. I haven't taken a life for standards, dwarf." Gyll's voice was gruff, angry. "I find that I don't like the feeling. I don't like it at all."

"Gyll—"

"Shut up, Motsognir." Gyll waved to the Hoorka—they came at a run, bearing a litter. One began attaching a portable med-pack to Helgin's chest, grimacing as she tore away the red-stained remnants of his tunic. They placed the dwarf on the litter. As it began to rise on its hover-tethers, Helgin beckoned to Gyll. "Is one of them Renard?" he asked.

"I wouldn't know. I've never seen him." There was a strange sadness in Gyll's eyes. He looked older.

"Yes you have." Helgin swallowed with an effort. He tried to turn on his side; one of the Hoorka gently nudged him back. "I talked with him this morning. The man who called. D'Vomiis."

Gyll's eyes went hard. He seemed to withdraw further into himself. "D'Vomiis," he said, detached, distant. "Neh, he's not one of them. No." He paused a moment. "I think you've a lot to tell me, dwarf."

"You won't like it." Helgin tried to smile. "Why don't we just take a walk instead. Let me hop off this litter—"

"I think you're going to talk to me." Gyll waved a hand at the Hoorka—the litter moved toward the groundcar. Gyll watched them leave. Doors slammed, the engine purred into life, its headlights carving the darkness. The beams swung as the driver turned and drove away.

Gyll walked slowly over to the body of the man he'd killed. He still held the sting, sprawled faceup, the eyes caught in eternal surprise. The man was young, good-looking in a rough way, perhaps still jussar. There was a lot of blood, black in the darkness; vibros were not clean weapons. Gyll reached down, squatting, and gently closed the eyes. "I didn't know you," he said quietly. "Enemies should always know each other." He spoke to himself, his hand still on the man's face. Sighing, he rose to his feet.

"But then," he said, "so should friends."

16

Gyll did not get back to *Goshawk* as quickly as he had expected or hoped. One of his aides drove up to him as he entered the field gates of Sterka Port.

"Sula?"

He inclined his head in acknowledgment. "Yah, Levitt? What is it?"

The young woman spoke over the purr of the groundcar's motor. "There's a group here to see you, Sula. They won't talk to any of the rest of us."

"Who are they?"

Her dark face remained noncommittal. "Hoorka," she said. "Neweden Hoorka." Her eyes tracked him up and down, taking in the smudged and bloody uniform, the quickly and inexpertly wiped face. He knew he should change.

"Thane Mondom?" he asked. He couldn't keep the hope from his voice. The intensity of it surprised him, but the beginning of Levitt's headshake quelled the optimism.

"Others," she replied. "Nine or ten of 'em. The one that does the speaking for the group is called Jeriad McWilms."

"Where'd you put them?"

"Out at the shuttle shelter—it'll be a bit before the shuttle gets back: we took the Motsognir right up to the ship."

"Take me out there, then." He swung into the open cab as Levitt accelerated away. He was tired; he rubbed at his eyes. *Too much happening at once, old man. They don't give you a chance to rest.* Gyll didn't want to face another crisis

175

tonight. All he wished was the oblivion of sleep. He felt sick, sick at having killed a man he didn't know, sick because Helgin was hurt, sick because there seemed to be duplicity all around him, even from the Motsognir, whom he'd trusted most of all. He approached the shelter with little enthusiasm.

The Hoorka-kin smiled as he entered, the smiles going flat as they saw him. McWilms, concern on his face, bowed low to Gyll, who returned the bow sketchily, perfunctorily. "I'm sorry, Ul..." McWilms stopped himself. "Sula," he corrected. "I didn't mean to have you disturbed at work. Are you all right? The blood..."

"It isn't mine," Gyll said wearily. "I'm just tired. What can I do for you, Jeriad?" He glanced at the others: Serita Iduna, Bachier, others he recognized, apprentices when he'd left the guild.

"We've left Hoorka," McWilms replied simply.

Gyll didn't know how to reply. He felt awkward, slow; all of his reactions, dulled. "Jeriad, you surprise me...." He brushed at his clothing.

"Sula, we're here to join you," Serita broke in. "Some new recruits, neh?" She grinned.

"Does Mondom know?"

The faces registered a varying range of emotions: neutrality, open distaste, hurt. McWilms seemed to be recalling something unpleasant; Serita's olive face still smiled, but the smile was forced now; Bachier frowned. "She knows," Bachier said. "She knows very well."

"The Thane was quite angry," McWilms interjected. "She made threats, she cursed us—and you. There was nearly a confrontation with the rest of the kin. It was rather ugly, Sula."

"Why did you leave?"

McWilms looked at the others. He rubbed his right arm: a nervous habit. "The Hoorka..." he said haltingly, "aren't what they once were. You knew that. It's worse now, Sula. Mondom's made a deal with the Li-Gallant; we're now a part of his rule-guild, under his control. It's not the same now. It's all cracked and changing. Why wait for it to fall apart?" He paused, shrugged. "We'd like to go with you."

"She's abandoned the code," he said, almost a whisper. Anger surged through him; he forced it down.

"At least parts of it, Sula. And who knows how much longer the rest will hold? We'd rather move with the opportunities you offer."

He should have felt some triumph. Instead, Gyll almost laughed, mockingly. This no longer mattered: the bright future he'd thought he was offering his old kin was tarnished now, blighted by the deceptions of Helgin, which in turn threatened further lies, other actions done behind his back by people he'd thought he trusted. If he hated what Mondom had done to Hoorka, he hated it because it had become something other than what he'd intended. But there was no deliberate deception there; simply a change in the framework in which she operated. It seemed that the Family Oldin might have misrepresented itself from the beginning.

He didn't know which was worse.

Gyll had little enthusiasm to give McWilms and his fellow defectors. He was too tired to think, too exhausted to deal with it.

"I'll tell my chief aide Fischer that you're here," he said at last. "He'll see to you all, make arrangements."

Gyll could see puzzlement and disappointment in McWilms's face, and he forced a wan smile to his lips. "I'm sorry," Gyll said to all of them. "I know you've all taken a huge chance on my recommendation, and now I'm not showing much enthusiasm for your courage." He ran a hand through his hair—it came away sooty. "I'm very glad you're here, but it's been a long, difficult, and strange evening for me."

"We understand," Serita said. "The woman—Levitt—told us some of what had happened. We're sorry that the Motsognir was hurt."

"It's very different, what we have to do for the Oldins," Gyll said. "I had to kill a man tonight, with no warning, with no honor. He was someone who was no personal enemy of mine, for whom I had no contract."

"He was attacking a friend," McWilms said. "That seems reason enough."

"It should be," Gyll answered, "but it wasn't."

177

17

The room was dark, the port partially shuttered, though in any case it showed only the salt-on-velvet of stars, looking toward the band of spilled light that was galaxy center. The gravity was set very low—Gyll had to watch his step lest he push too hard and flounder in air for an instant. The bedfield was a white mass in the center of the room, over which hovered the spiked bulk of a medi-doc.

Gyll paused at the door, hesitant. He did not look forward to this confrontation. He didn't want to hear the words.

"You look like you're waiting for a funeral, and I'm not planning to die. You want to come in instead? If you've got ale with you, I'll even give you a kiss." Helgin's voice was hoarse and weak. Gyll could see the dwarf, his beard dark against the sheets, eyes gleaming in starlight.

"No ale. Just me."

"Then no kiss."

"How you feeling?"

Even in the twilight, he could see that familiar, battered face shape itself into a scowl. "I'm just resting a moment before I get up and start dancing. How the hell *should* I feel, Gyll?" Above Helgin, a diode flashed amber on the medi-doc. Gyll watched the light with seeming fascination: amber, a flicker, then again green. "I've got a hole in my side, several smaller companions in the legs," Helgin continued. "I'm scraped up all over and I feel like a vampire's leftovers. And my hair's filthy and my beard itches. I'm feeling like shit, Gyll." Helgin fixed the older man with a sidewise stare. "So . . . when are we going to drop the inanities and talk about what's really bothering you?"

Gyll came fully into the room, letting the door close behind him. He walked all the way around the bedfield, touching the medi-doc tentatively; he lifted the shutters of the port and peered out at the folded curtains of stars. "I'm not feeling so well either, Motsognir."

"I haven't got a lot of sympathy to spare at the moment for simple mental anguish."

His back to the Motsognir, Gyll shrugged to the universe. "I can understand that." He let the shutters fall back with a clatter, turned, and leaned against the wall, hands behind him. "You lied, Helgin. Lied a lot."

"It's the way of the worlds, Gyll."

"It's not the way of friends."

"I suppose telling you that it was for your own good won't appease you either."

"I don't need any more lies."

"That's an excuse, not a lie. There's a difference."

"Who's Renard, Helgin?"

The Motsognir turned his head away at the question, his hair rustling against the pillow. "It matters that much, Gyll? You just can't ignore it, look the other way for a few days, and let me play out my own problems? I heard the news that you got a bunch of your precious Hoorka to take back with us—that wins you your bet with FitzEvard. Why can't you just worry about getting them ready?"

"Who's Renard?"

Gyll thought that Helgin would not answer. He waited; there was no reply but the Motsognir's slow, loud breath and a faint humming from the medi-doc. With a growl of disgust, Gyll thrust himself away from the wall. Helgin's voice halted him.

"He's a frigging bastard, a low-life whose loyalty is measured by the price he's paid. A piece of scum, stuff you'd get on your boot walking through Dasta."

"Who pays him?"

"You already know that answer."

"Tell me anyway," Gyll insisted.

"FitzEvard. Renard's an employee, just like you."

Gyll muttered a curse. The Motsognir heard; he laughed bitterly. "You can't tell me that you haven't known that since last evening, Gyll. It's no big thing—FitzEvard pays a lot of people. You're in good company as well as bad."

"Why'd the two of you fight?—FitzEvard pays *you*, as well."

Helgin sighed. One hand fluttered above the sheets. "We didn't like each other, first of all. And we have differing priorities. Renard doesn't care what he does as long as it creates chaos on Neweden. He'd love to kill *you*, Gyll, because of the uproar it would cause if done in the right place, at the right time. I wouldn't let him. And we also had a power conflict—who was in charge. If he killed me, it's almost as good as getting rid of you, because of the stink you'd raise." The long explanation seemed to tax him. The hand fell back to the sheet; the dark eyes closed and his head sank back. Lights shimmered amber above him.

Gyll knew that he should feel guilty, interrogating Helgin when he was in this condition, but he felt little but anger and sadness. "And now?" he asked.

"Now?" Helgin echoed. "Nothing, Gyll. Nothing."

"We could go to d'Embry or the new Regent."

"Why? The damage to Neweden's done. This world's been pushed over the edge of change, and we can't stop that now. And—you may have trouble with this, Gyll—I still wouldn't trade the Oldins for the Alliance. Not at all. I'd gladly kill Renard, but I'd go back to FitzEvard afterward, not d'Embry."

Gyll shook his head. "You're right. That's hard to believe."

"It's the truth. You're the one that desires truth, O righteous one." His voice was full of scorn.

"You're damned right," Gyll answered heatedly. "I'm frigging tired of this, Helgin. If I'm archaic and stupid, fine, but Neweden shaped me and I still believe in that outmoded concept of honor."

"Neweden lies worse than anyone, man. Look at the Li-Gallant if you want to see a slimy eel." Helgin lay back again. His hand lifted, then fell, as if he wanted to reach for Gyll but was afraid that the gesture might be misinterpreted or rejected. "Gyll, you can't go around bothered because the universe doesn't conform to your idea of morality. It doesn't work that way."

Fury was in Gyll now. A calm, distant part of himself recognized the anger for the catharsis it was; it boiled, driving his open hand against the medi-doc. The device rang with a metallic protest, shivering in its holding field. "Don't give me this philosophical shit, Helgin!" he roared, feeling the words ravage his throat. "I don't give a *damn* who's lying or why, I just need to understand. What are we doing on Neweden, what does FitzEvard want with it?"

Something had changed in Helgin's eyes. Under the hedge of his eyebrows, they had narrowed, gone hard. He twisted a strand of his beard between thumb and forefinger, lips pursed thoughtfully. "Want to know what else I've done, Gyll? It's more than just consorting with Renard. You remember Gunnar, Vingi's old rival, killed in a most un-Neweden-like manner by an unknown assassin? That killer was me, Gyll. Me. Acting on FitzEvard's orders. But then, you Hoorka don't blame the weapons, do you? You're just the weapons in someone else's hands. That was me as well: a weapon in FitzEvard's hands."

Gyll could not speak. He'd told himself that he would not be surprised by anything the dwarf could tell him. But this eight-standard-old confession startled him. "Why did you kill Gunnar?" he said at last.

"Me?" Helgin started to sit up on his elbows, but then grimaced in pain and lay back once more—a flurry of varicolored dots flickered with his motion. "I did it because FitzEvard asked me to do it. Not *told* me, *asked* me—we Motsognir have our pride, after all."

"Then what were FitzEvard's reasons?"

"I forgot to ask him," Helgin muttered, then shook his head. "Gyll, FitzEvard and d'Embry have had a running confrontation for decades. I don't think it insignificant that Oldin would choose to come to Neweden when d'Embry's Regent. Maybe that was entirely it—he wanted to cause d'Embry problems. Or maybe he really *wants* Neweden, for whatever purposes."

"It sounds damned petty."

"To you or me, yah. We ain't FitzEvard, are we?"

"What about the ippicator?"

"I don't know anything about it. Honestly."

Gyll's fist beat a rhythm on his hip, a steady *slap-slap-slap*. Suddenly he stopped and swiveled on his toes. He began to walk toward the door.

"Where are you going, Gyll? You didn't tuck me in."

The door slid open as Gyll touched the contact. The light of the corridor beyond spilled into the room, falling short of the bedfield and leaving Helgin lost in gloom. "Can't you ever be serious, Helgin?"

"I'm always serious. Where are you going?"

He answered truthfully, "I don't know."

"Shut the door. Please."

Gyll stepped back; the door sighed mechanically and abandoned the room to twilight once more. "Make this quick, Motsognir. I'm suddenly not much in the mood for talking."

"I just want to know what you're planning to do, Gyll. I ask as a friend, because I do care about you."

"I've declared bloodfeud against Renard, and any member of the Hag's Legion. I intend to follow that up."

Helgin nodded. "You're not going to quit Family Oldin, not going to try some heroics that'll just be used by both sides?"

"I don't know what I intend to do. I'll think about it, first. What worries me most isn't you or me or the frigging Oldins. There are ten Hoorka here on the ship, ten of my old guild-kin, who came because they trusted me. I can't leave them, and Mondom won't take them back from me, not if I know her at all. I trapped them here."

"I wouldn't phrase it quite so pessimistically."

"I would."

There didn't seem to be anything else to say. Gyll waited; Helgin lay still. The medi-doc purred to itself, and Gyll went back to the door.

"You gonna tell them?" asked Helgin, behind him.

"Who?" He did not turn.

"Your Hoorka foundlings. You gonna tell them about all this?"

"No. At least not yet."

"You see, you're learning it too, Gyll—it's better sometimes to lie or omit the truth." There was no triumph in Helgin's observation.

"You might be right." Gyll punched at the contact with a forefinger; the door opened. "But I hope you're not."

He left.

Gyll sat at his desk for a long while, turning the thoughts in his mind like spadefuls of earth. He stroked the bumblewort in his lap, his feet on the desk—orangish fur floated through the room.

"Fischer," he said at last to the empty air.

A click as a speaker activated: "Sula?"

"Get me Thane Mondom in Underasgard."

"Yes, Sula." The speaker snapped off.

Gyll swung his feet from the desk—the bumblewort chirruped in irritation. He tried to dump the creature off his lap, prodding the soft shell of its back. The wort braced its legs, not wanting to leave. Sighing, Gyll let it remain where it was, scratching its earflaps absently.

Click. "I have Thane Mondom, Sula."

"Thank you, Fischer." Gyll activated the camera and flat-screen. Mondom stared out at him, the broken walls of the caverns behind her. The view gave him only head and shoulders—a dark, wrathful woman. "I assume you've called to gloat," she said before he could speak.

He'd expected the bitterness, but had expected it to be encapsuled in the Neweden circumspection. He hadn't thought she'd be so blunt. "Not to gloat," he said. "Just to tell you that they're here. And to give it one last chance with you."

"You still have the bumblewort, I see."

Gyll glanced down—the wort had put its front paws on the desk, peering up at the screen. Gyll rubbed its nose, and the wort ducked away with a shake of its head. "Yah, I still have the wort, and you're evading the question."

She nodded. "You've told me all I need to know. They came to you. If you're not gloating, I don't see where we have anything further to talk about."

"Will you take them back, if they decide to return?"

Her face changed with that. She became suspicious, puzzled, her lips drawing back slightly, her nose wrinkling. "Don't you want them now that they're there? No, I won't take them back. They've made their choice; let them die with it."

"Let's at least be reasonable about this, Mondom."

"Reasonable?" She laughed, her face twisted. Her eyes seemed large, touched with moisture; the skin under her eyes was dark with a lack of sleep. "You've done the cruelest thing you could do to Hoorka, Gyll. You crippled us—who knows, maybe it's the mortal wound you were after, but it'll be a while before we die. If you wanted to watch Hoorka suffer, this'll do it. All I have left are the dregs of the full kin and the apprentices. I haven't enough people for a viable rotation; that means we might have trouble with some contracts. I may lose kin to thievery or lassari-traits—some of those I have left are damned close to that now. The new Regent won't even talk with me, much less try to open offworld options." She seemed to run out of steam, her vehemence collapsing. Her shoulders sagged; the focus of her camera shifted slightly as she leaned away.

"You're allied with Vingi now. You won't starve."

Her eyes widened. She shrugged. "I had to do it."

"That has destroyed Hoorka more than anything I've done."

"You're not Hoorka. Don't let it bother you."

Gyll snorted derision. "If I were staying longer, I'd dismantle the Hoorka myself—I could do it; go to the Li-Gallant, offer him the services of the Trader-Hoorka at a break-even rate, guarantee the death of a victim. I could even make it a point of our agreement that he outlaw the assassins' guild called Hoorka. He'd do it, Mondom."

"If you've become that vicious, you've changed a lot in the time you've been gone, Gyll."

"Oh, I've changed, Mondom. Very much." He looked away and back. "And I hate the Hoorka, Mondom. The guild has outlived its usefulness. The society changed around it, and it's no longer viable. Give it up."

"And come to you?"

"You'll be nothing but a tool for the Li-Gallant if you stay." *Neweden is gone*, Helgin had said. *I still wouldn't trade the Oldins for the Alliance*. The wort mewled at him. He stroked its shell.

"And whose tool would I be there?" Anger colored her cheeks. "The Sula isn't content with his small victory," she said, breaking into the impersonal mode. "He wants everything."

"Mondom, don't cut me off like this. Let's at least talk."

She had turned away from him. "The Sula is an ass. I don't hear him anymore."

"Mondom . . ."

But her hand had already reached out. The screen went dark.

* * *

"Gods, McClannan, certainly you're not serious?" D'Embry was startled into a half-shout. She could not believe what he'd said. "You're talking about a man's life, not some silly game."

McClannan shrugged. They were in her office, now rather bare. The d'Vellia soundsculpture was packed and crated, silent. The animo-paintings swirled unseen in boxes. Only the desk remained. The carpet was dying; she'd let her daily maintenance lapse since McClannan had mentioned in passing that he intended to have it removed after she left. He stood in front of her desk now, immaculate, wearing the robes of office that she'd always eschewed as too ostentatious, the sunburst symbol of the Alliance golden at his throat. He looked the proper image of a regal Diplo—the very type she'd always abhorred. He brushed at his lower lip with a thumb.

"I didn't expect your approval, m'Dame."

"That's good. Then you won't be disappointed. Why even tell me? I can't even fathom your reasoning, man. A Hoorka contract for Sula Hermond's life? It's absurd."

"I don't think so."

A spasm of pain shot through d'Embry's chest. She closed her eyes against the stabbing hurt. These attacks had come more and more frequently over the last week, and the symbiote on her back seemed less quick to cope with them. *Getting old and worn-out, woman, and McClannan's taken away the reason you kept fighting: cause and effect.* She wondered as well if the symbiote wasn't wearing out, thinking that it would be like a Trader item to do just that. D'Embry grimaced, knotting a tiny fist on her lap. She could feel McClannan's gaze on her, definitely less than sympathetic, somehow predatory. She bid her eyes to open, made her hands relax. "What good is this supposed to do, Regent?"

"The Li-Gallant tells me that the Alliance needs to show that it is better for Neweden than the Family Oldin, that we're stronger."

"And this contract is supposed to prove that? Excuse my stupidity, but somehow the logic escapes me." A cold amusement rippled through her; she found it difficult not to laugh, scoffingly. "Not even a fool like Vingi would believe that kind

185

of crap—and in any case, the Sula will simply buy out the contract. It will never be run."

"I don't think he'll pay it off." He seemed too calm. That worried d'Embry, made the pain of her body recede.

"He'd be crazy not to do so. The Oldins are easily rich enough, no matter how expensive you made the price. All you'll prove is that the Oldins are as wealthy as the Alliance."

"I have additional information, m'Dame." Smugness tightened his smile. He waved a negligent hand. "It's a calculated risk, admittedly, but I think he'll run."

D'Embry shook her head. "McClannan, you're talking about murdering a man."

"I'm talking about letting Dame Fate decide. That's the way it works here, isn't it? Let Dame Fate decide if he's to live or die."

"It's still a life."

McClannan adjusted the collar of his robe. He brushed at imaginary lint on the silken sleeve. "How many people will die if the Li-Gallant boots the Alliance off-planet? Given a free hand to deal with the lassari as he sees fit, how many will die? Let the Oldins do what they want, and how many more will go to see the truth of Neweden's afterlife? You've said it yourself, m'Dame: wherever the Oldins go, turmoil and death follow. I'm trading one life against several."

"All your altruistic excuses aside, it's *still* a life." She could feel the beginnings of the pain again. She ignored it, breathing deeply despite the agony that caused her. *Damn you, symbiote, take care of this. Do your frigging job.* "And it still comes down to speculation on your part. You *think* this, you *believe* that. Are you willing to gamble for a life? I wouldn't. I repeat—it's not a game."

"Game or not, it's already done."

"You can still cancel the contract. All that costs you is money; McClannan, I'll pay that out of my pension if the expense worries you."

He hesitated. She saw it in the set of his chin, the slightly open mouth. She attacked before he could answer, sitting forward in her chair. "Do you really want the Sula's body dumped at the gates of Diplo Center?" she asked. "That may work here, but *you've* never had to kill a man, never seen the blood. Hell, man, our whole thrust is that we offer peace and security—civilization. How would Niffleheim view this contract?"

"Niffleheim allowed you to let the Hoorka work offworld."

"Not often, and only with great reluctance. After Heritage, never."

McClannan scoffed, his composure returning and confidence coming back to his voice. "Come, m'Dame. You stopped the offworld Hoorka contracts because of Niffleheim's pressure, not your own altruism. So don't lecture me about ethics and morality. Neither one of us is an expert in those fields."

She knew that she should not be angry, not if she wanted to convince him. She had to remain calm, yet control eluded her. She didn't know why—the influence of the symbiote's chemicals, a lack of patience that had increased as her health deteriorated, whatever... She could hear the snappishness in her voice; she immediately regretted it. "What field *is* your area of expertise, McClannan? Lying? Going over your superior's head? Or are you just looking to increase your skill with murder?"

McClannan drew himself up to his full height, glaring down the length of that classic nose at d'Embry. "I told you not to lecture me, old woman," he said, his words clipped. His facade of respect for her was gone; what she saw behind that abandoned facade appalled d'Embry—*Gods, I didn't know he hated me that much.*

She softened her tone, trying to recover some of the ground she'd lost to anger. "I'm sorry, Santos. You're right, that was uncalled for. Let's talk about this rationally."

It did not mollify him. "I've no interest in talking any further, m'Dame. I'm the Regent; please allow me to make my decisions without interference."

She sighed; the pain was arcing through her and she felt nausea boiling in her stomach. "I'm just trying to show you that you're making a decision you'll regret. Santos, I *do* have the experience—it's sometimes worth listening to."

"Tell me you've never made a decision you've regretted."

She kneaded her stomach. "I wouldn't make that claim," she said. "You know that."

"Then don't claim that your advice is so valuable." McClannan nodded to her. "I think you've said enough." For an instant, his face showed concern as he looked at her. "You're in pain. Should I call the Center doctor?"

"No, thank you."

"Then I'll be about my business."

He turned and left the room. D'Embry waited until he was gone, then doubled over, "Oh, *damn!*" she muttered through clenched teeth.

18

The apprentice had a look of joy as he handed the flimsy to Thane Mondom. "A contract," he said, smiling.

She didn't look at it. She stared at the apprentice in reproof. "You don't need to be so happy about it," she told him. "The Hag will smile at you one day—those that gloat at death, She keeps. She of the Five will never snatch you back."

The apprentice ducked his head. "Go on, get back to your post," Mondom told him. As the boy left, she unfolded the flimsy, read the words there. She glanced up, still holding the paper, and seemed to gaze into an unseen distance.

"What is the man thinking of?" she said in a whisper. "Gyll won't run. He won't run."

19

Steban was awed. The port overwhelmed him with noise and fury—open spaces and huge machines. And his contract was even more unusual: the creator of Hoorka, that figure of the full kins' tales. Steban had never met him; Gyll had gone before the Hoorka chose Steban from the ranks of jussar applicants. There was a certain thrill knowing that he would meet the man soon.

It had taken time, longer than any contract he'd initiated before. First he'd had to pass the port's Diplo guards, polite but insistent on knowing his business. He'd had to wait until one of them called Diplo Center and received clearance. Then, with a badge clipped to his nightcloak as a pass, he'd gone to the shelter beside which *Goshawk*'s shuttle rested. He contacted the unbelieving people there, insisting that he would speak fully only with the Sula. It was his first view of Traders—they seemed normal enough, burly men and women whose main tasks seemed to be moving boxes and taking inventories. They'd radioed the ship, evidently quite pleased to pass the responsibility upward. Then had followed a long wait; he'd watched the shuttle depart, and spent an hour talking with the Traders—he did not believe half of what they told him, tales of offworld sights and pleasures. He'd nodded politely, but kept a skeptical grin on his face.

And now he stood before Sula Hermond himself. Steban arranged his face in the neutral aloofness Thane Mondom had taught him, and bowed deeply to the man. Sula Hermond didn't appear overly prepossessing; he was old, to Steban's eyes, his hair gone mostly white. His eyes were more sad than anything else, as if some old mood had settled there, wrapping itself in folds of quiet and sorrow. Still, the body was lean, taut with well-toned muscles, and there were tracks of old knife scars on his hands. Steban felt that he'd probably like the man. He could understand why Thane Mondom had once been his lover. "Sula Gyll Hermond?" he asked when their gazes met.

"Yes," the old man replied quietly. A strong voice, Steban thought, but I doubt that he raises it often. A man who rules by strength of friendship rather than fear. Steban glanced down at the bio-monitor on his belt—a light glowed green: positive ID.

"Your life has been claimed for Dame Fate and She of the Five, Sula. We of the Hoorka have received a contract naming you as the victim." Steban's voice was dispassionate, made distant by the rote recitation of memorized, well-rehearsed

189

words. His eyes were half-closed, as if he rummaged in his head for the text. "You have several options—"

Sula Hermond had raised one hand, a gentle interruption. Steban wondered—this is the man who created the assassins, gave them their skills, had killed more himself than any of the rest, more even than the famous Aldhelm? Sula Hermond acted like a shy teacher. "I know the routine," he said, and he smiled. "You say it well, too—you've done the lessons properly."

In confusion, Steban smiled back, then immediately replaced the smile with the mask of Hoorka aloofness. He knew that Sula Hermond saw the slip and was amused by it; the man's smile grew larger. "Do you wish to negate the contract, Sula?" Steban asked. Thane Mondom had told him to expect payment. Steban was already fumbling for the pouch on his belt in anticipation.

"I think not." Softly, always softly.

Steban looked up, bewildered now. He let the flap of the pouch drop. The old man still smiled at him, sad and gentle. "Sula, I thought—"

"—that I would pay," Gyll finished for him. "I know."

Steban did not understand. From the tales he had heard, from what he'd seen here today at the port, the Family Oldin was wealthy. Surely the Sula misunderstood him. He shook his head. "Sula, if the contract is paid out, you will not be hunted."

The smile was still there, but harder-edged now, the eyes gone distant. "I realize that, son. Don't forget who wrote the code." The man took a deep breath, straightening and stretching, and Steban realized that, despite the Sula's age, he would be a formidable opponent. He looked quick and devious. "It would be amusing," the Sula continued, "to ask Thane Mondom what she would do if I were to simply take this shuttle back to *Goshawk* and sit. Would she rent a shuttle herself and come knocking at the door? Do the Hoorka have the powered suits and heavy artillery she'd need to breach the hull? Boy, I tell you, the Hoorka wouldn't have the money, the people, the equipment, or the expertise. *I* could do it, she could not. The sunstar would rise laughing at the guild-kin."

Sula Hermond had become more and more perilous to

Steban's eyes as the old man spoke, less the kindly teacher and more the vaunted assassin of Hoorka tales. Now he sighed, a long exhalation, and leaned back against the rough wooden wall of the shed, arms folded at the chest, and he was once more the gentle elder.

"But I won't do that," he said. "You'll tell Mondom this, boy: I've neglected the gods of Neweden long enough—*my* gods, whether I want them or not—and I intend to do penance for that neglect. I'll put my life in Dame Fate's hands. I will run—tell Mondom that it will end in the hunt of knives, and that I quite intend to see the sunstar rising tomorrow. Tell her that—you can remember it all?"

Steban nodded. He'd forgotten the Hoorka mask again; his mouth hung open.

"Good. You've done your duty then, boy. I know the rules of this game, if not some of the others I've been forced to play recently. At least I should be good at it. You have some tracer-dye with you. Use it, and you can go."

Sula Hermond extended his hands toward Steban. The apprentice fumbled again under his nightcloak, pulling forth a small vial. He touched the cap—a fine mist covered the hands, a quickly drying dew. "Fine. Now give my words to the Thane."

As Steban turned to leave, Sula Hermond called after him. "Tell her one more thing, apprentice. Tell her that he who creates has leave to destroy, as well. I don't like what Hoorka has become. This will be the last hunt."

"Sula?"

"Just tell her that."

Steban left the shelter. He was confused, his mind a tumult. He could not decide what he had just seen, which Sula Hermond was the true one: the harsh assassin, the gentle old man.

They stayed—a static triangle—as far apart in the room as they could. Gyll was seated behind his desk; Helgin, looking battered and bruised, was in a floater snuggled in the corner nearest the door; McWilms, his attention divided between the other two and the view of Neweden through the port, stood, arms akimbo, leaning against the outside wall.

"It was a good little joke, Gyll," Helgin said. His voice

was hoarse, his face—what could be seen of it under the beard—was mottled with a gold-brown bruise. He twisted his beard around a finger. "A wonderful little joke. Hah, hah," he said with leaden precision. "Now please tell me that you weren't serious."

"I am. I'll run the contract."

"Don't push the joke too far, Gyll; I might not think it's funny anymore. I might even start believing that you're telling the truth."

"I know it surprises you when people do that." Gyll glanced at Helgin. The Motsognir stared back, impassive. "It's the truth. I want to go through with it."

"Mondom will be one of the Hoorka, Sula." McWilms spoke, shrugging away from the wall. He didn't look comfortable to Gyll, as if the fit of the Trader-Hoorka uniform bothered him, or as if he were forced to be privy to a private quarrel in which he had no part. "We, ahh, didn't exactly leave her with many good full kin. She'll be one of those hunting you, almost certainly."

Gyll frowned. He'd suspected that such would be the case, but McWilms's words made him face the truth of that speculation. "I wish that didn't matter to me, Jeriad. But it does. It fails to change the essence of my decision, though."

McWilms looked through the port at the expanse of Neweden, as if fascinated by the cloud patterns. "I wasn't trying to change your mind, Sula, just pointing out something you might not have known. I understand your decision quite well, myself, unlike others."

"*I* don't," Helgin grumbled. He glanced at McWilms, scowled at his back, and turned to Gyll. "I don't understand at all."

"You're not from Neweden," McWilms commented, staring at the world, "and you're not Gyll. You're not *anything* like Gyll."

The dwarf shot a glance of venom at McWilms. Gyll spoke hastily, seeing the irritation in the dwarf—he knew the short-fused Motsognir temperament. "You know how the Hoorka are set up here, Helgin. A victim won't die if it's not his time to do so. Dame Fate rules Hoorka."

"That's superstitious rationalization that you don't believe much more than me. And you also set it up to buy out the contracts."

"There were always some of those who could afford to pay off the contract, and who still chose to run."

"Yah, the idiots with death wishes, or fools who felt themselves invulnerable, like childish heroes."

"Which am I, Helgin? Idiot or fool?" Gyll felt his own temper rising, his voice gaining volume to match the thunder of the Motsognir. McWilms had turned to watch them, his face grave, his left hand very near his vibro hilt.

Helgin gave each of them a look of disgust. "And people complain about *my* temper," he said. "You're neither one, Gyll. You're my friend, whether you let yourself believe that now or not. The Motsognir don't give friendship outside our race easily. I speak to you as I would one of my own: what the hell do you hope to accomplish?" Around and around: his finger toyed with his beard.

"I've no idea, Helgin." Gyll took a deep breath. "It could be a whim, I suppose. But too much has gone on around me lately. You know what I'm referring to. Now someone's gone to the trouble of signing a contract for my life. I want to know who that is—and there's only one way, by my old code, to gain that information, and that's to die. I don't intend to do that, but neither do I want to feed Hoorka's purse. That's not all," he said, raising a hand to silence the protest he saw forming on Helgin's lips. "The reasons are all small and all internal." *Yah, killing that unknown man, finding that I've been splendidly lied to, seeing the manipulation going on behind my back, even the finding of the ippicator.* "I'm not sure I could articulate them very well, but they add up to this—I want to take the chance. I want to see where I stand with Dame Fate."

"It sounds damned silly to me."

"Helgin—"

"I mean it." The Motsognir lurched to his feet. Unsteadily, limping, he strode over to Gyll's desk. "People don't play frigging games with their lives. Not if they're sane."

Gyll rose as well, leaning on the desk, hands on the wood. "And you don't tell me what I can or can't do." He stared at the Motsognir, but he could feel McWilms's gaze on him as well. "I'm well aware that this isn't a game."

"I know what you're after, Gyll—a sign from the gods that you've been doing the right things, that you've done all you could. You're looking for absolution. If the answer's 'yes,' then you live; 'no,' and you die. Very simple."

"And my business."

"*No!*" The dwarf stamped a bare foot into the rug. "It's not just your business. You've given allegiance to the Family Oldin. You owe them your services as Sula—you owe that to the Neweden Hoorka that have joined you."

McWilms stirred. "Those Neweden Hoorka will, to a person, understand what Gyll is doing, Motsognir. Leave us out of your arguments."

"The Oldins lied," Gyll said stiffly. "That makes me wonder about loyalty."

Helgin shook his head. "You're stubborn, the lot of you. The Oldins didn't so much lie as they did leave you out of their machinations."

"Lies of omission," Gyll half-shouted.

"Kindness to your frigging sensibilities, you mean," Helgin roared back.

For a long minute, no one said anything. McWilms returned to his survey of Neweden. Gyll and Helgin stood in poses of defiance. Then Helgin, with a curse of disgust, spat on the floor and turned. He stalked from the room without looking back. Gyll watched the door close behind the Motsognir, his feelings twisted.

McWilms moved away from the wall. He smiled at Gyll with compassion. "I'll bet he's a real bastard when he's mad."

Gyll's face was still downturned with anger. "You can be certain of it." Then he forced himself to smile in return—the effort was not entirely successful. "I'm sorry you had to watch this, Jeriad, but I wanted you to know what I intend to do. It doesn't endanger your status here; Helgin will make sure of that, once he calms down."

"I understand, Sula."

"Helgin doesn't." Again, the frown. "He thinks I'm crazy. There're times I'd like to wrap that beard of his around his throat."

"Whenever you want to do it, let me know. I'll give you a hand."

Despite himself, Gyll chuckled. "Did you manage to find out anything in Sterka?"

"I checked around, as you asked, Sula. I think I have good news for you. Let me go and get the map I drew."

Gyll nodded. McWilms reached out, grasped Gyll's bicep with a firm hand. "We could wait until morning to do this, Sula."

"If Dame Fate wills it."

"She does. I'm certain."

Gyll smiled. "I'm glad you think so. But no, we do it now."

Outside her window, the sunstar was setting behind Sterka Port, sinking into a cushion of low clouds and touching the sky with a ruddy orange—not an overly pretty sunset, but adequate. M'Dame Tha d'Embry stared into the last light of the day, shielding her eyes with a hand tinted the shade of the sunstar itself. She could see that the Trader shuttle had left the port—and she wondered whether it would return.

A spasm hunched her over, her fingers clenching the sill with whitened knuckles. *Falling apart, aren't we, symbiote, just like this world. Falling apart, and all we can do is delay the inevitable.* She felt the release of the symbiote's chemicals into her bloodstream, allowing her to slowly straighten. The sun had dipped lower, wrapping itself in the clouds, its light gone muddy.

Well, go ahead and make the grand gesture. It won't do any good, but you'll be able to tell your conscience that you tried. She sighed, and made her way back to her desk. She was conscious of her walk, that it was stooped and slow—an old woman's walk, an invalid's hobble. She lowered herself down on the floater's cushions, her arms supporting her. The effort made her wheeze asthmatically. She waited, felt her breath come slowly back. *So tired; gods, is it worth it?* And, as always when she had those thoughts, the symbiote—its survival dependent on hers—slipped a mild euphoric into her. *So you can sense the despair, symbiote? Too bad you can't communicate—what a strange existence you must have, a leech listening to the maunderings of a worn-out mind.* She could feel the parasite lurking, just below the threshold of her thoughts, as if she could, in some deep concentration, reach out and speak with it.

She stretched out a tinted hand, touched the contact that activated her com-unit. It swiveled slowly up from the desk. She laid her fingers on the keyboard and stared for a second at the contrast of her wrinkled skin against the smooth and perfect keys. *The machines stay young while we fall apart.* She tapped out the familiar letters of her key entry, then asked for the line to Diplo Center on Niffleheim. She thought for a moment that McClannan had been smart for once and canceled her validation code, but the screen lightened with the menu of access codes for Niffleheim, as well as the local time there: 2:04 P.M. That meant, if she was lucky, that Arthol would be back from lunch. Maybe. It would be safer to wait, but she was afraid that she'd be too tired later.

She was always tired.

502G3486DC: ARTHOL PETTENGILL. She keyed in the code deliberately, one-fingered, pressing needlessly hard. The screen went into a flurry of static as the tachyon relays kicked in, and she heard the ocean roar of interference. A minute. Two. She thought of canceling the call, of trying again later; then there was the distant click of connection. A faint, shrill burring rode in the interference, and then a wavering, static-pocked face stared out at her; mustachioed, balding, but with surprisingly young eyes in the pudgy face.

"Tha! Good to see you...well, perhaps not so good, is it? Trouble, it has to be trouble or you wouldn't look so serious, and you wouldn't be wasting good Diplo money on the relay."

She had never been one to mince words—she knew Pettengill would not expect it now. "Do the Diplos want to be called murderers?" she asked dryly. "If that's trouble, then yes, you're right, Arthol. And you're looking good, young man—a credit to your teacher, I hope."

Pettengill chuckled at the contrast between the two halves of her speech. "You were a tough one to follow, m'Dame, but I try. I try. Now, what's this about a murder?"

"Your little Regent McClannan took out a Hoorka contract on a Trader—and an Oldin at that—Sula Gyll Hermond."

In the welter of interference, Pettengill frowned. "Hermond

was the head of your assassins' guild, wasn't he?—the one we think killed Guillene on Heritage?"

"Yah, and he's been with the Oldins for the last eight standards. McClannan, over my protest, bought a contract on the man—a damned ugly way for a Regent to deal with his problems, if you ask me. I want McClannan taken out of here, Arthol. He's not competent. If you have to have him as a Regent, put him somewhere else. Not here. He'll botch it, I guarantee you." She paused for breath, ready to resume her commentary against McClannan, but she waited too long.

"And put yourself back in as Regent, Tha?"

He said it gently. It stopped d'Embry in mid-word.

For a moment, she was silent with shock, both at the soft accusation and at the fact that she'd not anticipated it, when it seemed so logical a conclusion to make. "Arthol, I think you know me better than to sling that particular piece of mud at me," she said carefully. "My interest in this is the image of the Alliance, as damnably altruistic and self-sacrificing and false as that sounds. And in any case, I think . . ." She halted again, realizing that what she was about to say was the truth. *So you've come to that decision at last. Good.* "I think that my health would preclude any reappointment. Hell, Arthol, I'm all done, both with Neweden and the Diplos. All I care about is making it through the next day. I'm an old woman, good for the occasional lecturing and speechifying, the relic you'll drag into your classrooms once a standard for the entertainment of the current batch of bright young hopefuls." A breath, again, and this time Pettengill did not interrupt. "Just let me do one more thing for the good of the Alliance, my friend. Bounce McClannan out of here. Put him somewhere safe. Make him rescind the frigging contract. It's not the way we should deal with crises, this method of his."

She sat back, waiting. Beneath the view of her screen, his hands would be moving, clasping, unclasping—nervous habits she remembered well. His face shuddered with some vagary of the relays, breaking apart and reforming. "As I understand the Hoorka, Tha, the victim can pay off the contract. The Oldins are rich enough. Why not bleed their pockets a little?"

"McClannan—for some reason or other—thinks Hermond will run. And in any case, that's not the point. We're talking about a moral position, Arthol, not a game of chance. And I wouldn't be surprised if FitzEvard regards the contract as a violation of the Alliance-Trading Families Pact. He may even be right. You're likely to have to fight a long legal battle, whichever decision Hermond makes."

A hand, wavering in the mediocre transmission, came up to run a thumb along the line of his cheek. *That's bad—he's got that frown to his mouth. You've lost, old girl. It's just going to be words from here on unless you can come up with something good.*

"I don't think you've judged the situation correctly, Tha." She strained to hear him against the storm of the background. The friendly warmth seemed to have seeped from his voice, though it might have been only her own perception. "Again, as I recall *your* Hoorka"—he stressed the word—"the signer of a contract is revealed only if the contract is successful, the victim killed. I think we all agree that this is unlikely to go that far, in which case, all FitzEvard has are his suspicions, and he's not going to waste a lawyer's fees on those."

"So you're willing to take the risk as well."

"I think so."

"If we were to lose Neweden, we lose the ippicator bones as well as the other resources of this world."

"We won't lose Neweden."

She sighed. "What if Hermond should die, Arthol? What if it was learned that you'd been informed in advance of the contract? When FitzEvard raises the stink you know he'll raise, your career will go down with McClannan's, and you've got a lot farther to fall. You'll lose everything."

That threat was not a gambit she liked to play, both because it was weak and because it would lose her whatever affection the man might have for her. But she had no more strings to pull, no more favors to call in. All she had were empty bluffs, and a knowledge of a bureaucrat's instinctive fear for his reputation.

Pettengill's eyes had narrowed—in his fleshy face, that looked almost porcine. "I didn't think you'd stoop to threats, m'Dame. It's not like you. Why don't we just forget you said that?"

Arthol, I'm sorry for what I'm going to do. Really I am. "Why don't you worry about your future a bit?" she replied.

"Diplo Center has a log of this call—that's automatic. Even if I'm gone when the investigation starts, they'll start checking the texts of all the incoming relays from Neweden in the past few months, and they'll find that I just told you about the whole problem—unless you are going to say that you'll erase the recordings after I sign off. In that case, Arthol, I'd ask you to consider that I could be making a copy here myself."

There was no expression in his eyes; they'd gone distant and unreadable. "That's a disgraceful attempt at blackmail. It shames you."

"It does indeed," she admitted. "Nevertheless, I'm doing it—call it trying to right a larger wrong with a smaller one. What are you going to do about it, Arthol? Are you going to play a game like McClannan, and let your career rest on the chance that Hermond won't run, or that if he does, he isn't killed? Let me remind you of another statistic—only about twenty-five percent of contracted victims escape the Hoorka if they run. That's pretty low, isn't it?"

When he hesitated before answering, she allowed herself a moment of hope, diluted by the manner in which she'd gone about it. But he shook his head at last. "You can't bluff me that way, d'Embry," he said, and even through the static she could hear the coldness in his voice. "Thank you, but I think I'll decline your little scheme. We have to trust the people we put in charge—I think you've used a similar argument when people here have tried to have *you* removed, after the Heritage incident, for example. Listen to your own advice, m'Dame. Let McClannan make his own mistakes."

"He's already made them. You'll find that out. Leave him installed as Regent, and you'll lose Neweden within a standard."

"That's supposition only, and one that might easily be attributed to jealousy." The speaker in her com-unit hissed and crackled. "And I think that Regent McClannan would be distressed at the cost of this relay. Unless you have further arguments, m'Dame . . ."

She did not. It was over. "You've just made a mistake, Arthol. It will be a big one. Remember that I told you that."

"I'm not likely to forget this conversation at all. And I have a meeting in a few minutes."

D'Embry nodded wearily. She made a curt good-bye and switched off the com-unit. She sighed wearily, sinking back in her floater, her eyes closed. "Well, old girl, you tried. At least you tried."

20

He'd sent McWilms on before, following him by a few hours.

When Gyll stepped from the shuttle into the cool Neweden dusk, he scanned the flat expanse of the port. He put himself in the role of the apprentice who would be watching for him, charged with the task of keeping the contract victim in sight until the full kin took up the hunt near midnight. *Remember, it doesn't matter if the victim knows he's being watched, but don't expose yourself to danger. Observe, but stay your distance.*

Gyll saw the apprentice almost at once. The boy leaned against an empty trailer, making no attempt to conceal his presence. Gyll could see the red slash on the nightcloak even through the murk of gathering night. He bowed in the boy's direction; Gyll could not be sure, but he thought he saw an answering inclination of the hooded face. Gyll stretched unnecessarily, letting the boy see that he carried nothing but a sheathed vibrofoil—no suspicious bulges, no pack that might conceal sting or other weapons, not even the thick belt of a bodyshield. The apprentice would convey that information to Underasgard and Thane Mondom. The full kin would be armed accordingly.

Gyll waved to the shuttle pilot and strode over the tarmac toward the gates nearest Diplo Center. Behind him, he could hear the footsteps of the apprentice. Gyll walked slowly, staying to the middle of the pedestrian lane, making no attempt to elude his shadow. The last glow of evening was in the sky, the first stars trying to overcome the lights of Sterka. The port beacons were on, turning the area into a glittering maze. There had been times when Gyll would have tarried to gaze at the scene, but he had no eye for aesthetics tonight. He gave his identification papers to a sleepy Diplo guard who perused them haphazardly and then waved him through the gates. Gyll went across the way and into Diplo Center, startling a night receptionist who had just come on duty and who seemed to have nothing better to do than to be certain that his hair was arranged satisfactorily.

"I wish to see former Regent d'Embry."

"I'm sorry, she . . ." the receptionist began, and only then looked up. He swallowed his words abruptly and set down his comb. "Excuse me, Sula. I'll ring her." He had a brief, energetic conversation under the security hood of his comunit, then turned back to Gyll. "She's in her office, Sula. You may go right in." Gyll nodded. He glanced back to the entrance of the Center; the shadowy form of the apprentice stared at him through the glass. Gyll made his way to d'Embry's office.

It had changed since the last time he'd seen it. Only the desk was still uncovered, the remainder packed for shipment. D'Embry was in her floater, the room lights dimmed. Only her eyes moved when he entered.

"Sula Hermond," she said. He was surprised at how weak her voice had become, at how frail she appeared to be in the cushions of her chair. Her skin seemed gray and almost translucent—under her tunic, the hump of the symbiote bulged. It seemed larger than before.

"M'Dame d'Embry."

"I can't help you, you know. I tried, but they wouldn't listen, not McClannan, not Pettengill; no one. Except for McClannan, they all said that you wouldn't run." Her eyes closed slowly.

"Then McClannan was right," he replied softly.

"Which proves that there is a first time for everything." Her eyes opened again. She lifted a hand in a half-wave: flesh tinted ice blue. "Take a seat, Sula."

Gyll went to the front of the desk, pulled a hump-chair from the floor, and sat. "You seem awfully damned relaxed for a hunted man," d'Embry commented.

"The contract run is something I know, if always experienced from the other side before now." He shrugged. "At least I know the rules of this."

"But not of other things? Such as the role of a Sula?"

"I thought I knew them, m'Dame. It seems I might have been mistaken."

She nodded as if she knew what he meant, or perhaps she was merely indicating that she had heard him; Gyll wasn't certain. This was not the d'Embry who had been Regent. This was a slow old woman who lacked the flash and fury of the Regent. Defeated, he thought. The fight's left her, and she's given up. The realization forced Gyll to alter his planned speech—he wondered if he shouldn't just forget this and begin the run now, save his breath for the hunt.

"It's FitzEvard's doing," he said baldly. "All of it: Gunnar's death, Renard, the Hag's Legion, probably the ippicator as well. Oldin's behind all the problems Neweden's had recently. I don't know his reasons—maybe just to spite you, m'Dame, to cause you difficulties."

She smiled at that. "The difficulties I've had aren't Oldin's doing. I managed them myself."

"M'Dame, Renard is in the pay of FitzEvard. The man's been here a decade or more, off and on. Renard organized the Hag's Legion, he's made sure that the lassari stay discontented and angry. As for the killing of Gunnar, that was done by an Oldin assassin. And, m'Dame, when Kaethe Oldin was here, she once showed me an ippicatorian embryo engineered from a tissue sample in the Oldin Archives."

Nothing. Nothing. Gyll had been certain that the revelations would goad her into rage, would rekindle the cold anger he'd seen in her before. It did not; she only nodded and clasped hands underneath her chin. "Why do you tell me all this now?" she asked, too quietly, too softly. "Two weeks ago... perhaps less..."

"M'Dame—"

"Sula, my access codes have all been canceled as of four hours ago. I can't contact Niffleheim except through slow-time channels. McClannan wouldn't know what to do with the information you've brought even if he were willing to listen to me. He'd most likely accuse the both of us of concocting the whole tale to discredit him."

The blank hopelessness on her face appalled him. "I'm sorry, m'Dame."

"Oh, so am I," she said tonelessly. "Tell me, Sula, are you leaving the Oldins?"

He shook his head. "No, I don't think so. I came here to repay the Oldins for lies spoken to me; I wanted to hurt them, to show them that I was angry. And I had a question to ask of you—I'd hoped that this would guarantee me the truth."

"And the question?"

He'd been thinking of it since Helgin had told him of the deceptions, since McWilms had arrived with his contingent of Hoorka. Gyll leaned forward, intent. "Do the Hoorka have a future here—on Neweden, with the Alliance?"

She smiled faintly. "It would be simple to lie to you like all the rest, Sula. That lie would hold the satisfaction of hindering the plans of someone who's given his allegiance to FitzEvard. You're so open that you'd believe anything I told you, Sula. You should learn to curb that inclination; it may kill you someday." She started to laugh, coughed once, then with a racking spasm that drained her face of color. When she had recovered, she shook her head at him. "But I'm not going to lie to you, Sula, and you'll just have to accept that I'm not going to tell you the truth, either. I'm not Regent. I can't answer your question anymore. Nor am I Thane Mondom, who holds the other half of the answer."

"You know McClannan, know how he'll react."

"Sula, I never thought McClannan would betray me the way he did. So much for thinking that I know the man. All I know is what's happened to me. I've grown old and decrepit in a world that's changed. Maybe Hoorka's done that as well." She looked at him, her gray eyes rheumy. "And maybe not."

"You won't answer."

"I can't."

"I think I knew the answer before I came here." Gyll glanced around the room, not wanting to look at her. "M'Dame, if you could find a way to tell your superiors what I've said, the regency might well be yours again."

"And then you could ask your question. Again."

"I know you didn't step down voluntarily."

She laughed, dry and hoarse. "Still after your revenge,

Sula? You do tempt me, but as I told you, I've no authority here, and I find that I'm glad it's gone. Sula, if you're going to continue with this nonsense of running the contract, then you'll have your questions answered for you. I just pray that you'll enjoy the solution. Or you can go to McClannan with this story of yours, but I think I should tell you that he's the signer of the contract against you. He's not going to believe you; he won't want to. He'll shake his head and smile nicely at you. He'll see nothing but a potential trap, and he'll laugh you from the Center."

"So it's McClannan's contract." Gyll smiled sadly. "Thank you for telling me—I would have always wondered. It makes sense."

"McClannan's a fool. I told him he couldn't win this way. If you live, you add to the reputation of the Oldins; if you die, he stands a good chance of being removed by Niffleheim. I told him that; he wouldn't believe me."

"You seem to have good reasons for disliking the man, m'Dame. I trust your judgment. I won't go to him."

"But you'll run." D'Embry shook her head wonderingly. There was a slight tremor to the movement, a palsy.

"I'll run."

"You're crazy, Sula." She stared at him. "You come here with a tale all wrapped up like a present, FitzEvard caught in the bow. Yet you're going to go back to that same man as one of his captains, *if* you manage to live through the night— because of a contract you could void in a moment. Sula, if you haven't paid off the contract because you don't want to take Oldin money, take mine. I won't need it."

"M'Dame, it's neither money nor misplaced pride."

"Then what?"

He shrugged. "I'm playing by my old rules once more before they're no longer valid. I'm letting Dame Fate have Her way."

D'Embry sighed. She looked down at her hands. "Sula, I never thought you really believed in that theology, or that, if you had, your recent standards away from Neweden would have destroyed your faith."

"I thought the same." He rose, with a groan of effort. His legs ached, as if already fatigued from the night's run.

Her gaze had not followed him. "I find this foolish and wasteful."

Gyll didn't answer. He moved toward the door, opening it. "Sula?" she said behind him.

"Yah?"

"Good luck."

The apprentice still waited by the main doors. Gyll passed the boy, who moved back away from him, then followed behind. The sky was almost fully dark now, the stars at the horizon obscured in skyglow. He moved at an easy pace toward Sterka's busy streets. Gyll made his way toward the Street of Singers as Sterka changed from evening to night around him.

He came to the Street of Singers at an intersection a few blocks above Oldman Church. There, a figure in dark clothing, a bulky pack beside him, waved to Gyll.

"You're late," McWilms said, nodding to Gyll and watching the apprentice dodge into shadow—he knew that the boy would be calling for advice from Underasgard.

"There was something I had to do," Gyll said curtly. He glanced down the street toward the church. "Are they there?"

McWilms nodded. "Four of them, counting Renard—I was lucky; I watched them going in."

"What's our best approach?"

"I don't know, Sula. There's a rear door and two side entrances, plus the windows. They can't watch them all, but there's no way of knowing what they might have in the way of traps or alarms."

"Then we'll find out. You brought the equipment?"

McWilms tapped the pack beside him. "It's all here."

"Good. Follow me, and keep to the shadows as much as you can."

"And your apprentice tagalong?"

"If Mondom's taught him well, he'll stay out of the way. Let's go, Jeriad."

McWilms shouldered the pack. Gyll in the lead, they made their way back to the avenue paralleling the Street of Singers. The apprentice ducked back between two houses as they passed. Gyll and McWilms moved quickly down the street, ignoring the stares of the residents, watching from

porches and steps. "One of them, any of them, might be
Hag's Legion, Sula. They could give a warning to Renard."

"It's a chance we take, Jeriad. You can leave if it worries
you too much. This is my bloodfeud—you don't have to be
involved."

"It's my quarrel as well, Sula. Renard killed Ric, ultimately; who knows how many other kin have fallen to him?
I'm going with you."

At the end of the street, they turned between the
buildings into an alley once used by Helgin. Oldman Church
sat before them, dark-shuttered and quiet. The structure
looked empty, deserted, like the houses nearest it. McWilms
set his pack down once more, rummaged through it to find a
bio-meter. He set the controls, checked the range; diodes
flashed on the monitor. "I'm getting four readings, Sula," he
whispered. "It should be the same ones."

The apprentice turned into the alley behind them, halted
in a scraping of gravel. Gyll turned, scowled at him. "Keep
out of this, boy," he growled harshly. "It's none of Hoorka's
business. Just be quiet." Wide-eyed, the boy nodded, his
gaze more on McWilms than Gyll. McWilms nodded to him.
"You heard the Sula, Steban," he said. "Do as he says—what
we're doing has no effect on your contract." Again the nod;
Steban slunk back into shadows.

They turned back to Oldman Church. "I like the nearest
side entrance, Jeriad. No windows nearby—if we can get in,
we might be able to surprise them."

McWilms raised a shoulder. "One way's as good as
another."

"Get out the snooper and bodyshields—leave the rest of
the pack here for now."

They buckled on the bodyshields, checked that their
vibros were loose in their sheaths. Quickly, with all the skill
of silentstalk, they slipped unseen to the side of the church.
His back against the paint-peeling wall, Gyll used the hand-
code. *Snooper.* He gestured at the door.

McWilms aimed the snout of the device at the wooden
door. A dot of scarlet showed on its face—he held the monitor
toward Gyll, who sighed inwardly. Going to one knee, he
examined the door carefully. He found nothing to indicate the

alarm detected by the snooper. *It's inside*, he signaled to McWilms.

Other door?

No. Gyll hesitated, weighing his options. The likelihood was that all entrances were guarded or alarmed—it was just as likely that there was no way around it short of sophisticated electronics which would take hours to receive from *Goshawk*. Time was a commodity he did not have. At the same time, those inside would be expecting nothing: Renard, from what Gyll knew of him, was arrogant enough to expect no trouble from Gyll despite the declaration of bloodfeud; the man would not be here otherwise. And his contacts were probably good enough that he knew of the contract against Gyll. He, like the rest, would be expecting Gyll to be sitting safely in his ship. *Other side*, Gyll signaled to McWilms. *Give me a feint, then leave.*

McWilms looked at Gyll askance. *Dangerous.*

Do it. The gesture was harsh. Gyll's eyes brooked no further argument. After a moment, McWilms slid away around the far side of the building. Gyll waited, his vibro now out but unactivated. A minute, two: he heard a crash of splintering wood and the distant burr of the alarm. On the second floor, lights flashed on. He heard the sound of running footsteps, moving away from him. Gyll moved back a step, kicked—the frame gave way, the lock still attached, the door swinging open. Gyll switched on his bodyshield and moved inside.

Adrenaline surged through him, excitement raced in his head. He felt young again, invincible. He felt good.

A set of stairs led upward down a short corridor, light spilling down the steps. Gyll moved toward them, staying close to the wall. There were no shadows on the stairs—no one standing at the top. Gyll moved up them quickly, pausing on the third step to raise on his toes and scan the landing above him. There, the stair opened out onto a balcony that circled the church, a few doors opening off it. Hoverlamps, all lit, were spaced at intervals around the balcony. One of the doors to his right was open; in the light of the room beyond, shadows moved. Two people, he estimated. He moved toward the door.

When he was next to it, he put his back to the wall, reached in his pocket for a coin. He flipped it over the balcony's edge; the coin clattered on the floor below. "Micha?" someone called from the room. It was a deep voice, one that Gyll recognized: Renard. Gyll waited. He could hear the sound of a whispered consultation in the room; if Renard was the type of leader Gyll thought him to be, it would not be Renard that went to investigate the noise.

A man stepped out; a thin, wiry lassari. Gyll moved, hammering at the man's throat with the hilt of his unactivated vibro. The man choked, gasping, his knees buckling as Gyll shoved him aside, switching on his vibro as he moved into the room.

Renard was waiting. The sting fired even as Gyll moved. The Trader-made shield, far more supple than those the old Hoorka had employed, went rigid only for a second as slugs hammered into the walls and tore the life from the man Gyll had disabled. Then Gyll could move again.

He faced Renard.

The man's smile was nearly a grimace, showing teeth white against his skin. The plant-pet was coiled around massive shoulders, the sting held in large hands, its muzzle trailing a thin line of smoke. The man was bearlike, imposing. Renard threw the sting aside.

"The bodyshield indicates a lack of trust, Sula," he said, moving away from Gyll as the Sula advanced. Renard pulled his own vibrofoil from a sheath on his belt; the air was loud with the double howl of the weapons. Renard went into a guard of two—foil down and to the right of center: an unorthodox guard, one designed to throw off an opponent's timing. "You require a warning when such weapons are used on Neweden, don't you? I'm afraid I neglected to post it."

"Distrust works when one deals with a dishonorable opponent, Renard."

"Honor is a manmade virtue, Hermond. It has no existence by itself. I deal with my enemies by whatever method works."

"This method failed, Renard. I intend to settle our bloodfeud now."

Renard circled to the center of the room, Gyll moving to keep him away from the door. The foil was still down, waiting for Gyll's move. Gyll thrust with deliberate slowness; Renard's blade whipped up and slapped the thrust aside with a screeching of metal. Renard immediately riposted, a straight counterthrust. Gyll backed a step, batting Renard's foil aside as sparks flared. They halted, Renard's foil back in guard two, Gyll's up in a more traditional guard of four.

Gyll thrust once more, and this time when Renard parried, Gyll went around the movement in a circular parry, down and then over as he advanced. Renard backed, his vibro flailing. The weapons screamed. Gyll did not let Renard rest this time. He went into a compound attack, never letting the other man take the initiative. Twice he thought he had the man, his foil piercing Renard in the forearm, nicking his chest. Blood showed on Renard's shirt, ran down his arm, slowing his movements. Gyll advanced, confident.

And Renard again did the unexpected. With his free hand, he snatched the plant-pet from his shoulders and whipped it into Gyll's face as he stepped forward. Gyll ducked away too late—the animal's spines lacerated his cheek and temple, narrowly missing his eyes. Gyll blinked away blood, trying to watch Renard's weapon.

The plant-pet flailed at Gyll again. Gyll blocked it with his left arm, barbs digging into his forearm, letting Renard's momentum carry the man toward him. He brought his foil up; Renard's blade deflected the thrust and Gyll's vibro only nicked Renard's side. They were now nearly corps-a-corps, the vibros thrumming madly. Gyll leaned back, kicked. His foot found Renard's knee. The man howled in pain, staggering and dropping the limp body of the plant-pet. Gyll thrust at the man through Renard's frantic defense. The vibro found Renard's chest; Gyll leaned into the thrust, pulled back, lunged again.

Renard moaned, spitting a foam of blood. He fell backward, collapsing into a sprawl, his vibrofoil chattering on the floor. Gyll picked up the weapon, turned it off.

There was a sound behind him; a footfall. Gyll whirled, vibrofoil moving. Sparks flared with a clattering of blades. "Sula!"

Gyll stepped away, seeing McWilms. "Damn it, I told you to leave—you could have gotten yourself hurt."

McWilms flicked his vibro off, sheathed it. Gyll did the same; the room was suddenly very still. "The two that came after me were easy," McWilms said. "One was a woman, who was the better of the two, and a foolish man who kept getting in her way. I thought I'd see if you needed help. I notice you don't. That's Renard?"

Gyll wiped at his face with a sleeve—it came away scarlet. Blood dappled his hands. "That's Renard," he acknowledged.

"Your face looks awful—some of the cuts are deep. Should I call the ship?"

"I have other things to do tonight. The cuts can wait."

"All Neweden will thank you for that man's death."

"He didn't die for Neweden." Gyll looked about the room. He found paper, took a stylus from his pocket. *I, Sula Gyll Hermond, did this*, he wrote, as Neweden law required. *My declaration of bloodfeud is over.* He laid the paper on Renard's corpse. "Bastard," he said. "Cowardly, dishonorable offworlder."

Still looking at the body, he spoke to McWilms. "Thank you, Jeriad," he said. "I know you didn't have to help me with this. Go to the Assembly and notify them of the outcome. I'm sure the Li-Gallant will be anxious to hear the news." He turned, wiping a trickle of blood from his eyes. "And do me one more favor. Give me your tunic."

"Sula?"

"There's a homing dot under the collar of mine—I found it before I left *Goshawk*. Tell Helgin for me that this is none of his business."

"As you wish." McWilms pulled his tunic off, handed it to Gyll. "Sula, none of the kin will think less of you if you come back to the ship now."

Gyll did not answer him. He stripped off his tunic, put on McWilms's.

"I'll be back after dawn," he said.

21

Gyll suspected that there were now two apprentices—Steban behind, and one other ahead of him with the detector for the dye on his hands: in accordance with the code, the detector would function only when Gyll was more than two hundred meters distant from it. Closer, and the detector ceased functioning, giving him the chance due him by Dame Fate. Fine; they would know in what direction and how far away he was if they lost him—unless he could get beyond the unit's range. As he remembered, they were not exceedingly powerful, perhaps twenty or thirty kilometers at best.

Gyll began to increase his pace; he heard Steban shift abruptly into a trot to stay with him. Gyll swung around the first corner, turning right and breaking into a run. Startled pedestrians stared as he jostled his way around them—a gray-haired man, his face scored and bloody, dressed in dark Trader costume. Gyll turned right again, then settled into a walk once more. That feint should have drawn in the other apprentice—Steban would have relayed the news of the sudden flight. Yes, there she was across the street, peering desperately about in the inviolate circle the Newedeners habitually gave Hoorka. She saw him in the same instant; Gyll saw her whisper into the relay button on her collar. A few seconds later, he heard the panting approach and sudden stop of Steban. *Good. Now they'll both stay closer, afraid they'll lose me again.* Gyll resumed his leisurely strolling, moving slowly toward the center of Sterka. He glanced at a time display in a storefront: 9:37. In a little more than two hours, the full kin would take up the hunt.

For the next hour and a half, Gyll made a sauntering tour of the city, stopping first at a public facility to clean his face and stanch the flow of blood. He bought a flavored ice from a street vendor, sat on a bench and watched a juggler perform, shopped in several stores. Now and then he would

211

turn abruptly, move at a trot for a brief time, darting and turning but always stopping after a few minutes. He faked weariness then, pausing as if short of breath in full sight of the apprentices. They stayed very near him, especially in crowds, sometimes both abreast of him, sometimes behind, but always within a few quick steps. Gyll saw no other Hoorka—he once made a dash when both apprentices were momentarily obstructed, knowing that they would call in any third, unseen watcher. They did not. He wondered what they were thinking, his shadows, of this crazy old man who sometimes seemed to forget that his life was dependent on the whims of Dame Fate, and who did not have the breath to elude them for long.

11:15. By now, the full kin would have been wakened and made ready. A flitter would be sitting near the dawnrock, ready to take them to Sterka and a meeting with the apprentices. He had to make his move now.

A mistake common to most victims was that they, oddly enough, became complacent under the loose and benign surveillance of the apprentices. They would try to elude the shadows at first, but after a few failures, simply stop trying—most of the apprentices were used to that pattern. Gyll had followed it as well; all his runs had been earlier in the night. For the last half-hour or more, he'd simply walked. He knew he could not outrun the girl, who was faster than Steban. Still, Steban most likely had better wind than Gyll. So a straight course was out of the question. Gyll needed to be able to dodge and twist, confuse them, present them with too many variables. The best place for that was in the streets nearest Market Square, bordering on Dasta. Faster now, he began heading in that direction.

Opportunity came early. The apprentices moved closer to him as the streets became narrow and more crowded. Ahead, the avenue rose in a series of long steps, curving to the right and, at the top, passing over another street in a low bridge. Suddenly Gyll broke into a run, heading toward a knot of people around a fruit stall. The apprentices moved behind him halfheartedly, waiting for him to run out of breath as he had every time before. Gyll halted, leaned over as if catching his breath, watching as the apprentices slowed to a walk. Then he pumped into a full run, shouldering his way through the customers around the stall. Shouts of anger pursued him. The apprentices were caught flat-footed, additionally hampered by the annoyed crowd. Gyll saw a side street, ducked into it, and then into a shop where a bemused clerk glanced at his scratched face quizzically. Gyll moved back into the dark recesses of the shop, followed by the gaze of the curious clerk. He pretended to examine merchandise—sexual toys—while keeping the window in the edge of his vision.

"Many of our customers like our stock of masks, sirrah. They can keep an, ahh, overzealous partner from making too visible a mark." The clerk stared at Gyll's face, a smile touching his lips.

"No, thank you." Steban trotted past, glanced quickly through the window of the store, but missed Gyll in the shadows. Gyll moved toward the door. He peered out, up and down the street.

"There's no need for shame, sirrah," the clerk said behind him. "We cater to a natural function. No one here will think less of you whatever your preferences for stimulation."

Gyll laughed. "Then I'll be back," he said, stepping into the street. The apprentices were not in sight. Gyll backtracked, staying close to the buildings in case he needed to hide quickly. He vaulted the low bridge, landing easily on the street below. At a jog now, he made his way back to the wealthier business sectors.

His luck held. He saw no sign of the Hoorka apprentices. Hopefully, they would spend the next several minutes looking for him in Market Square before the tracer told them that he was no longer close. By then, it would be too late.

Forcing himself to move calmly, to meld with the people around him as best he could, he went to a transit stop and boarded a public tram, taking it from central Sterka to its last stop on the southern outskirts of the city. Overhead, he knew, a Hoorka flitter would pass the tram, moving toward Sterka and the apprentices.

Gyll left the tram, moving from the small secluded station that served the farmlands around Sterka. A flitter-rental outlet stood nearby. Gyll rented one of the machines—an old flitter well past its prime—and flew south across the fields toward Underasgard, perhaps five kilometers away in the hills. He put a hand in his pocket, fingering the small round pellets there that had come from his ship's armory. *I'm sorry, Mondom, but it's time to end this farce*. By now, the full kin would have learned from the chagrined apprentices that Gyll was gone. The tracer would be used to find him—if he was very lucky, he was already beyond its range, and the Hoorka would have to guess which way he'd gone. Given that, Gyll could, by lying low and continuing to move, most likely elude the Hoorka without confrontation and greet the sunstar free and alive. He did not count on that luck, though; if he was still within the detector's range, they knew which way he was heading, and he had only a small time in which to do what he intended to do. He raced the flitter as fast as it would go, landing finally in a clearing near Underasgard.

The cavern mouth looked as it always did. The dawnrock stood impassive under the stars, Gulltopp's light throwing its shadow across the grass. The cave entrance yawned darker than night under a wrinkled brow of rock. Gyll knew that the guards would be there and watching—after his last visit here, the vigilance would be tighter. He knew that the old trick he'd employed then would not work again. No—this time it would have to be a headlong confrontation; Gyll would need luck. He muttered a brief prayer to Dame Fate, the old words passing his lips strangely. *Praying again; next you'll be bowing low to full kin and getting out of their way like a lassari*.

He made a circuitous approach to the mouth of Underasgard, moving as quickly as he could without making excessive noise. It took all of his standards of expertise in the skills of silentstalk, but at last he crouched behind a boulder just outside and to one side of the caves. He took a deep breath, held it, listening intently: no talking, but he could hear two shallow breaths, amplified by stone. Gyll reached into his pocket once more, took out a vial wrapped in cotton. He removed the protective covering and tossed the vial into the cave mouth. A tinkling of glass, a sharp hissing: Gyll waited a few minutes, then swung over the boulder and darted into the cave. Two apprentices lay slumped on the ground there, breathing deeply in sleep. Gyll smiled and moved deeper into Underasgard.

He knew the ways well. He slipped easily past the

inhabited sectors into the less-traveled corridors. He broke the seal on a glow-tube, following its bluish light over the rough trails of broken stone. Slabs tilted beneath his feet, falling back with an echoing, dull clank. The noise did not bother him; there were no listeners here but the cave animals. He passed through a cavern where the light of the glow-tube failed to reach the walls, leaving him surrounded by leering darkness, where a cold wind blew past him like Hag Death's breath. He came, in time, to the cavern of the headless ippicator, and there he stopped, shock and anger welling inside him.

Bones were missing; not many, but a few. Gyll's eyes narrowed, and he walked nearer the skeleton. It was not disturbed or defiled—whoever had removed the bones had been reverent and careful—and by the tracks, the intruder had worn boots, such as those the guild-kin wore.

Abruptly, he knew who it had been, and knowing that, why. "Mondom," he breathed. "Is it so bad that you'd sell what is sacred to the kin?" A chill not of the cavern went through him. D'Embry had said that he would have his answer if he ran the contract—he knew now. The code was cracked and broken, a vestige that would soon be gone entirely. Dead, like the ippicators themselves. "Mondom, She of the Five will leave you with the Hag forever for this," he whispered, then straightened, inhaling. *No time, no time— do what you came to do.*

He set the glow-tube down and pulled a handful of dark pellets from his pocket. Frowning, he took each one between thumb and forefinger and twisted. Small, dry clicks accompanied the rotation; he counted them carefully. When each pellet was timed and armed, Gyll took two of the seedlike objects and dropped them carefully near the entrance to the ippicator's cave. "Rest forever, Old One," he whispered. Then he left, going back the way he'd come. As he neared the Hoorka caverns he placed more of the pellets, then—stealthily— set them around the Hoorka lair itself. He used the old apprentice backtrails to move toward the kitchens. There, in the greenish illumination of the glow-fungi, he saw Felling, the Hoorka's cook, sitting in his room off the kitchen, reading.

"Felling," he called softly.

The man looked up, his mouth agape in a rotund face.

His pudgy fingers dropped the reading wand. "Ulthane?" Felling stuttered with nervous laughter. He wiped his hands on his pants, his mouth undecided between smile and frown. "Gods, you startled me. I thought one of the little apprentice bastards... Well, you're certainly a surprise. Thane Mondom's out on a contract tonight, if you wanted her...."

Gyll leaned against the wall. He smiled. "I know," he said. "She's hunting me. I'm the victim."

Felling started to smile, changed his mind. His gaze skittered about the room, nervous. "But..." he began, then shook his head. "You pick a funny place to hide."

Gyll laughed softly. "I'm not here to hide, old friend. I need you to do something for me."

"Ulthane, if you're being hunted—"

Gyll waved him silent. He moved away from the wall, taking a step toward Felling, who backed away. "Get everyone out of the caverns. You have about ten minutes. The kin are to leave everything and run. Anyone left here will be food for Hag Death."

"You can't mean that."

"Oh, but I do." He still smiled. "Underasgard will be filled with rock in ten minutes, buried and gone. Unless you want the kin to be part of it, get moving." Then, more softly: "I'm sorry, Felling. I truly am. Tell Mondom this for me—tell her that from here on it will be the hunt of knives. I leave my fate to the Dame." He gestured harshly. "Now *move*, man!"

As Felling fled one way, Gyll went the other, out from the caverns, sowing his pellets and lastly putting one beside the dawnrock. Then he moved away from Underasgard at a run, angling deeper into the folded landscape of hills and forest.

Minutes later, he felt more than heard the explosions. The rumbling added speed to his feet, and he prayed that Felling had gotten all the kin outside.

Gyll knew that they followed.

He could feel it in his stomach, twisting with worry—he'd seen the flitter from a vantage point on a ridge near Underasgard, seen the noisy apparition wheel across the sky with its flickering riding lights, sliding behind the trees below him near the wreckage of Underasgard. The flitter's presence

meant that someone in the caverns had the presence of mind
to contact Mondom before his explosives had brought down
the rock. Which meant, also, that they would know he was
near, that the detector would point toward him like a deadly
finger. Gyll rubbed his hands; ill luck, that. Had the Dame
been mindful of him, Mondom might never have known of
Underasgard's destruction until the dawnrock failed to chime
at the sunstar's arrival. With luck, they'd have been scouring
the land around Sterka for him. With luck.

But perhaps the myriad gods of Neweden had wanted to
see the excitement of a close chase, the furious, frightened
scurrying of the hunted quarry. Perhaps the Dame still
intended for him to live.

Gyll was moving through a stand of trees newly shed of
their leaves, moving diagonally up a steep slope. His boots
were muddy to mid-calf, and he pulled himself up, gripping
at branches and the trunks of young trees. The night was
fairly bright. Both Sleipnir and Gulltopp were up now, and
the woods shimmered in their double glow. Gyll struggled to
the top of the rise, panting. *Worn out in truth this time, old
man, and Mondom and her companion will be fresh and
anger-driven. Better find your reserves soon.* He crouched,
head down, his breath loud and vsible in the chill air. Sweat
made his spine cold beneath his clothing; the dampness had
gotten into his boots, numbing his feet.

Crack!

The sound was sharp in the stillness. It made Gyll draw
in and hold his breath, brought his head up sharply, narrowed
his eyes. Luck, his luck this time; across the valley he'd just
left, two figures in nightcloaks moved. They'd been on the far
side of their ridge when he'd made his climb. If he moved
quietly now, the noise of his passage would be masked as he
moved down into the next valley. The Hoorka—too distant to
see who they were—moved slowly, obviously casting about
for signs of Gyll's passage. He was within the near limits of
the tracer; they knew he was close, knew basically which way
he was moving. But the luck was still holding. They were
moving at a slight angle to him, away from the obvious tracks
he'd made getting down from that last ridge. It had rained
recently, and the earth was soaked. Except under the carpet
of dead leaves (and sometimes even there), his trail was

painfully visible; if they found it, they would not need the tracer any longer. Gyll looked to the moons—it was around three, as near as he could tell. Dawn at Underasgard would be just after six—three hours. Even if they found his trail, he had a chance. His breath had returned. Gyll thought that he could keep the distance between them. To stay close, where their detector would be useless, gave too much to chance; a misstep, a sound, or a moment when he was not hidden, and they would be on him.

Crouching, he slipped over the top of the ridge and started down the far side.

There was a creek at the bottom, thin ice at the edges of noisy water. He stepped carefully across it, hoping that none of the rocks in its course would tilt and shout alarm to his hunters. The next hill was bare except for dry meadow grass; Gyll decided to move down the creekbed toward another stand of trees. The wind picked up a bit, blowing in his face—bad; it would carry sound behind him, but there was nothing he could do about the wind. He was almost to the trees. He glanced back over his shoulder. What he saw froze him for an instant. Against the night sky, a figure stood on the hilltop. It pointed at him. Another figure came up beside it. Together, they half-ran, half-slid down the slope.

A shiver ran the length of Gyll's spine. For a second, he could not move. Then, with a curse for the vagaries of his luck, he turned and fled into the trees, seeking height and shelter. As he ran, he put himself in his pursuers' place, trying to decide what they would do. One would be certain to follow his trail, but the other . . . that one might take the easier route through the tall grass, figuring that Gyll would make for the top of the ridge—a pincer trap, with the quarry between. Gyll pulled his vibro from its sheath but did not yet activate it. He retraced his steps a few meters, trying to stay in his tracks, then swung himself up onto an overhanging branch. Crouching against the bole of the tree, he waited. *Don't let it be Mondom. Please don't make it be Mondom. And keep me hidden.*

The Hoorka was a man, alone. Gyll thought he recognized the face, much younger in his memory, as a surly apprentice named Meka Joh. The Hoorka made his way through the stand of trees, his head—despite Hoorka training—

down and intent on the trail Gyll had left. *Boy, you should have learned your lessons better. Use all of your vision—keep the trail low in your sight and your head up.* Gyll waited until Meka was underneath him. His muscles tensed for the leap.

He hit Meka just behind the head, flicking his vibro on at the same time. Gyll fell heavier than expected, twisting to face the Hoorka. Meka was slow, stunned, but his weapon—a Khaelian dagger—was out in a defensive position, instinctively. Gyll moved with a grunt of effort, his vibro moving past the dazed man's guard easily, warding off a slash of the dagger. The foil slid easily into Meka's midriff. With a low moan, the Hoorka doubled over. His head up, he stared at Gyll with wide, pain-stabbed eyes. His mouth worked but no words came out.

He fell.

Blood steamed in the cold; from Meka, from the gore covering Gyll's foil.

He felt very little: no guilt, no remorse, just a cold satisfaction that he was still alive, that he'd taken out his enemy. *Would it be the same if Meka were Mondom, if she were the one I'd given to the Hag?* He shook the thought from his head—he must move. Gyll slipped the vibro back into its sheath, took the Khaelian dagger from Meka's unresisting hand, slipped the homing device for the dagger from the body's waist. Then, grimacing, he stripped Meka of the Hoorka nightcloak. He put the cloak on, feeling the once-familiar weight of the heavy cloth, the old clasps, the fullness of the hood behind his neck. It fit him well. He shrugged the nightcloak into place around his shoulders and made the sign of the star over Meka's body. "Rest well, Meka Joh," he whispered. "May the Dame snatch you back from the Hag soon." He strode away in the direction he'd come, pulling the hood over his head.

Once outside the trees' shelter, he looked for Mondom. She stood at the top of the ridge, watching him. Against the sky, her hands moved.

? she signed.

Not there, Gyll answered with the hand-code, hoping that the nightcloak and darkness would allow his deception to work. Mondom was perhaps forty meters away, but her face was hidden in the shadow of her hood. *Go around,* Gyll told her, waving her toward the far side of the stand of trees. *Circle. Surround.*

Mondom hesitated. She seemed to regard him strangely. Then she moved, down from the summit and toward the trees. When the tangle of limbs finally hid her, Gyll put his back to the trees and ran upstream along the creekbed. *Be with me, Dame, and this will put an end to the night. Another soul's gone to the Hag by my hand, but it's not Mondom and it's not me. Give me a little more time, and she can't take me.*

Running, he did not see Mondom come back out from the trees, did not see her watch him and then—swiftly, lithely—begin the chase, keeping to the higher ground, moving parallel with him.

He could not run for long. His wind was low, his side ached with each breath, his legs were sore with fatigue. Gyll had put himself in good condition over the last few standards, but the night had taken its damage, as had age. He simply did not have the stamina of his youth. He forced himself to continue moving, if only at a trot, coming to an area of broken rock. He began to climb, seeking a hollow where he could rest in concealment for a while. He reached for an outcropping of rock with his left hand.

Steel grated against rock—his hand throbbed with stabbing agony. Gyll bit back a shout of pain and surprise. A Khaelian dagger impaled his hand. Like a live thing, it twisted and bucked, tearing flesh, grating against bone, blood spilling down his arm. It pulled loose even as he reached for it, a hissing coming from the tiny jets in the handle. The dagger turned in the air and was gone, spilling droplets of red. Gyll turned to watch it go, cradling his injured hand. Mondom was there, above and behind him, and the dagger was back in her hand. Her arm went back to cast it once more. Gyll twisted sideways, sliding down the rocks, his hand in torment, sharp outcroppings tearing at his clothing and skin. Mondom's dagger clattered against rock where he had been, falling and then leaping up again to return to Mondom. Gyll found his footing and ran, knowing that the range of the Khaelian weapons was very short, aware that the fuel for it was limited. *Run. She won't throw again until she's very sure of her target.* He couldn't move the fingers of his left hand, and the blood poured forth—he put pressure on the wound as he ran, trying to stop the flow, gritting his teeth against the hurt.

He didn't know why he hadn't used the dagger he'd taken from Meka. *Was it because the target would be Mondom, or did you simply forget with the pain and fear?* For the first time that night, he felt that Hag Death might be able to take him, and panic at that thought filled him with a new energy. He ran, knowing that Mondom and the Hag were close behind, each pursuing him relentlessly. If he had harbored doubts that Mondom could finish this task, they were gone now. She would. She would kill him.

The worst realization was that he was not sure if, to stop her, he could kill her first. Certainly he might be capable of it—self-preservation is a powerful motivator—but would he strike first with all his strength? To try to wound her, disable or disarm her, was to limit himself, to lower his odds. He knew he could not run long enough to avoid a confrontation. Already the new rush of adrenaline was gone. His breath was harsh and loud, his lungs cried for surcease. He had to turn, had to become the hunter instead of the hunted.

Damn Neweden, damn all of its gods: She of the Five, Dame Fate, Hag Death. Why did You bring me to this? The night could have gone easily, but You wouldn't permit it. Why, damn You? Why?

Ahead, the valley widened into a meadow dotted with large boulders. The creek meandered through the middle, glinting in moonlight. There was no cover here, but the walls about the valley were steep and high. Mondom would have to enter as he had, along the creekbed—she would be too easy a target if she attempted to descend the cliffs. Gyll crouched behind a scree of rock, trying to slow his breath. He heard her footstep and rose slightly, Khaelian dagger in his hand.

He threw it, knowing he could not miss. She was too close.

And he knew he had been abandoned by the gods. The dagger tumbled, awkward, like any plain dagger. Broken. It struck her fully in the chest, handle foremost. Mondom let out a cry and leapt back. The dagger flopped on the ground, the jets moving it spasmodically.

Gyll knew that dawn was close. It might as well have been hours away. If he ran, she'd use her own dagger again, and this time she would not miss. If he stayed, she would come to him.

"Mondom?" he said loudly.

He thought at first that she would not reply. Then her voice came from darkness. "You've destroyed the caves, Gyll. I hope it gave you pleasure—there's no home for the guild now. I'll have to go begging to Vingi, and we'll lose what little autonomy we had."

"You won't go begging if you've sold the ippicator's bones."

He heard her grunt of surprise. "So that's why you demolished Underasgard," she said. "Because of a religion you claim you don't believe."

"I would have done it anyway."

"Then you're simply vindictive and you deserve to die, Gyll. As for the bones—they would have staved off the inevitable. You've destroyed us, Gyll. The Hoorka have no future here, and your code and the guild will die together. I'll sell the rest of the bones if I can get to them, and we'll guarantee deaths, for the Li-Gallant at least."

You'll get your answer. I hope you enjoy it. "I'll smash the Hoorka myself, then. I told you that I could do it. Now I will."

"Hoorka wants your life. I'll have it, too."

"It's almost dawn, Mondom."

"What is dawn, if the code's gone?"

He felt a thrill of fear tightening his back. "You can't mean that," he said.

"Does that scare you, Gyll? Good. But you needn't worry. You'll never see dawn." Then she stepped out, kicking aside the dagger he'd taken from Meka. He could hear the whine of her vibrofoil, could see the glimmering of vibrowire in the moonlight, the luminous tip glowing. "You have a foil, Gyll. Use it, and see if She of the Five will forgive you." Mondom hefted the Khaelian dagger as well, holding it easily in her right hand. "Come out, or are you going to hide like a lassari?"

He'd finished tending the wound. Dame Fate had made her decree known. Gyll slipped his foil from its sheath, held it in his hand, unactivated. He ducked behind the rocks, moved a few meters to his left, then peered up again. Mondom was looking to where he'd been, the dagger ready. Gyll stood in a rush, flicking on his vibro. Mondom whirled and tossed the blade.

Gyll sidestepped, his vibro in front of him. He was lucky; he managed to touch the quickly thrown weapon; that, plus his motion, deflected it enough. The keen edge nicked his side, tore a hole in Meka's nightcloak. Gyll rushed at Mondom, who had transferred her foil to her other hand—their weapons met with a clashing. Brilliant sparks arced to the ground. Gyll tried to muscle past her defense; Mondom parried, riposting. Gyll countered the attack, still advancing. They did not speak. Their feet scraped on rock, their breaths loud and harsh, their gaze always on the other's foil.

Mondom had been good. She was better now. It took all of Gyll's skill to keep her back, to stop her from reaching him. The Khaelian dagger slashed through the air near him, hissing like an angry dragon, clacking against Mondom's homing belt. She took the dagger in her left hand as fear hammered at Gyll's chest—he could not watch two weapons at once.

Neither had noticed the rising sound through the clamor of their vibrofoils, but now thunder rushed by overhead: a flitter, low in the sky. Mondom's foil stopped in mid-attack, though she did not glance up at the craft as it passed them, nor did she let her guard drop to give Gyll an opening. Gyll had seen the insignia on the flitter's side: the taloned world of the Oldins. He lunged at Mondom, a straight thrust. She hesitated a fraction of a second too long; his foil nicked her shoulder as she knocked his blade aside. He could see her hand, just at the edge of his vision, tightening on the handle of the Khaelian dagger. He knew she was ready to use it, and he did not have enough hands or the two sets of eyes he needed to defend himself.

The flitter wheeled about savagely, dipping, then careened to a halt in the meadow near them.

Mondom, underhanded, tossed the dagger. The jets spat vapor, speeding the weapon unerringly toward him. Gyll tried to slap it aside with his foil. As he did so, Mondom thrust, lunging.

The dagger struck him in the stomach, burying itself deep, twisting as it entered. The vibro slid into his chest, striking bone and then slithering between the ribs.

"Mondom..." Gyll began. He could not feel his hands; he heard rather than felt himself drop his weapon. The vibro screamed against stone. Mondom stared at him and he found that, curiously, she seemed to be crying. He tried to smile to her, but the night was dimming. Gyll could not be sure, but he thought he saw Helgin step from the flitter. He would have spoken, but the ground swirled around him, lumbering, then slammed up at him. Gyll felt cool stone on his cheek. He knew that he should be hearing the grumbling of the flitter's engines, the keening of the vibros, but the sounds were gone. There was only silence and the chill of the rocks.

Then, nothing at all.

"*Back away!*" Helgin snarled. The sting he held was pointed unwaveringly at Mondom. "Turn the vibro off and toss it gently to one side, and back away from him."

Mondom turned to face the Motsognir. Helgin could see the glistening of her eyes; he could also see the blood on her foil. "The body is mine," she said, her voice steady despite the obvious emotion she was feeling. "It has to be given to the signer of the contract."

"And I'm telling you to get away from him, or you won't be killing anyone else in the future. I haven't got Gyll's sense of honor, lady, and that's my friend lying there—I'd love to see you pay for him. Now, move back."

She hesitated a moment, staring at the dwarf and the weapon he held. Then she switched off her vibro (though Gyll's still chattered on the ground) and moved away from the body. Helgin came forward, knelt beside Gyll, one hand at the sting's trigger, the other probing Gyll's neck for a pulse.

"Damn," he muttered. "Oh, *damn!*"

"He's dead?"

"What the hell do you think?" Helgin said throatily. The dagger was still in the body, its fuel exhausted. Helgin took the weapon out, threw it down on the stones. He picked up

Gyll's vibro, flicked it off, and put the weapon in his belt. "Help me put the body on the flitter," he said.

"The body's mine, Motsognir. You know the code. Go against Hoorka, and we'll be hunting you."

"Where? I'm not like Gyll, Thane. I'd sit in *Goshawk* and laugh at you. And I've got the sting."

"You can't hold it and the body, too."

Helgin scowled. He rose to his feet, legs well apart. He lifted the sting, pointed it at her chest. "I can move him myself if I have to, Thane, but I won't leave you standing there to stab me in the back while I do it. It's your choice. Frankly, I hope you don't decide to help me."

Neither of them moved for long seconds. Then Mondom sighed. She shrugged. "All right, Motsognir. What's the difference now, neh? The code's junk, and there'll be no more contracts—I'll be killing those pointed to by Vingi. I'll help you." She looked at the body, the nightcloak tangled around it.

As they lifted Gyll's limp body into the passenger seat of the flitter, she leaned over it, feeling for the pulse. Helgin watched her, impassive. "You don't trust me, Thane? Did you think I'd lie to you?"

"I'm surprised you'd want the body, Motsognir, that's all. And it's my duty to see that Gyll's dead. The last duty."

"Gyll was my friend, and friends do what they can for each other. I couldn't get here quicker, but I'll take him back to the Oldins." False dawn touched the eastern sky. Shadows had become more distinct, color had returned to the landscape, the stars had fled.

"He was my lover."

"You certainly have a touching way of showing your affection."

Mondom hissed, a sharp intake of breath. Her hand went to her vibro sheath, found it empty. She stepped back from Helgin, her hand fisted at her side. "Gyll would have done the same to me," she said.

"Keep telling yourself that. Maybe someday we'll both believe it."

Helgin swung into the pilot's seat. He revved the engines— the rotors whined as a harsh wind sprang up, billowing Mondom's nightcloak, ruffling her short hair. Helgin leaned from his seat, bellowing against the roar of the engines, his beard flying. "Thane, I'll give you a chance you don't deserve, because *he* would have done it. You can come with me, go back to the ship. We'll make a place for you."

She hesitated only a moment. "No," she shouted back to him. "I can't."

Helgin grunted. "Good." He reached for the flitter's controls and wrenched the craft into a quick ascent, circling the meadow as he rose.

Mondom watched until the flitter was gone behind the hills, until the morning stillness had returned. She stared for a long time at the blood spilled on the stones.

Then, the clouds touched with light, she made her way back to the ruin of Underasgard and her kin.

ABOUT THE AUTHOR

STEPHEN LEIGH has been selling short stories to SF magazines (*Analog, Isaac Asimov's Science Fiction Magazine, Destinies*) since 1976. Although he has a Bachelor's degree in Fine Art and Art Education, he makes his living as a bass guitarist and singer for a couple of rock groups. He is married to Denise Parsley Leigh, who is active in SF fandom, and they presently live with their daughter in Cincinnati, Ohio. He has written two previous books about Neweden, *Slow Fall to Dawn* and *Dance of the Hag*. He is currently at work on his fourth novel.

OUT OF THIS WORLD!

That's the only way to describe Bartam's great series of science fiction classics. These space-age thrillers are filled with terror, fancy and adventure and written by America's most renowned writers of science fiction. Welcome to outer space and have a good trip!

FANTASY AND SCIENCE FICTION FAVORITES

Bantam brings you the recognized classics as well as the current favorites in fantasy and science fiction. Here you will find the most recent titles by the most respected authors in the genre.

SPECIAL MONEY SAVING OFFER

Now you can have an up-to-date listing of Bantam's hundreds of titles plus take advantage of our unique and exciting bonus book offer. A special offer which gives you the opportunity to purchase a Bantam book for only 50¢. Here's how!

By ordering any five books at the regular price per order, you can also choose any other single book listed (up to a $4.95 value) for just 50¢. Some restrictions do apply, but for further details why not send for Bantam's listing of titles today!

Just send us your name and address plus 50¢ to defray the postage and handling costs.
